Farmer's market #4

A KILLER MAIZE

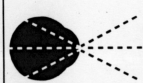

A FARMERS' MARKET MYSTERY

A KILLER MAIZE

PAIGE SHELTON

WHEELER PUBLISHING
A part of Gale, Cengage Learning

GALE
CENGAGE Learning·

Detroit • New York • San Francisco • New Haven, Conn • Waterville, Maine • London

LIBRARY OF CONGRESS CATALOGING-IN-PUBLICATION DATA

Shelton, Paige.
  A killer maize / by Paige Shelton. — Large Print edition.
    pages cm. — (A Farmers' Market Mystery) (Wheeler Publishing Large Print Cozy Mystery)
    ISBN 978-1-4104-5840-7 (softcover) — ISBN 1-4104-5840-7 (softcover) 1. Labyrinths—Fiction. 2. Murder—Investigation—Fiction. 3. Large type books. I. Title.
PS3619.H45345K55 2013
813'.6—dc23   2013008781

Published in 2013 by arrangement with The Berkley Publishing Group, a member of Penguin Group (USA) Inc.

Printed in the United States of America
1 2 3 4 5   17 16 15 14 13

For my grandpa, Stanley Grzyb, who, when I was a little girl, always took me to the Fourth of July Carnival. He would give me two stacks of quarters and help me bet on the Money Wheel. Then we'd ride the Ferris wheel twice and have to go home because he always had to get up at 4:00 A.M. the next morning to get to work on time. Those were the best forty-five minutes of every summer.

ACKNOWLEDGMENTS

A special thanks to:

Bonnie Mills Schelts and Laine Barash for the idea of adding syrup to Becca's product line, and for helping me and Becca with the recipes.

Jenny Hanahan for her South Carolina real estate advice.

There is a group of people who are dedicated to a job that is painstakingly tedious; they are copyeditors. Thank you to Caroline Duffy for the blood, sweat, and tears you've shed while copyediting the Farmers' Market Mysteries. You are invaluable.

My agent, Jessica Faust, and my editor, Michelle Vega. Geez, I'm lucky.

My supportive and enthusiastic parents.

My guys, Charlie and Tyler, who help with every book in different ways. This time, as I was working on the recipes, I overheated some oil and the entire house became quickly filled with smoke. They hurried in to clear out the smoke and then helped me fix the recipes, all without one word of complaint. Geez, I'm lucky again.

Spider Symbolism from Wikia.com: Linked to treachery and death in many cultures, the spider was seen as a "trickster" in ancient Africa and a "spinner of fate" in ancient goddess cultures; in ancient Greek myths, the goddess Arachne was turned into a spider by her jealous rival Athena. Christian cultures have viewed the spider as an evil force that sucked blood from its victims and, alternately, embraced it as "good luck" because of the cross on the back of some species. The Chinese have welcomed the spider descending on its thread as a bringer of joys from heaven.

Corn Maze: A thing that I have no desire to ever enter. Ever. Sincerely, Becca Robins.

ONE

I love a good Ferris wheel, so much so that even as I stared up at this one, I was willing to tell myself that it really didn't look like it might fall apart at any minute. I wanted to hop onto one of the swinging seats and ride the never-ending circle. I wanted it to stop when I was at the top, so I could look across the countryside and see . . . well, from there, I supposed I'd only get a glimpse of more countryside, but it'd be a nice view.

It probably wasn't the best idea, though. Maybe it was the strange noise the engine made when Virgil, the operator, pulled the handle. Clunk, clunk, buzz, whoosh didn't instill the confidence that a smooth engine rev would have. Maybe it was because the swinging seats didn't seem to swing quite right. At least two of them didn't appear to be swinging at all but were instead frozen in an uncomfortable leg-up position. Maybe it was because I'd noticed that at least a few of the security bars didn't look like they could lock into place; they bounced open and closed unless someone was holding them down.

Maybe it was how the Ferris wheel was decorated, but fake spiderwebs only added a sense of the season, not something ominous. No, those were the least of my concerns. I liked the way they enhanced the spirit of the mid-October Swayton County Fall Fair and Festival.

Even with all of my doubts, I loved Ferris wheels. I was sure I'd ride this one at some point. I just had to work up the courage.

"You sell jams and preserves?" Virgil rejoined the conversation after he set the wheel in motion. There were only two riders, teenage boys who either didn't have much else to do or were related to someone who worked at the fair and were still young enough to feel invincible.

"I do. I make them first, then I sell them." I leaned against the tall measuring stick that illustrated the height requirement for the Ferris wheel. I was short, but at least I was tall enough for all the rides, I'd noted to myself. "I have a small farm. I grow strawberries and pumpkins."

"That sounds interesting," Virgil said.

Virgil Morrison was somewhere north of

sixty, but not far. He'd told me that he'd been working at the fair since he'd moved to Orderville, South Carolina, twenty years earlier. It was one of the many odd jobs he worked to pay the bills. Over the past few days I'd asked him a number of times about his other odd jobs and his life before the last twenty years, but he'd ignored the questions with either silence or a change of subject. His thinning gray hair was so short that it required only a washcloth to groom. His eyes were dark and seemed pupil-less until you looked really closely. When I first met him, I thought he might be angry about something, but that was just the way he held his face: scrunched and strained, uncomfortable and suspicious. After talking to him a few times, I decided that he didn't know how his face looked and he didn't much care anyway.

Virgil also had a tattoo on the side of his neck. It was this, even more than the Ferris wheel or our common wardrobe of overalls, that drew me to him. I was fascinated by a senior citizen with a tattoo on his neck. It was small and only a simple black ink spider, but it had piqued my curiosity. I'd initially thought it might be just a temporary addition, something to go along with the fake spiderwebs. But I was now pretty sure

13

it was permanent. What was the story behind it? I hadn't come out and asked directly. After all, I couldn't even get him to chat about his life outside the fair and festival; I didn't think he'd be willing to tell me about the tattoo. Yet.

"It is interesting," I said. It was the first time Virgil had asked me something personal. I thought I might finally be making headway, and I hoped to ride the wave a little longer. "I'm really lucky to be able to do what I do, even though it is a lot of hard work. Stop by my booth, I'll give you a free sample."

I had plenty of jars of jams and preserves. I might have sold three since we'd set up temporary stalls on Monday. Today was Thursday, which meant I needed to sell at least one jar today to keep at a one-per-day pace.

The Bailey's Farmers' Market owners had requested that Allison, my sister and Bailey's manager, round up some market vendors to sell their wares at the Swayton County Fall Fair and Festival. The annual event was full of the things a fair should be full of: rides, albeit I wasn't sure of the safety of any of them; games; baking contests; butter sculptures; and some wonderful and adorable animals to peer at and pet. It was also the rev-up and kickoff to the opening of South Carolina's biggest corn maze.

The fair ran from the second Monday in October to the third Friday, with the maze opening on Wednesday during the second week. The deluge of activities was a great way to both offer some family fun and gently shift everyone into fall and the upcoming Halloween holiday.

I'd been asked to donate some pumpkins for a decorating contest that would be a part of the maze's opening day. I was happy to donate a whole truck-bed full of pumpkins to the cause, but I was currently doing everything I could to stay as far away from the maze as possible, and it wasn't even open yet. I wasn't a maze person, but that was only because I wasn't the sort of girl who enjoyed being in spaces where I couldn't see a way out, couldn't see over the top, or might end up hopelessly stuck at a dead end.

Plus, the whole corn-as-part-of-a-horror-story idea was well rooted in my psyche.

Fortunately, the temporary stalls set up for me and the three other Bailey's vendors were on one side of the fairgrounds and the far-stretching field of corn was on the other side, past the Mad Maniacal Machine, aka the old, small roller coaster. But no matter

15

where I was, at my tent, or visiting the rides, food carts, or some of the animals in the two small barns, I could glance out and see the large hand-painted sign that stuck up from the middle of the maze. It was a cartoonish but eerie portrayal of a house that apparently used to sit on the property. Whether the actual house had been as spooky as the one in the illustration, with its big gaping windows and leaning walls, I wasn't sure, and I hadn't had much luck finding out. Every time I tried to get more of the house's story, my questions were met with either shrugs or comments like "I dunno" or "Ah, gypsy magic." The reactions only added to the atmosphere, though, so I'd begun to think that the people I'd asked were being purposefully mysterious.

So, not only did I avoid the maze itself, but I also tried to avert my eyes from the sign. I did think that business might actually pick up once the maze was open.

The fair owners had been mostly honest when they told the Bailey's owners that their annual event had become less and less popular over the years and needed some help. They thought that the popularity of Bailey's products might attract more fair attendees.

The fair, however, seemed not merely

"less popular" but rather, pretty close to all the way dead. Bailey's might have made a great name in the world of farmers' markets, but we weren't doing anything to help the fair's attendance numbers.

"That'd be great. I love peanut butter and jelly sandwiches," Virgil said to the offer of samples. "Thank you."

I smiled. We were finally getting somewhere.

"Becca!" called a voice from somewhere behind me. I thought I recognized it, but I couldn't be sure.

"You've got to be kidding," I mumbled as a mental image of a face formed in my mind.

"Uh-oh, that doesn't sound good," Virgil said.

"Is a tall blond man with a cowboy hat walking — with bow legs — in this direction?"

"No cowboy hat, but yep to the rest."

"Is he wearing jeans with holes in the knees and a T-shirt that's seen better days?"

"Yep."

"Oh no. How did this happen?"

Virgil stepped forward. "You want me to get rid of him?"

I didn't know exactly what he meant. Would he tell him to go away, or would he

get rid of him permanently? It was a tempt-
ing offer either way.

I reluctantly shook my head and then
turned around.

"It is you!" said the man in worn jeans
and ratty T-shirt as he pulled me into a hug,
lifted me up, and twirled me in a circle. "It
is damn great to see you, sweetheart."

"Hey, Scott," I said when I landed again.
I didn't want to smile, but his enthusiasm
was infectious, and even though I'd never
fall for that off-center grin and those overly
happy green eyes again, it *was* kind of good
to see him. That very same infectious
enthusiasm had been the reason I'd stayed
married to him about a year too long.
Despite his many faults, he'd always been
fun to be around.

"How are you? You look great, the same
as when you dumped me, actually. Becca
and I were married," he said to Virgil.

"That right?" Virgil said, his face breaking
with its own smile. He was amused. I liked
seeing his stern features soften. I felt a pull
at the corner of my mouth.

"I'm fine, Scott. What are you doing
here?" I asked.

"The shooting gallery, right over there.
Come over, I'll give you some free shots."
He held up an invisible gun and shot it off

18

to the side. "Boosh, boosh."

"Really? What happened to the dealership job?" When he and I had divorced, he'd left for Charleston and a mechanic's job at a Toyota dealership. It was the best job he'd ever had.

"Ah, lots has happened since then. The shooting gallery helps me be my own boss some of the time, Becca. You know all about that, right?"

"Sure."

"I own it." Scott crossed his arms in front of his chest and winked. " 'Cept between you and me and you, sir" — he looked at Virgil — "we picked a bad gig. This place is a graveyard."

I looked at Virgil. Though I'd yet to crack his concrete-wall exterior, I knew he had pride invested in the Swayton County event. Perhaps the feeling was simply the result of having worked there so many years, but I could tell he liked the fair. He liked working the Ferris wheel. He even liked the frightening and disconcerting noises the engine made. It wasn't hard to see that he took his job seriously. The expression on his face told me I was right on target. His dislike for Scott was quick and obvious.

"I dunno," Virgil said. "We get to work outside. We get the chance to meet some inter'sting people. Some of us, like you, young man, get to have access to guns. It's a win-win, the way I see it."

Scott blinked. He verged on annoying most of the time, and he wasn't great at holding down jobs, but he wasn't stupid. He knew he'd insulted Virgil, a man who, though older than him, was built wide and solid like a good pickup, and had a spider tattoo on the side of his neck. Scott didn't want to mess with Virgil, and he knew he just had.

"Sorry, man. I just meant . . . shoot, I didn't mean to insult you. You're right, this is a great place. I hope it picks up, that's all."

Virgil stared at Scott for a beat or two too long. If Virgil had continued to stare, I might have had to jump in and defend my ex and his copious talking skills. I'd done plenty of that when we were married, and I hadn't wished for the opportunity to present itself again. Fortunately, Virgil let another smile sprout as he turned and pushed the lever so that the teenage boys could begrudgingly exit the ride.

"I'll see you later, Virgil. Come by for some jam." As I spoke, I put my hand on Scott's arm and directed him away from the Ferris wheel.

20

"I didn't mean to insult the guy, Becca. What is he, the owner of the fair or the land it's on or something?" Scott said when we were far enough away from Virgil that he could neither hear us nor read our lips.

"I don't know who he is," I said. "I've been trying to figure it out."

"I'll go talk to him later, spread some of my Scott-charm. I'll have him eating out of my hand by the end of the day."

His Scott-charm wasn't quite what he thought it was, but he could be likeable enough, especially if you remained more an acquaintance than a good friend, or a wife.

"Do you have a few minutes to walk with me? I need to check on my stall. Want some crackers and jam?"

I could have been rude and told him I needed to get back to work. But as I'd watched him aggravate Virgil, something became clear in my head: I was kind of interested in how he was doing, even if we hadn't been able to stay married. I didn't know if some preordained amount of time needed to pass before you could have a mostly clean slate with an ex, but this felt about right. I was also just plain curious; what had he done with his life since me?

"Love some. Just like old times."

The Swayton County Fall Fair and Festival was located about half an hour from my hometown of Monson, South Carolina, right outside the even smaller town of Orderville. Monson wasn't in Swayton County, but close enough that the hilly green countryside, now covered in the reds and yellows of changing leaves, was just like what I was used to.

Scott and I wove around a few other quiet or mostly empty rides, a cotton-candy stand, and a goldfish toss. In the last week, I'd spoken to a number of the fair workers, but the only one I'd wanted to really get to know was Virgil, so the free moments that I'd had — and there had been many — were spent chatting with my fellow Bailey's vendors or trying to engage Virgil in a conversation.

"How long have you been here, Scott?" I asked. I waved to the corn-dog vendor, who I thought was named Jerry, as we stepped around his small trailer.

"Just set up yesterday," he said. "Really, I had no idea how bad this fair was. I don't think I'm going to stick around if it doesn't pick up in the next day or so."

"The other Bailey's vendors and I have been talking about that, too. We've been here all four days, and are supposed to be here through the weekend and all of next week except Monday. I feel bad for the organizers, but us being here isn't helping anyone. Potential fairgoers couldn't care less about us, and we're losing money by not being at Bailey's. I plan on bringing out some pumpkins Wednesday for the decorating contest, but I could easily come back just for that."

"Who else is here?" Scott asked. During our marriage, he'd met a number of the Bailey's vendors. He'd become friends with a few of them, too. I hadn't seen him visit Bailey's once since our divorce, so I didn't know if he'd kept in contact with any of them.

"Remember Brenton, who makes and sells dog biscuits? He's here. So is Stella, the baker, and a new vendor who is all about squash. His name is Henry, but I still don't know him well. He's quiet."

"Henry . . . squash? Is his last name Dennis?"

"I think so. You know him?"

"Yeah, I do. He's a former mechanic, too. Small world."

"I'd say."

As we approached the short line of Bailey's vendors, I observed some less-than-happy friends. Brenton leaned back in his chair, his hands on top of the baseball cap on his head and his eyes tightly shut. Stella had her hands on her round hips as she surveyed her table full of fresh bread. She'd brought less to sell today than the previous days, and it looked like she might still end up going home with too much inventory. Henry, the new vendor, seemed to be texting, the look on his face telling me either that he wasn't sending happy words or, perhaps, that his thumbs were too wide for the tiny keyboard.

"Scott, is that you?" Stella said as we approached. She looked at me quickly as if to see if it was okay to be friendly to him. I smiled. I didn't relish the idea of hanging out with either of my ex-husbands, but I didn't despise either of them either. I'd been the one to end both marriages, but neither Scott One nor this Scott, Scott Two, had been too heart-broken with the decision.

"Stella, Stella, the most beautiful baker to any fella," Scott said as he reached over her display table and hugged her tightly.

"Oh, Scott." She laughed. "You haven't changed a bit."

"Well, I hope I've changed a little. Maybe grown up a bit, but I'll always be me, I suppose." He looked at me.

I didn't think he was searching for my approval, but I gave him a half smile anyway.

"Scott, is that really you?" Brenton leaned out of his small stall.

"Brenton, buddy," Scott said as he sauntered over and shook Brenton's hand.

"I haven't seen you for some time. What're you doing . . . ?" Brenton looked at me. "Are you two back — ?"

"No, heavens no," I said too quickly. I cleared my throat.

Scott laughed. "No, sir, we're way over." He winked at me. "I own the shooting gallery stand over there. I'm working the fair just like the rest of you."

"Are you having any more business than we are?" Brenton asked.

"No, this place is as dead as a snake on the highway. I don't understand why they even opened the gates," Scott said.

Henry had come out of his stall and stood next to me. I didn't know if he was shy or just needed to get the lay of the land before he contributed to conversations, but he seemed comfortable just to stand next to me and listen.

"Yeah, we were talking about leaving, but we might be stuck," Brenton said. "We're not sure if Allison wants us to stay no matter what."

"I've got a call in to her," I said. "I'll give her the scoop. We'll know soon."

Scott looked at Henry. "You might not remember me, but we worked together at a dealership in Charleston."

For a moment, Henry studied Scott doubtfully. He spoke right before his silence became uncomfortable. "Sure, sure, I remember you. You were great with brakes."

"I do have quite the brake reputation," Scott said proudly, but I thought he might be mocking himself slightly. If that was the case, then maybe he had matured.

"Didn't you leave to — ?" Henry began.

"Well, I'm most definitely buying some bread, Stella. What'ya got?" Scott announced, cutting off Henry's question. I wondered what that was about, but I didn't ask.

"Ms. Robins, Ms. Robins." A harried voice turned the group's attention to a quickly approaching young woman.

Lucy Emory was somehow an important part of the Swayton County Fall Fair and Festival, though she'd never made it clear just exactly what her role was. She carried a clipboard and always had a writing implement in her hand or threaded atop her ear. She rarely smiled and had one answer to almost every question: "I'll check on that and get back to you."

I didn't think she was much older than

me, and from the first moment I met her I felt an immediate connection to her denim wardrobe and makeup-challenged ways. Her hair was brown, though, and cut even shorter — boyishly, in fact — than my blonde hair.

"Hi, Lucy," I said as she stopped next to Brenton.

"Ms. Robins, I've heard you are all leaving the fair. Is that true?"

I looked around at my fellow vendors and Scott. Either we had been overheard, or someone had told on us. I didn't like that neither Allison nor I had had a chance to talk to Lucy before she got the information elsewhere, but the damage had been done.

"Lucy, I'm sorry you heard that news through the grapevine rather than directly from us," I began. I debated asking to speak to her privately, but it didn't seem necessary. This was one of those moments that made me wonder what Allison would do. She could handle any situation with professionalism and grace. I wasn't as polished, and I worried I'd offend someone, but I did my best. "We have discussed the fact that we don't seem to be helping your business much. Maybe it would be better if —"

"No, no, no, you can't leave. You just can't. I know we've been slow, but things will pick up."

I exchanged a silent look of doubt with Stella.

"Does the fair usually start off like this?" I asked.

Lucy's eyes flashed, and she bit at the inside of her cheek. "Sometimes, yes, but tomorrow's Friday. It always picks up on Fridays."

"That would be good," I said as I looked at my comrades. No one was convinced.

"Lucy," Stella interrupted, "Becca's being polite. I'm afraid I'm not on my best behavior, so I'll just jump in here. We'll stay tomorrow, but if things don't look to be improving, we won't be back. Even with Monday off, a whole other week of business this slow isn't good. I'm sorry about that, but Becca's right, we're also not helping the fair a bit. I'm mystified as to why y'all even wanted us here. I'm certain we haven't brought one extra fairgoer."

"But you're all part of Bailey's, and Bailey's is so popular."

"Maybe your customers aren't the same as our customers. I don't know what it is. Please don't take it personally. We all have businesses to attend to. Not only are we not helping you, but our businesses are suffering, too," Stella reiterated.

Lucy cringed. "Yes, I understand, but I would appreciate it if you do give us tomorrow and then reconsider the rest of next week."

"Absolutely," Stella said as she looked at the rest of us. "I'm sorry, Lucy."

"We're all sorry it's not working out," I added.

"Sure. Sure." She smiled weakly until her eyes landed on Scott. "Shooting gallery guy?"

"Yes, ma'am."

"You'll probably be leaving, too?"

"I'm gonna try and stick around," Scott said enthusiastically. I could tell he felt her pain.

Huh. Maybe he really had matured. The Scott I'd been married to would have just said, "Yep, I'm outta here."

Lucy looked as though she wanted to say something else but couldn't quite find the words. Piped-in organ music played cheerfully in the background and mixed with the whirr and rumble of the less-than-reliable machinery of the rides. A wave of corn-dog-scented air made me suddenly hungry.

"All right, then. I guess I'll let them know," Lucy said before she turned and hurried away.

I'd asked her a few times who she meant

whenever she said "they" or "them," but she'd yet to tell me. I assumed she meant her bosses, perhaps the fair organizers or owners, or perhaps a manager. I thought about following her and talking directly to "them," but it wasn't going to change the outcome. Even though I hadn't talked to Allison yet, I knew we would have to pack up. It wasn't fair to my fellow vendors. In fact, I suddenly wished I hadn't agreed to stay through Friday. There was still a lot of Thursday left to suffer through. My gut was telling me that the next day and a half was going to be long, awful, and bad for everyone's business.

There were many reasons I'd come to wish I'd listened to my gut. The next day and a half was pretty awful, but not because our businesses suffered. In fact, Friday, early afternoon, business started to boom, and by then we all wished it hadn't.

TWO

"Thanks for taking me today, Becca," Stella said.

"My pleasure. This works out."

Stella and I had decided that carpooling to the fair on our last day would be wise. We were both taking only a small amount of inventory, and everything fit nicely in the bed of my old truck, still leaving plenty of space if either of us happened to win a giant stuffed animal or something. We'd discussed whether or not to believe Lucy's assurances that business would pick up today. We both thought it might, but not enough.

"Oh, hey, I have a question," I continued.

"I'm listening."

"Have you heard anything about 'gypsy magic' or something like that?" I asked.

"Actually, I have. It's strange, isn't it? I've asked people about that big billboard out in the middle of the maze. A couple have just said the words 'gypsy magic' and then hurried away or changed the subject, but . . . oh, I think it was the corn-dog vendor, his name's Jerry, told me that legend has it that a gypsy woman used to live on the property and her sprit watches over the citizens of Orderville. He couldn't remember her name, but he said that people are superstitious about uttering it aloud." Stella laughed, but it was slightly strained. No matter what you believed, spooky superstitions could still leave an impression.

I wasn't superstitious about or bothered by legends and such, but the fair's setting amid a corn maze had given me a few goose-bump moments.

"Maybe he *did* remember it but didn't want to tempt fate by saying it aloud," I said with my best mock-scary voice.

Stella laughed again. "I don't know. He only recently moved to Orderville. Shoot, I can't remember what he said, a couple months ago or something. Nice kid. Maybe he can tell you more about her."

"I'll ask him."

"Hey, I'm sorry if I was rude to Lucy yesterday," Stella said a beat or two later.

"Oh, I wouldn't worry about it. It needed to be done. I talked to Allison last night, and she said she'd try to get us out of today and next week if we wanted to. I felt like we should do what we told Lucy we would do, so I spoke for all of us and said that we'd go in today and think about next week, even though we all are pretty sure we won't come back."

"Good. We did commit. We need to be there today." Stella sighed.

"Allison also wanted me to apologize to everyone for her. She didn't know it would be such a bust."

"We'll be fine. One week isn't going to kill any of us. It's the strangest little fair or festival or whatever, though, isn't it? Of course, I would never let my children ride any of those rides, but the animals are cute and well cared for."

"I love Ferris wheels, but I'm going to have to double-dare myself to ride that one. I will ride it, though, before the day is done. I vow," I said weakly.

"I'll join you. Why not, no one's been killed yet."

A few minutes later, as I pulled into the parking lot, Stella said exactly what I was thinking: "Uh-oh."

The lot was a big dirt field, but at its far end, three small buildings marked the fair's entrance. Two were ticket booths, and the third was a trailer into which Lucy sometimes disappeared. It was probably where her mysterious bosses were located.

There were only a few parked cars and trucks in the lot, but the three buildings were partially obscured by four police cars, three of them with their lights flashing. The fourth police car wasn't from Swayton County, but from my hometown, Monson. My good friend and the man I'd recently kissed without warning, Sam Brion, was a police officer in Monson. I wondered if, by chance, he was there, too. But mostly, I wondered what was going on.

"This doesn't look good," I said as I steered the truck toward the police cars. As we approached, we saw a crowd of people right inside the front gates. It was only seven in the morning, too early for any fair attendees, so I assumed most of them were fair workers and vendors. I searched for Brenton, Henry, and even Scott, but I was suddenly so worried that my eyes only skimmed. I hoped they were okay. I hoped everyone was okay.

I parked the truck in the dusty lot, and Stella and I hurried through the front gate. I recognized several faces among the gathered group, people I didn't really know but who I'd seen and waved to over the last week. We finally found Scott on the edge of the crowd, standing away from everyone and staring out at the unpopulated fairgrounds.

"Hey," I said as I touched his arm.

He flinched slightly before absently saying, "Becca, Stella."

"What's going on?" I asked. I saw a bruise on the arm that I touched. I also noticed a tear in the front of his T-shirt. But neither of these things seemed as important as finding out whatever had brought out the police, so I didn't comment on them.

"Someone was killed," Scott said as he crossed his arms in front of his chest, covering only part of the tear. "Murdered."

"Who?" I asked.

"The guy who ran the Ferris wheel."

"Virgil?" I said.

"Yeah, the one I was rude to yesterday."

"Oh no!"

I had to sit down, but there wasn't a chair close by. I sank to the ground. I felt like I might faint, but I didn't want to. I focused on staying conscious. Scott and Stella crouched next to me.

"We were both talking to him yesterday," Scott said to Stella. "Were they better friends than I thought?"

"I don't know. You okay, Becca?" Stella asked.

I was too busy focusing to answer, but I managed a nod as I tried to take a deep breath and force my vision not to tunnel.

Scott watched me closely, and Stella put her hand on my shoulder. I was grateful that they were both silent as I worked through the initial shock. It took a few moments, but soon I felt steady enough to speak.

"We weren't really friends," I said. "I've been trying to work up the courage to ride that bucket and a half of bolts they've been calling a Ferris wheel. We chatted but never really became friends. I think I just had plans . . . maybe had plans to get to know him better. He was . . . interesting. It's just such a shock to hear that he was killed. I'll be okay in a second."

Scott rocked off his knees and sat next to me. Stella patted my shoulder and smiled sympathetically.

"Do you know what happened, Scott?" I asked.

"Yeah, it's not pretty, though."

"I can take it. Like I said, it was just the initial shock."

"He was found hanging from the top chair of the ride, by his own belt, but he was shot first. It was awful," he said thoughtfully. He'd been supportive of my anguish, but I could tell he was trying to hide his own.

"Did you see him?"

Scott nodded. "I'm the one who found him. I was here early. The shooting gallery was acting up last night. It needed some tweaking. I came in early to take care of it."

"Oh, Scott, I'm so sorry."

Scott shrugged and smiled at me. "S'okay. You know how tough I am."

"Still," I said, "that had to be rough."

"Becca?" a voice pulled my attention up and away from Scott.

I had to shade my eyes from the first rays of the early morning sun. I could only distinguish the person's outline, but I knew who it was. "Sam?"

"I should have known you'd be around here somewhere. There's been a murder."

"Sam," Stella said. "It seems we haven't seen you since the last dead person." She extended her hand, and he helped her stand.

He reached for my hand next. I took it and stood up next to Stella. Scott made it up by himself.

Stella was right. I hadn't seen Sam since shortly after the last murder that had occurred in the Monson vicinity. In fact, I was certain he'd purposefully been ignoring me the past several weeks. Our last conversation had gone something like this:

"Sam, I'm sorry about the way I handled

my feelings for you. I shouldn't have just kissed you out of the blue like that, particularly when I was committed to Ian."

"So, the kiss was a result of your feelings for me?"

"Yes."

"Are you still with Ian?"

"We haven't broken up, but I told him about the kiss."

"How'd that go?"

"Not well."

At that point, Sam had sighed. "Becca, I'm pretty sure I told you I'd consider even a dual with Ian if it came to that. I wasn't kidding, really, though what I meant was that he and I could fight it out on even ground — we could both puff up our feathers and you could choose one of us. I don't want to break anyone up who doesn't want to be broken up. Please figure out what your heart wants. When you know that, you will either never break up with Ian or you will. Let me know when you know."

And that had been it. That had been the last time we spoke. Ian and I weren't officially broken up yet. Though we still saw each other, we weren't officially much of anything at all. He was mostly busy with his new land and lavender farm. I was mostly busy with my market stall and my extra business at five Maytabee's Coffee Shops. We were busy, and busy had been a great excuse to not face reality head-on. I felt stupid and immature about the whole thing. I thought I'd known exactly what I wanted, but when it came down to it, I only knew I wasn't sure about anything except that my behavior made it pretty clear that maybe I didn't deserve either of them.

Now that I was standing, the sun was no longer blinding me and I could see Sam clearly.

He hadn't changed over the last several weeks, but he wasn't in his uniform. His brown hair was free of whatever slick gunk he put in it when he was on duty, and he wore a simple black T-shirt and jeans.

His eyes were the same clear blue that seemed to change temperature more than color with his moods. Right now they were warm and friendly. He smiled, which made me smile, too.

"Sam, what're you doing here?" I asked.

"The local guys were concerned they couldn't round up enough officers to investigate the murder. Turns out they were fine. I'm on my way out. You want to walk me to my car?"

"Sure."

Scott cleared his throat.

"Oh, sorry. Sam, this is one of my ex-Scotts . . . I mean, one of my ex-husbands . . . that sounds horrible. Sam, this is Scott Triplett. He and I were married at one time." I had never once, before attending the Swayton County Fall Fair and Festival, had to introduce one of my two ex-husbands when they were in an "ex" status. It was awkward duty, probably because they were both named Scott, or maybe because there were two of them.

"Actually, we sort of met earlier," Sam said. "However, I didn't know about you two being married."

"I didn't get your first name. Sam?" Scott reached for a handshake.

"Sam Brion. I'm an officer in Monson."

"Nice to meet you officially or, I guess, unofficially."

"Nice to meet you, too," Sam said.

"How about I get you to the car, Sam?" I said.

"Sure, okay."

"I'll be right back," I told Stella and Scott.

We threaded our way through the crowd and back to the parking lot. For a few steps, neither of us said anything. I was glad when he was the first one to finally speak.

"What're you doing here, Becca?" he asked. He seemed to be keeping a bigger

40

distance from me than he normally would. It wasn't much, but I noticed it.

"The event organizers asked Allison if she would ask some vendors to set up here. They thought it would be good for the fair and good for us. As far as I can see, we haven't brought them one extra person. And our businesses are suffering. This is our last day probably, except that I'm donating some pumpkins for their maze opening next Wednesday."

"And your ex-husband — one of them at least" — he smiled — "what's he doing here?"

"He owns the shooting gallery stand. We ran into each other just yesterday. In fact, I was talking with Virgil, the man who ran the Ferris wheel, the man who was apparently killed, when Scott came up to me." We'd stopped next to Sam's police cruiser. I put my hands in my overalls' pockets and peered up at him as he peered down at me. October in South Carolina could still have extra-warm moments, but usually, the mid-autumn temperatures were perfect for enjoying the outdoors. I felt somewhat chilled this morning, though, but that might not have had anything to do with the temperature.

"He found the victim. He was pretty upset earlier."

"I imagine he was. Who wouldn't be?" I'd found my own fair share of dead bodies. The experience didn't have a calming effect.

Sam nodded. "Did you know the victim well?"

"Yes and no. I didn't really know him, but I had been stopping by and talking to him. I love Ferris wheels and wanted to ride that one, but I needed to find a good dose of courage first."

"You were afraid?"

"Did you get a close look at this one, or a close listen? No, probably not. It's not . . . well. I figured I should make sure my will was in order before I hopped aboard." I smiled weakly. Sam smiled, too, which made me smile a little more.

There was way too much smiling considering the circumstances.

"What did you know about Virgil?" he asked.

"He didn't talk much, and he had a tattoo on his neck. In my imagination, he was part of some violent Russian mob group and his tattoo was for some crime he had to commit to become a part of the gang. He escaped and has been in hiding in South

Carolina doing odd jobs here and there."

"That's a pretty good imagination."

"Did you see the tattoo?"

"No, I didn't even see the victim. I got here after they'd taken him down and away."

I looked back toward the fairgrounds. "That had to be quite the challenge." I swallowed. "Wasn't he hanging from a top seat of the ride?"

"That's what I heard, but your ex, Scott, turned on the ride and brought him down to see if there was anything he could do for him. He ended up having to climb part way up to gather him, so, well, so the body wasn't . . ."

"Really? He climbed up?" I thought about that a moment. I supposed that's what I would have done, but I wasn't sure. "Were they angry he didn't call the police first?"

"No, not angry. They were just hoping someone else could confirm Scott's story."

"They doubt him?"

"I don't know, Becca. I don't think so." Sam sighed and rubbed his hand over his chin. "Here, I thought, was a potential murder you might not feel the need to get involved in. Then when I show up, not only do I find you, but I also find that someone you care about is connected to this mess, too."

"That's past tense . . . well, I suppose I do still care about Scott's well-being. I don't want anything bad to happen to him, but he doesn't take up much space in my thoughts and hasn't for quite some time."

"Strange that he's here, though. I mean, was it a surprise to run into him?"

"Completely."

Sam nodded and then looked toward the fairgrounds.

"So . . ." I began.

"What?" Sam asked, his eyes now locked on mine.

"Sam, are . . . you . . . are we okay?" Normally, I wouldn't ask such a question, but I hadn't seen him for a long time, several weeks, and no matter why he was there, it was really good to see him and I didn't want the moment to pass without at least trying to make things better between the two of us.

Sam stared at me a long moment. "Becca, I've decided I'm not going to be that easy for you. I know where this is headed. I also know that you and Ian are officially still together. What I said the last time we spoke still holds true — I'm not interested in being a part of breaking up any couple. I think it's pretty clear where I stand. You have to be the one to let me know. I'm not going anywhere."

I suddenly remembered the time I thought Sam was dead. I shivered.

"If and when you're ready," he continued, "just give me a call and ask me out. Take me out on an amazing, unforgettable date and we'll see how it goes. For now, though, will you try to stay out of this murder? Your ex seems like a pretty good guy. He might need a friend, but I don't think he's under suspicion for the murder. You won't need to investigate."

"I see." I swallowed my embarrassment. "Well, today's my last full day here, I'm pretty sure. I was shocked about Virgil, but I didn't *know him* know him. Even if Scott was under suspicion, I doubt I would feel compelled to clear his name." I paused. Actually, I might, I realized, but I wasn't going to tell Sam that. "I'm going back to Bailey's tomorrow and sell my jams and preserves and stay out of all this."

"Sounds smart." Sam put his hand on his car door. "You've got me curious about the tattoo, though. I'll look into it and stop by Bailey's tomorrow or the next day if I think it's okay for you to know the details."

"You will?" Before I'd accosted him with the kiss, he'd stopped by Bailey's a lot. We'd become friends, and more than anything I missed our friendship. Well, *maybe* that's what I missed most. I knew it would be fun to have the old Sam back if that was possible, but I'd thought about the kiss way more than I should have.

"See you later, Becca. Stay out of trouble."

I waved as he drove out of the parking lot.

I turned toward the fairgrounds once again. There'd been a gruesome murder, and I'd spoken to the victim — as small a conversation as it had been — just the day before.

Any joy I'd just felt over reconnecting with Sam washed away and was replaced by an only slightly diluted version of the shock I'd felt when I first heard about Virgil. I wanted to get out of there. I wanted to go home, back to Hobbit my dog, and back to Bailey's. I wanted to see Ian and Allison and tell them what had happened, but my recent experiences with murder told me the police would probably want to talk to me and the other vendors about what, if anything, we'd seen, or knew about the victim.

The air smelled earthy, only slightly crisp with fall, and with a hint of the greasy fair treats that I loved so much. No one had their machines or stalls up and running yet. I wondered if the "show would go on" or if they'd all just shut down. I hoped Lucy and her bosses wouldn't care when the Bailey's vendors left, which I thought would be about two minutes after the police dismissed us.

"Let's get this over with," I mumbled to myself as I made my way back to my friends, and my second ex.

THREE

The police interviews went as I expected: slowly, stretching throughout the entire morning. Though the only person who knew where I was in the middle of the night and before I picked up Stella from Bailey's was my dog, Hobbit, the police didn't seem to think I was a killer. And Stella had her entire family to support her alibi. Henry and Brenton were equally unconcerned about whether the police thought they might be involved. As far as I could see, no one was arrested, so either they didn't find the culprit or didn't have enough evidence yet to arrest someone.

Once we were done, Lucy gathered everyone together and announced that the search for initial evidence was complete and that the fair could resume normal operation. Similar to what happened at Bailey's when one of our market vendors, Matt Simonsen, was killed, the fair workers were concerned there might be a killer in their midst. But Lucy allayed their fears much more adeptly than I would have expected given my earlier interactions with her. She told everyone to be cautious, and she announced that she would be hiring a team of security guards to patrol the grounds and escort people to their cars if they chose.

Not one local fair vendor thought the fair should close. Henry, Stella, Brenton, and I couldn't wait to get out of there, but we were the only ones. Even Scott wasn't in a huge hurry to leave.

I tried to put myself in their shoes, and I realized that I'd have to just chalk it up to the "old hometown spirit." Besides, they didn't have a Bailey's to go back to, a place they knew was better. If business had been slow before, it was bound to be even slower now, if there was any at all. The thought that we should invite all the fair workers to bring their attractions to Bailey's or set up shop in Monson crossed my mind, and then left it. Of course, that wasn't a viable idea.

But then I got the biggest surprise of all. Murder turned out to be very good for fair vendors, it seemed — with the obvious exception of Virgil. After the police interviews, at around noon, my fellow Bailey's crew and I came together a distance away from our stalls to plan our escape — I mean, our return home. As we conferred, the noise level around us rose to a notch I hadn't heard at the fair until that moment. Suddenly, there were people everywhere. I stood on my toes and looked out toward the parking lot; it was filling from a line of vehicles that started so far down the state highway that I couldn't see the end of it

"If you kill someone, they will come," I said. The only one who heard was Stella.

"Uh, that seems strange," she said. "Do you suppose that's just the normal Friday bump in traffic that Lucy spoke about or . . . something else?"

"I have no idea, but look" — I nodded toward her stall — "you've got a line of your own forming."

She turned and looked and then turned back to me with panic in her eyes. "I don't think I brought enough bread."

Someone tapped on my shoulder.

"You make jams?" asked a middle-aged man holding a kid's hand with one of his and a cone of cotton candy with the other.

"Yes, sir."

"I'll take some."

Instead of making the quick getaway we'd hoped for, we manned our stations.

For the next couple hours, we were

swamped with customers. There wasn't time to further consider why the crowd had grown; we just had to take care of everyone to the best of our limited inventories. We all sold out way too quickly, and Lucy was none too happy with any of us.

"I told you things would improve," she said, seeming to have recovered from the trying morning.

"We're sorry, Lucy. We really are," I said, because I couldn't think of anything else to say.

"S'okay. I'd really like for you to come back again tomorrow and next week though. I think we'll be just as busy. I think you'll all sell a lot."

Considering the circumstances, it suddenly felt wrong to tie our commitment to the fair to our bottom lines. It's what we'd done only the day before, but now things were different.

Stella and I looked at each other, both of us uncertain how to handle Lucy's request.

"Please. I'll be honest with you," Lucy said. "I don't think you being here brought us any extra business, but we've received a positive response anyway. Just today, I had two people tell me they loved buying your dog biscuits." She looked at Brenton.

Brenton smiled sheepishly. He was so

easygoing that he'd never want to cause waves.

"Please," Lucy said again.

I didn't get it. Even if she had heard positive responses, why in the world was it so important that we stay?

"Give us some time to discuss it. I'll find you," I said.

Lucy smiled. "Thank you!"

"She really wants us around," Stella said as Lucy disappeared into the crowd.

"I know. I can't quite figure out why she's so adamant, though," I said.

"We offer something different," Henry said. It was always a surprise to hear his voice. "We're not fried in grease, we're not a clunky old ride, we give a fresh feel to the fair."

"You're probably right," Brenton said. "I'll do whatever, Becca. The whole thing only lasts one more week, and we'd already planned on not being here Monday. We could make Saturday or Sunday our last day, or see how it goes and then commit or not commit to next week. I don't think Lucy would mind if we played it day to day; at least it seems like she'd be okay with that. I can stay or go, but I have a built-in Internet business. I've got orders coming in that I can easily fulfill in the evenings, so this isn't my only way to pay the bills. It's up to you all."

"I can stay," Henry said as he looked toward the quiet Ferris wheel. The ride was the only thing that had been officially shut down. "I think we should stay."

"Stella?" I said.

"I'm fine coming tomorrow and seeing what happens, I suppose, but I do feel kind of rotten about doing a one-eighty after business picked up. How bad would it be, Becca, to come tomorrow and then decide on next week from there?"

"I think it's okay. These are business-people. They get it, I'm sure." I looked toward the Ferris wheel, too. For an instant, my imagination turned it into a big, dark, steely monster that was capped with even darker storm clouds. In truth, it was just a big old machine that glowed in the waning sunlight of a beautiful fall day. "Okay, I'll let Lucy know. I'll be right back, and then we can leave for Monson."

Switching gears again wasn't comfortable, but it only made sense that we stayed. We'd told Lucy we were leaving because of the poor business. It was as if she'd stepped up to the plate and given us what we were looking for — a bigger crowd. I suspected the bump in traffic had everything to do with

53

the murder and nothing to do with it being Friday, but it wouldn't hurt us to stick around a little longer and see what happened. So, unless Lucy was Virgil's killer, she probably didn't have much to do with the rush.

"Oh goodie!" she said as she hugged me. I was caught off guard by her enthusiasm, but glad she was pleased. "You won't regret it, I promise. And I bet you'll enjoy it so much that you'll change your mind again and want to come back next week, too."

I nodded agreeably but didn't say anything for fear she'd take it as further commitment.

As I made my way back to the temporary stalls, the hairs on the back of my neck rose and rippled. I stopped and turned around, looking for whoever was watching me. The area was so crowded that it was impossible to pinpoint a specific voyeur. Perhaps my instincts were off.

"Hey," a voice called from somewhere to my left. For some reason, I knew the call was for me.

I turned to see the corn-dog vendor leaning out the front window of his small, closetlike trailer. "Your name's Becca, right?" he said. My mother would have described him as a "nice-looking young man." He might have been thirty, but probably not quite. His curly brown hair was shaggy, but he was clean shaven and his smile was the youngest thing about him.

"Yes."

"Cool. I'm Jerry Walton. I was talking to Scott, and he said you liked to play poker."

I laughed. I hadn't played poker in years, but it was something that Scott and I had enjoyed together. "I suppose."

"We got a game together for tomorrow night. You up for it?"

"Me?"

"Yeah. Scott will be there. He told me to talk to you, but I think you might be a ringer. We only bet with licorice and peanuts. It's more for fun than anything else."

I laughed again. A poker game on a Saturday night didn't exactly fit with my current lifestyle. I knew Ian and I were going to try to spend some time together this weekend, but we'd talked about Sunday night or Monday, and as with all our other recent plans for spending time together, we hadn't been specific about details. I had no desire to hang out with Scott, but there was something appealing about the unpredictability of it all. I thought I might regret it later, but I said, "Sure. What time?"

"Awesome. We'll play under that pavilion over there. Fair shuts down at ten, game starts at five after or thereabouts."

I had an urge to retract my knee-jerk-like acquiescence, but I held back. What would it hurt to join in a poker game on a Saturday night?

I waved farewell to Jerry and veered to Scott's shooting gallery.

It was booming — actually, the "guns" made more of a popping sound than a boom. The booth was wide, easily accommodating the five rifles tethered to the front area by cords. Metallic critters on a chain mechanism provided the targets as they rolled across a painted backdrop, popping up as they passed and falling down with the ding of a bell when the laser dot from one of the rifles hit them. I found it all a bit gruesome — not that it was bloody or anything, but the whole idea of shooting at bunnies, squirrels, and foxes did not appeal to me. Every gun had a shooter, though, so what did I know?

I was surprised to see that Scott wasn't manning the booth. Instead, a seemingly uninterested teenager sat on a stool to one side of the activities. He went through the motions of taking money and handing out small prizes, but I could tell he'd rather not be there.

"Where's Scott?" I asked him when he

had a brief break.

"Doing something with the Ferris wheel," he said without looking at me.

"Really?"

"Uh-huh."

I knew Scott enjoyed tinkering with mechanical things, but the Ferris wheel? He often said that a motor was just a motor. They had some differences, but for the most part they all worked the same way. Without bothering to tell the teenager good-bye, I turned away and went to find Scott.

It didn't take long. He was crouched down, most of his body hidden behind the open door of the case that covered the Ferris wheel's motor. I saw only the bottoms of his shoes.

"Scott?" I said as I stepped over the rope someone had put up to indicate the ride was closed.

"Hey, Becca," he said as he peered out.

"Did you offer to do that, or did they ask you?"

"I offered. I didn't promise I could make it work any better, but I thought I could at least take a look at it. It wasn't working quite right, you could just tell by listening to it."

"What do you think? Can you fix it?"

"Maybe. It hasn't been well taken care of.

If someone had just done some regular maintenance, it might still work smoothly. I doubt they'll power it back up, but maybe I can guide them on how to care for it until next year's fair."

"That's pretty considerate of you," I said.

Scott shrugged. "Nah, when you have my talent, you can't keep it to yourself." He laughed.

"So, are you staying? With the big jump in attendance — are you sticking around?"

"Yeah," he said, his head back in the motor case. "There's enough business to make it worth my while, though I can't say I don't feel a little guilty about it. Profiting from someone's death is wrong and not my style, but I'm trying not to look at it that way."

"What way are you trying to look at it?"

"A coincidence. I'm hoping that business would have picked up anyway. Maybe. Why not?"

"Got it."

We were silent a moment as he worked and I thought about what else to say.

Scott leaned back again, still on his knees, but pulling himself into full view, and looked at me. "How's your family, Becca? Your parents, sister, everyone?"

"Good. My parents are in Monson for a while, though you never know when the road trip bug will hit them again. Allison, Tom, and Mathis are great, too. Everyone is healthy and fine."

"That's good news." He hesitated a moment. "Is it weird if I ask about your love life? Just curious, you know."

I laughed. "Only if I can ask you about yours."

"I'll go first." He put his hand on his chest. "I'm remarried."

"That's terrific," I said and I meant it. I was suddenly pleased he'd moved the conversation this direction. There was zero physical attraction between the two of us. Whatever we'd had together had been replaced by a platonic familiarity, and though not forgotten, locked away in one of the compartments labeled "Another Life." "Tell me about her."

"She's my — our age. She has a five-year-old son who has changed my life in so many great ways. Her name is Susan; his is Brady. They're in Florida right now visiting her family, but I hope you get to meet them someday."

"I do, too. I'm happy for you, Scott."

"Thanks. What about you?"

"Ah. Me. My love life is complicated at the moment. I'm sort of with someone named Ian, but I have my concerns about whether it will last. I seem to be doing everything I can to sabotage it."

Scott's eyebrows rose. "Really? That doesn't sound like you. I was the one to sabotage us — well, my immature behavior was. You were the levelheaded one. I can't see you sabotaging anything."

I decided he didn't need the details.

"I have a dog, a great dog. Her name is Hobbit," I said. "She's almost a golden retriever but with about three-quarter-sized legs." I'd acquired Hobbit from the same 7-Eleven parking lot where this Scott and I had last seen each other. As he'd driven away, a kid held up this small, long-footed puppy and asked if I wanted her. I had. It was one of the best decisions I'd ever made.

"You really wanted a dog. That's good."

"So, what do you think happened to Virgil?" I asked.

Scott looked up at the top chair. It rocked slightly, stirred by either a small breeze or some random vibrations. "Dunno. He wasn't all that friendly."

"My police officer friend, Sam, said he'd check into the tattoo and see if he could find out more about it."

"Really? That's pretty cool. You must be good friends." Scott's cell phone buzzed in his pocket. He pulled it out and looked at it. "It's Susan. Give me a minute." He stepped over the rope and walked to an area behind the Ferris wheel where a few trees provided some privacy, if not total peace and quiet.

Curiosity sent me toward the motor casing. I would have no idea what I was looking at, but not because Scott hadn't tried to educate me. To this day, whenever my truck started acting up, I would open the hood and just stare at its innards. It was habit, even if my eyes glazed at the sight.

This motor was just as confusing, though it did look smaller and perhaps simpler than the motor in my truck. I had no idea which of the parts did what, but all of it was most definitely dirty. Oil and soot filled the casing and covered the mechanisms, and it smelled dirty, too. Even though I wasn't sure what I was looking at, it was clear that Scott had been right: the motor hadn't been well taken care of.

As I scooted backward, I caught sight of something just outside the right wall of the casing. I peered around and saw a wallet sitting on the ground. I immediately knew it was Scott's. There was something familiar about the light brown leather and the way it was worn and curved slightly. It probably wasn't the same wallet he'd had when we were together, but it was the same style. I reached to grab it only so I could give it back to him, but my fingers accidentally grazed the wallet's outer edge and flipped it open, revealing inner pockets overly stuffed with credit cards. The dollar bills, if he had any, were probably behind the card pockets in a larger back space. I also noticed a small, folded yellow piece of paper — perhaps a large sticky note — had slid to the ground when the wallet opened.

I reached for the paper and was going to put it back into the middle of the wallet, close it, and take it to Scott, but something else got my attention. Written on the paper was the word "Virgil."

I didn't even think about the fact that I was invading Scott's privacy; I unfolded the paper to inspect it more closely.

It was exactly what I thought it was: a large yellow sticky note, the sticky part dirtied with small particles of dust and lint and no longer very sticky.

Written on the note, in handwriting that I would have recognized anywhere, were these words: "Virgil Morrison. Ferris wheel. One down!!!" The exclamation marks were heavy and bold, as if drawn in anger.

In the span of about a second, my mind tumbled over the millions of things the note could mean. The only thing for certain was that Virgil's name was part of it. Other than that, it was unfair to speculate. It could mean . . . well, lots of things. For the briefest of instants, for a miniscule passing of time, I did wonder if this note indicated that my second ex-husband, Scott Triplett, had been the person to kill Virgil Morrison. It was ridiculous to attach such a serious event to the simple words on the paper. It was paranoid and misplaced. Scott wasn't a killer. Well, the Scott I'd known wasn't a killer.

I re-folded the note, put it back where I found it, and closed the wallet. I grasped it just a little too tightly as I stood and turned.

Scott had just finished his call and was walking toward me again. The look on his face was difficult to interpret, but he seemed to be suddenly stressed about something.

"Here," I said too forcefully as I held out the wallet.

Scott's eyes widened as he patted his back pocket. "Holy . . . where was that?"

"Next to the motor."

"Dang, Becca. Thanks. I don't remember taking it out of my pocket. I'm not sure I would have even looked over there again today."

"No problem. Everything okay?"

He glanced at his phone. "Oh, sure, all's well."

"Good. Hey, I'm playing poker tomorrow night."

"That's good. I told Jerry he might get you to join us," Scott said distractedly. He looked at the wallet still in his hand and then up at the top seat of the Ferris wheel. I followed his gaze. The seat was still swinging gently, perhaps because of a nudge from Virgil's ghost. "Excuse me, Becca, but I have to go. I have something I need to take care of."

"Sure. See you tomorrow?"

"Yeah, yeah. See ya." Scott closed the door to the motor casing and then hurried purposefully away.

I hesitated only long enough to give him a head start — I didn't want him to notice I was following him. But even if he caught me, I wouldn't have to come up with a creative excuse. I could be going anywhere. If he left the premises, I'd probably have to give up the chase, but on the fairgrounds every place was a possible destination.

Scott didn't look back once as he hurried through the still-expanding crowd — the influx that had begun earlier in the day had not yet abated. He didn't acknowledge anyone; he just kept moving purposefully and quickly toward the front of the fair-grounds.

"Shoot," I said. His leaving seemed like a real possibility. There was no way I could hop into my truck and follow him.

Fortunately, I didn't need to worry. He stopped at the front trailer. He wiped his hand on his thigh before looking around and then knocking on the door. A couple seconds later, the door opened and Lucy stuck her head through the opening. She furrowed her brow at the sight of Scott, glanced behind him, and then opened the door further.

She stepped back, and he disappeared inside the trailer.

I stopped and thought about what I'd just seen — nothing really, but it still seemed . . . funny . . . off.

I suddenly wanted to know much more about my second ex-husband than I ever thought I would.

FOUR

My first idea was to pretend to confirm with Lucy that we, the Bailey's vendors, would definitely return to the fair on Saturday. She might think it strange that I was confirming so soon after initially telling her, but I didn't care. I also didn't care if Scott thought I'd seen him enter the trailer. I boldly stepped up the two attached metal stairs and knocked on the somewhat flimsy door.

And no one answered. Less than a minute had passed since Scott stood in this very same spot.

I knocked again, rattling the door even more. Again, no answer. I tried turning the handle, but it was locked. It wouldn't take too much to break the mechanism, but I wasn't that desperate. Yet.

I stepped off the small platform and pondered just why Lucy and Scott weren't answering the door. My mind couldn't conjure anything that wasn't salacious or illegal.

"Calm down," I said quietly to myself. "You don't know anything. It's no use making wild guesses. Just talk to Scott later."

I peered out across the fairgrounds and caught sight of Jerry, the corn-dog vendor, who seemed to be in the middle of a quiet moment. I hurried to his trailer and asked for a pen and piece of paper.

"I've got sticky notes," he said. "Will that do?"

"Of course," I said after a beat.

He looked at me funny. Perhaps he'd heard the suspicion in my tone.

" 'K." He handed me a pen and a square blue notepad. "What? You look disappointed."

I forced a laugh. "Sorry. Yellow's my favorite color. I was hoping . . ."

"Yellow's too girly." He smiled quizzically.

Fortunately for both of us, a young boy with a handful of wadded-up money walked up to the trailer. He looked longingly at the picture of the corn dog on the outside wall and said, "One please."

His dad wasn't far behind and greeted my smile with a quick one of his own.

I wrote to Lucy that we'd *for sure* be back tomorrow and asked her to give me a call when she got the note. I gave the pad and pen back to Jerry and hurried to the trailer. I knocked again but received the same non-response, so I stuck the note to the small glass window — a window I couldn't see through because of tightly shut mini blinds — and hurried back to the Bailey's booths.

The drive home to Monson cleared my confused mind. By the time Stella and I pulled into Bailey's and she took off in her own truck, I decided that there must be nothing, or close to nothing, to the note I found in Scott's wallet or his disappearance into the trailer. They probably weren't even connected in any way.

They couldn't be.

Scott wasn't a killer. He didn't have a violent bone in his body. And he wasn't a cheater either. Neither of us had betrayed the other when we were married. Sure, he'd found a new girlfriend about thirty seconds after I told him I wanted a divorce, but I didn't know who she was, and by that point in our relationship I didn't care.

The cushion of distance from Orderville, Virgil's murder, the corn maze, and the fair seemed to lessen my "need to know" at least a little. I'd figure it out tomorrow. For now, I had a dog waiting for me, plants to attend to, and hopefully a sort-of boyfriend to call.

Since neither Stella nor I had taken enough inventory to last until the fair shut down at ten o'clock, I was home by four. I decided Hobbit and I would visit Ian. Though he and I hadn't spent a lot of quality time together lately, something about talking to Sam today made me want to make seeing him a priority. A sense of needing a stronger resolution to my confused love life had been niggling at me all day; seeing Ian would surely help.

As I drove down the state highway toward home, I called Ian but had to leave a message. This probably meant that one farm machine or another was too loud for him to hear the phone. Between crafting metal yard art and cultivating his lavender farm, he was usually polishing or cutting, or tilling or leveling, and all those activities were noisy.

My short-legged, long-footed best friend greeted me happily as I pulled the truck onto my long gravel driveway. Since finding a body in my kitchen a few months earlier, I'd been hesitant to allow Hobbit to stay home alone, but the killer was safely behind bars and we'd never had any issues before that unsavory incident. No matter the strain between us, Ian always offered to keep Hobbit with him, and his landlord, George, always welcomed her, too, but she'd missed home and her porch whenever I'd taken them up on their invitations. She'd been happy to fall back into a seminormal routine that included her pillow on her porch.

I'd practiced the doggy door with her a number of times. I hoped she understood our long talks and my instructions that she should never play heroine, that she should run and hide if someone else murderous or just a plain old stranger showed up at the house. I was worried about the teenagers Lucy was sending out to help harvest the pumpkins for the maze-opening festivities. Either I or someone else Hobbit knew would have to be there to introduce Hobbit to them.

As I scratched her neck, I glanced around the property. The converted barn that housed my kitchen was locked tight. My dad and Ian had fixed the lock that had been broken in the aforementioned "incident," replaced the main dead bolt, and attached an extra padlock to the outside. My crops, though mostly done for the year, looked fine, ready for the final pumpkin harvest. The ranch-style house appeared normal and untouched, too.

"Good day?" I asked Hobbit.

She nudged my hand with her nose. I wasn't scratching hard enough.

After we checked inside and found nothing needing attention, we hurried back outside into the South Carolina late afternoon. There was neither a better time nor a better place to be. I spent so much of my life outdoors that I was continually aware of the temperature, and I very much welcomed the transition from the stifling heat of the summer to the current autumnal perfection.

I took Hobbit for a run up the slope of land behind and to the side of the house and then around the back of the crops and down around to the side of the barn. After a few laps, we both drank hefty gulps of water.

The pumpkins were ready to harvest and would be perfect for the decorating contest. My strawberry crop had been great again this year, but I wanted an even larger yield; though the plants were self-propagating, I would still have to add seedlings in the spring. I'd need to prevent any strawberries from growing on those new plants the first year to hopefully boost the size and sweetness of the subsequent crops' fruit. I'd have to keep them separated from the established crop and snip off any buds before they matured into fruit. I'd already tilled and nourished a plot of land in preparation; come spring, the ground would be ready for the strawberries.

I had no pressing chores at the moment, but I could always find something to do, so I dug, tilled, trimmed a little, and pulled any weed that dared show its unwelcome head. I actually whistled while I worked. Hobbit reclined outside the edge of the plants, her ears perking at my happiness.

"Sorry, girl, can't help myself," I said.

She panted.

My head was clear by the time I was done, but Ian still hadn't returned my call.

I hadn't planned on it, but it looked like I had time to work on my latest fruity creation, a concoction that had risen from pure disaster.

Syrup was an unintended result even an expert fruit canner/preserver could end up with if they mistakenly boiled their fruit for too long — maybe a phone call interrupted operations, or maybe they got caught in a conversation with the mailman who they hadn't seen in ages and who wanted to visit for a minute or two.

Let's just say that it hadn't been my intention to make a batch of boysenberry syrup, but both a phone call and a chat with the mailman had turned my preserves into a runny, sticky mess that just happened to taste pretty good on pancakes and waffles. I had tried the recipe again, overboiling on purpose and adding some sugar and lemon juice, and ended up with a new product line. My grape syrup had been selling like . . . well, like hotcakes at Bailey's. In fact, the five Maytabee's Coffee Shops that were selling my jams and preserves had started requesting the syrups, too. I hadn't included them with the items I took to the fair, but I thought I might add a few jars to tomorrow's inventory.

I'd purchased some of the most beautiful apricots I'd ever seen or tasted from a fellow market vendor, and I had a healthy supply of apricot syrup that I'd made the previous week. I packed twenty jars of it along with lots of jars of jams and preserves. For the first time since the fair began I was concerned about not having enough inventory.

By the time everything was packed it was seven. Ian still hadn't returned my call, but it wouldn't take long or much gas to check the usual places, and I was becoming increasingly curious about what he was up to.

After a quick shower, I locked up the house, loaded Hobbit into the truck, and set off. Just as I pulled onto the state highway that led to Monson, my cell phone buzzed.

I answered with, "Good timing."

"Hey, Bec. Sorry, it's been crazy. Where are you?" Ian said.

"On my way to find you," I said.

"I'll make it easy. I'm at the farm."

"Hobbit and I are on the way. Should I pick up food?"

"That'd be great. I'm starving."

Just as I was going to ask if he wanted pizza or Chinese, I heard another voice in the background.

"Thanks, Ian. See you later." It was a female voice. One that sounded familiar but not enough that I could immediately identify who it was attached to.

"Oops. You with a client?" I said.

"No. No, just someone who stopped by to talk about lavender."

"Oh."

I wasn't the jealous type, never had been, but something about the tone of her voice — and his — piqued my curiosity; shoot, more than piqued it, punched it hard to full attention. I wanted to know who she was, but I didn't want to show my insecurity by asking. Fortunately, Ian jumped in to save me from further personal torture.

"Uh, that was Betsy. She's looking at some different recipes for Bistro. Recipes that use lavender." The way he said it, as though he was hiding something, knocked me off kilter.

I'd met Betsy only recently. It had been her boss that I'd found dead in my barn. The resulting events led to Betsy and me kind of becoming friends, or at least becoming friendly. Ian and I had gone to Bistro, the restaurant that Betsy now owned, a couple times. I'd noticed her talking to Ian with what seemed like avid interest, but I hadn't thought much of it. Ian was good-looking in that exotic artistic way. He was also intelligent and thoughtful. He was hard to resist. I couldn't blame Betsy for a little flirting.

"Oh," I said. "Too bad I'll miss her. So, Chinese or pizza?" I asked.

"Pizza sounds perfect. See you in a bit?"

"You got it."

I stopped at the small pizza parlor in town. It was a carryout place only, so once I ordered, I sat on a bench and told myself not to stew over Betsy being at Ian's. There was no reason to be bothered. The pizza took a long ten minutes, and then Hobbit and I were on our way again.

Wondering about Betsy's visit to Ian's farm somehow caused me to once again replay "the kiss" in my mind. In a moment that, unfortunately, I couldn't define as "weak," I'd kissed Sam Brion. He'd kissed back but only with his lips. He'd kept his hands to himself. I'd decided the kiss had been the culmination of a number of experiences Sam and I had shared. We'd been in some pretty hairy situations, literally life-and-death moments. We'd become close because of those moments and my continual efforts to throw myself into the middle of murder investigations.

Unbeknownst to me, my father had witnessed the kiss. Even in my midthirties, I'd needed his prompting to remember that I had to face everything with honesty. He, as usual, had been right.

So I'd told Ian about the kiss, but his reaction had caught me off guard even more than my own behavior had. He hadn't been happy. He'd been hurt, and a dark anger had clouded his eyes but it had dissipated quickly. Ultimately he'd been pleased that I'd 'fessed up. He'd said that he wasn't surprised that Sam and I had become close because of what we'd been through together, that having those sorts of feelings was only natural, but he'd also been very firm that he wanted me to make a decision regarding how I felt about him. I'd tried to be as honest as I possibly could. I'd told him I was still crazy about him but didn't want to lose my friendship with Sam.

He'd laughed a strained laugh, and said, "You know, I like Sam, too. I'd like for us to remain friends. Maybe we'll just have to see what happens next. If you get the urge to kiss Sam, though, I think you should probably talk to me about it first. I think that'll be a sign that something else is happening, something more than just a close friendship. Just promise me that you'll do that."

I'd promised him. And since then, I felt like we were all still in limbo, waiting for something to nudge us all in the right direction. Probably waiting for me. This sense of being at loose ends only affirmed my frequent thought that I didn't deserve either of them.

And then my chance meeting with Sam this morning had made me realize a few things: (1) I was happy to reconnect with him, (2) I wanted us all to get along, and (3) I really thought that since I was in my midthirties and I had been married twice, I should probably know how to better handle the entire situation.

Ultimately, I hoped it came down to everyone just wanting everyone else to be happy. Allison had set me straight on that confusion, though. She'd informed me that while I might be spending my time being wishy-washy and trying to figure out my own feelings, neither Sam nor Ian truly wished the other happiness if that happiness depended on me being in the other's life. She said that though they might be behaving like mature adults, neither of them probably wanted to, and at some point one or both of them might give in to the frustration that I was one hundred percent responsible for causing. She warned me that an ugly scene could be in my future.

I felt bad. And even more confused.

I sighed, and Hobbit whined as she put a paw on my leg. She was sympathetic, but I thought her patience might be wearing thin, too. Soon, even she would start rolling her eyes at me.

Ian had purchased several acres coincidentally located only a short distance down the road from my childhood home. He'd been preparing the soil, building the warehouse and living space, and obtaining permits for all sorts of things that I didn't know required permits. It had been mostly smooth going, but he'd run into a few surprises along the way. The previous owner, Bud Morris, hadn't ever connected his small shack into the available underground plumbing system. No one had offered to make the system available to him, and he'd never asked for help. Instead, he'd used his own well for water, and built his own outhouse. These were decisions he'd made without consulting county building officials, and said officials hadn't been happy to find that they'd been remiss in catching Bud's jerry-rigged and illegal system. It had finally taken a field trip by a county manager to Ian's farm to prove that Ian would, indeed, need some plumbing assistance. The underground system would need to be made available. Unfortunately, that entire process took numerous phone calls and more weeks than it should have to complete.

Through all the hassle and hard work, Ian had managed to continue to create his amazing yard sculptures, though he was making fewer than he used to.

Every time I passed the small white house I grew up in, I felt a tinge of nostalgia, but that tinge dimmed a bit each time I saw the current residents. This evening, the mother of the family was out on the front lawn with her two small girls. Though the scene brought to mind memories from my childhood of me with my own mom and sister, there was no doubt that the house clearly belonged to the new family, not to those old memories.

As I parked the truck in front of Ian's farm, I marveled at how much he had accomplished over the last few weeks. The dim sunset light was augmented by two tall poles to which Ian had attached huge clip-on lights. The newly built structure that would house his warehouse and retail and living space now had walls and windows. Only a few weeks earlier the frame had merely hinted at the future possibilities.

Hobbit peered out the car window and barked. Once I opened the door, she leapt out and hurried to Ian. They greeted each other with mutual enthusiasm.

"She hasn't seen you for what, a week?" I said as I carried the large pizza box toward a worktable and chairs. They were covered with sawdust, but we'd previously decided that adding sawdust to meals was just another way to get some extra fiber.

Ian smiled. "I've missed her, too. Both of you." He leaned over my slobbering dog, took the pizza, placed it on the table, and then kissed me — a quick light kiss. "You doing okay? I heard about the murder at the fair."

"I'm fine. Creeped out but fine. This time, at least, I didn't see the body."

"That's good. Do the authorities know what happened?"

"Not yet, I don't think. Hopefully soon." I thought about sharing with Ian what I'd found in Scott's wallet and his disappearing-into-the-trailer act, but I wasn't ready to sound suspicious of Scott. There was something else I wanted to talk about first anyway.

"So," I said, "Betsy was here?"

Ian smiled. "I suppose we should talk about that."

"Really? Why?"

"We made a promise to be honest with each other, right?"

"Right."

"I should probably tell you about Betsy's visit. I didn't kiss her or anything, though, so no worries there."

I suspected my hollowed-out gut was close to what Ian had felt when I told him I needed to tell him something about Sam and me. It wasn't fun, but I sensed that whatever he was going to say was real and not simply payback for my own indiscretion.

I sat down and smiled weakly. "Should we talk over dinner?"

As we ate, we watched Hobbit chase moths and discussed what had happened between Ian and Betsy.

And I didn't like it one bit.

Apparently, Betsy had called Ian twice to ask him out. He'd declined both times, telling her that he and I were still a couple. Betsy had insisted that the real couple was Sam and me, that she'd seen it and knew it was bound to happen. She'd told Ian he would be wise to face the truth now and move on before he got too hurt.

I had no idea Betsy had been paying attention to the dynamics between Ian and me and Sam and me or that the dynamics were so obvious to someone who was mostly an outsider. I didn't recall that Betsy had been around the three of us very often and I knew she didn't know Sam well. The whole idea of her having "observations" made me deeply uncomfortable.

Ian was ten years my junior, but he was wise in ways beyond both our years. He was like the math he was so good at: logical and consistent. Two plus two always equaled four. He was the voice of reason when I wasn't, and I wasn't, plenty.

Betsy had visited today under the pretext of discussing lavender, but Ian's first batch wasn't going to be available anytime in the near future; it would be at least a year, maybe two, before he had a viable crop.

Betsy hadn't called first but had driven from Smithfield and found Ian working on the warehouse. Once they'd established that it was premature at best to discuss Ian supplying Bistro with culinary lavender, Betsy shared an idea she'd had with him. She'd said, "I have a plan. I will host a dinner for you and Becca and Sam. We can talk this out like adults."

"What did you say?" I asked as I swallowed the chunk of now-tasteless pizza.

"I told her that it wasn't going to happen. I told her that whatever happened between you and me was between you and me. We weren't going to have dinner and decide who would be best with whom."

"Good answer."

"When I pointed that out to her, she did realize that her plan was poorly thought through, and she apologized for mentioning it."

We looked at each other.

I finally said, "Do you . . . what, like her? Are you attracted to her?"

Ian laughed. "Becca, whatever romantic feelings I have, they're for you. Now, I admit, I'm not sure if both of our feelings are strong enough to keep us together. But I promise you, I haven't had one romantic thought about another woman since we've been together."

"I so don't deserve you."

"I disagree. I just think you are who you are, that's all. You've always had some difficulty in the romance department. I feel fortunate that we're together, even if we don't last forever. I think we've been good for each other."

"I so don't deserve you. Again."

Ian looked at me, his dark eyes twinkling with the bright light atop one of the poles. "You know the best part is our friendship. No matter what, and I know people say this crap all the time, but I don't ever want us not to be friends."

It was pointless to repeat again how much I didn't deserve him.

"Guess who's at the creepiest fair I've ever attended or been a part of?" I said, hoping to change the subject to something lighter.

"Who?"

The rest of the evening was one of the best Ian and I had spent together in a long time. There was a noticeable difference in our relationship; it wasn't good, it wasn't bad. It just was, my hippie parents would say. "Was" or "is" is always better than something forced or phony.

I told Ian about the dubious rides, the corn maze that scared me, and the silly talk of gypsy magic. I told him about Scott, the note in the wallet, and the disappearing act into the trailer. I was surprised when he didn't tell me I might be overreacting. He thought the gypsy magic was far-fetched, but he didn't think I was off base wondering if Scott might be up to something suspicious.

"There's been something strange about the fair the whole time," he said. "No business, and now suddenly lots of business, business that might have picked up because someone was killed. And then there's the fact that Scott found the body. I kind of wish you hadn't committed yourself to going back. In fact, I don't think it would be a bad idea not to go back, no matter what you told them. I'm actually surprised it wasn't shut down, by the fair operators or the authorities. Strange."

I thought about that a long minute. It was more than just me. Stella, Henry, and Brenton were also involved. I supposed I could call them all and discuss the need or their real desire to return to the fair.

"Tomorrow's Saturday. We'll see how it goes, and I'll talk to everyone else. We'll decide what's best. We won't be there when there isn't a bunch of other people around. Remember when Matt Simonsen was killed at Bailey's?"

"Yes."

"We didn't shut down any longer than it took to gather evidence."

"True." He thought a moment. "You want me to come with you tomorrow?"

For a second, I almost said yes, but I knew that his taking a day off from work would put him way behind. I knew Saturday was one of his busiest days because he always tried to spend a good amount of time at Bailey's in his yard sculpture tent.

"I'd love the company, but I've got it under control."

All in all, the evening Hobbit and I spent with Ian was perfect, but when she and I went home, the noticeable difference was more noticeable than ever.

Our kiss good night wasn't as full of passion as it was friendliness.

Not that that was all bad. It just was.

FIVE

"Oh my stars above," Stella said as she peered around her tent wall and into my stall. "What in the world is going on here?" She fanned her face. It wasn't too hot, but we'd been working so hard, she was flushed.

The four of us from Bailey's as well as the rest of the fair had been busier than any of the busiest days at Bailey's. Stella and I had driven separately but had rolled our product in together on matching red wagons. We'd had to start taking care of customers even before we could get everything unloaded and put on display.

"I didn't think there were this many people living in South Carolina, let alone in Swayton County. Where did they all come from?" I asked.

The mysterious and bizarre death of Virgil Morrison had hit every single South Carolina news outlet. In fact, the strange occurrence had even made the national news.

Suddenly, little Swayton County was on the tip of everyone's tongue, and they all wanted to see the amazing Ferris wheel that had — how did one of the radio stations phrase it this morning? — "magically come to life, picked up its operator, and taken him on his final ride. Perhaps the legends of Orderville gypsy magic were true." Yes, it had been that gory.

The gathering around the shut-down Ferris wheel was big and disturbing. A throng of people stood underneath the ride staring up as their cotton candy or the powdered sugar from their funnel cakes blew in the breeze. Every time I stood on my tiptoes and looked in that direction, I had to tell myself to quit imagining foreboding dark clouds. In fact, the sky was clear and bright blue, not a cloud, dark or otherwise, in sight.

I didn't know specifically what everyone was looking at, but I was just as guilty of searching for . . . something. Maybe if we stared long enough, we'd understand how what happened could possibly have happened. How did someone manage to be killed on the machine that was under his own control? Maybe if we waited patiently, the Ferris wheel would finally speak and tell us its secrets.

Henry, Brenton, Stella, and I had brought

plenty of product. The most intuitive of us, Brenton, brought three times his normal busy Bailey's day amount. He proved to be the smartest. Even though we all still had some goods left to sell, it was only mid-morning. If the pace continued, everyone but Brenton would be sold out by noon.

"Bailey's is getting lots of notice, too. This will be good for all of the vendors," Henry said as he peeked around his tent wall. He'd been much more exuberant and outgoing this morning. Being busy got everyone's blood pumping, but it seemed to boost Henry even more than the rest of us.

We all had card signs on our display tables that announced we were from Bailey's Farmers' Market in Monson. I wasn't sure how much the fair customers were really paying attention, but if we got only a few new shoppers, I guessed it would be a good thing for the market.

"Allison will be pleased," I said weakly. She would be, but mostly because we'd stuck it out. Even though she'd agreed that we didn't need to harm our businesses by staying somewhere that wasn't producing sales, she was very into sticking with commitments, even if a murder had occurred. Hopefully, everyone would end up better off.

I didn't know whether she'd been watching my booth or just happened to get lucky, but at the one moment that there was a slight lull in business, Lucy swooped in and landed right in front of my table.

"Hi, Becca. I got your note last night and tried to call but the number wasn't yours. You must have written down the wrong one."

"Really?" I had been a little rattled, but I was surprised to hear I'd written down a wrong number.

"Anyway," she continued, "isn't this business wonderful? I'm so pleased for all of us, but I really do hope you all will reconsider staying again. You can, of course, stick with the original plan of having Monday off." She laughed; she was plain giddy. "There's just one more week, and even if Tuesday, Wednesday, and Thursday are slow, which I don't think they will be, I'm sure next Friday will be just as busy as yesterday. You'll be here Wednesday anyway with the maze opening, and I just know that'll bring out even more people."

If this pace continued, I was going to have to buy some jars of Smucker's and sneak my labels on them, but I didn't say that out loud.

I sighed. "I promise we'll talk about it,

Lucy. But, I gotta know, why do you want us here so badly? These crowds have nothing to do with us."

Lucy cringed, but she recovered quickly and matched my sigh with one of her own. "I might as well tell you the real reason."

She paused long enough that I actually leaned closer to her in anticipation of the answer.

"Go ahead," I said.

"The owners" — she nodded toward the trailer, though it seemed an unconscious gesture — "are thinking of opening their own farmers' market. They want me to observe how you do things and try to monitor the response from the locals."

A part of me wanted to laugh, but another part of me thought the owners might be pretty astute. "But," I began, "having the four of us here doesn't give you much information."

"More than you might think. I've been able to see the way you set up your products. I've watched how you interact with your customers, which is different than the way we" — she waved to the goings-on behind her — "interact. We're much pushier than you are, and though that makes sense, it's been good to watch and learn."

I blinked. There was no reason to think

that whatever farmers' market the Swayton County event organizers put together would be viable competition for Bailey's, but I couldn't help but feel a tinge of betrayal and disloyalty regarding their motives. Lucy must have seen my misgivings in the scrunch of my forehead and the squint of my eyes.

"But you're benefitting, too, particularly these last two days. Right?" she said enthusiastically.

"Yes, we are and . . ." I was going to say that it was all fine because it truly was. There was just something uncomfortable about it, but not horribly so. "Yes, we are." I shook off any doubt. "And you know, Allison is very forthcoming with her knowledge. She's often asked about the organizational aspects of running a farmers' market, and she shares willingly. You could ask her anything."

"Really?" Lucy said.

"Yes, really. She's wonderful that way."

"That's great to know. I will most definitely put together a list of questions and call her," Lucy said before moving to make room for another customer.

I was far too busy to spend any time really thinking about what she'd said, but I did spend a minute or two worrying that the time I and my fellow market vendors spent at the fair might end up being a big waste for everyone no matter how much we sold. The expense of transporting our goods here and the days away from our stalls and regular customers needed to be accounted for. Lucy or anyone could have simply asked Allison for advice. Anyone could visit any market anywhere — in fact, the more the merrier — and observe how we operated. It wasn't a difficult business model to understand. But I thought that maybe, just maybe, Lucy had a point about observing the reaction the locals had to such a setup.

I suspected they were mostly just like everyone else though; a large chunk of the population liked to buy local, fresh products. It was the nature of the beast, and even though "organic" was the "in" thing at the moment, there had always been people who wanted organic and homegrown, and there always would be.

Of course if one of us was the killer, then plenty of harm *had* been done. Until that second I hadn't given one moment's thought to the killer potentially being a fellow vendor. For some reason and even with my now vast amount of experience with murder, I would never consider a vendor or close friend a murderer. I'd made this sort of mistake in the past; maybe I should learn to be more suspicious.

As I finished counting out some change, I leaned forward and looked at Henry in the stall to my left. I had only recently met him, but I knew he was an expert at growing squash, and I'd learned just the day before that he had once been a mechanic and worked with Scott. That was all I knew. Even working next to him for a week hadn't given me much insight into his character, and I knew nothing of his personal life. I made a mental note to ask Scott for more details about him.

Stella was to my right and busy with a line of three customers. If Stella was a killer, then reality as I'd always accepted it would change forever. She was one of the most devoted mothers, wives, bakers, and market vendors I knew. And basically, with all that going on, she was just too darn busy to kill anyone. I discounted her entirely. If I was ever proven wrong, I'd have to conclude that every decision I'd ever made had been somehow misinformed and off track. Then again, I had been married twice. And I was currently doing almost everything I could to make sure I never had a healthy relationship again.

But still, no, Stella wasn't a killer.

My last cohort, Brenton, was holding a miniature Yorkie that had been thrust upon him. Holding, petting, and admiring dogs came with the job. It was a good thing he enjoyed them so much. He often mentioned that his customers assumed that because he made dog treats, he was capable of judging the lovability of all canine creatures. When he said he thought they were all wonderful, he wasn't lying or laying on a sales pitch. He truly loved dogs; it was that love that prompted him to create the healthy, nutritious treats in the first place.

That was almost all I knew about him. I'd heard about a years-earlier divorce, but I had no idea if he had a girlfriend, a boyfriend, or whatever. He never talked about his love life, and I didn't remember ever seeing him with someone who might be considered a significant other. Of course, that didn't mean a significant other didn't exist.

But Brenton wasn't a killer either, I was sure.

The only fair worker I really knew anything about was Scott, and he seemed an unlikely suspect, too, no matter what the note had said or the way he'd behaved. Scott was too . . . Scott-like to be a killer. He had a good heart and a sometimes tiring tendency toward "life of the party" antics. I'd never once seen him be mean. Even when our divorce was in full swing, I hadn't witnessed much pain or anger. He'd been sad, but never despondent.

Because of his recent suspicious behavior, I wasn't ready to give him the pass I gave Stella and Brenton, but I really didn't think he was a killer. I hoped not.

I didn't have a real sense about any of the other fair workers, but from what I could tell everyone else was just working hard to do a job that took a lot of hours and a lot of energy.

Besides, the murder took place either late at night or early in the morning. The killer could be someone who had nothing to do with the fair.

I wished I'd talked to Virgil a little more. I wished I'd pushed for more information, like his marital status, was he a parent, did he have pets? But I had tried, I'd tried to get to know him, make him interested in getting to know me. His guarded behavior might have had something to do with why he was killed, though that was such an ambiguous clue.

I had a sudden impulse to call Sam and see what he knew, if he'd learned anything more about the murder, or just about the spider tattoo, but although we'd reconnected, I didn't feel right about following through on the idea. I sensed our amiable meeting hadn't taken us as far as casual phone calls yet. If he stopped by the market, he would know that we'd decided to stay at the fair. I'd talk to him when I got back to Bailey's.

"Excuse me, hello, these for sale?"

I was pulled out of my thoughts, back into the moment, and discovered a nice-sized group of customers standing in front of my display table.

"Absolutely," I said. "How many would you like?"

Six

The entire morning was busy with eager customers, and we Bailey's vendors weren't able to discuss our future fair attendance plans until things slowed down when fairgoers became more interested in eating lunch than in buying our wares. We purchased our own corn dogs, fried Snickers bars, and roasted corn on the cob and finally found an available picnic table a little too close to the corn maze for my liking, but it was the only table available for us to gather.

"Well, I'm game to do anything. I give up, she's won." Stella laughed. "We keep discussing this, and I think we should just commit and live with the results."

Stella wasn't the only one succumbing. We were all exhausted and our collective rebellion, weak though it had been, had lost steam. We hadn't really done anything different from what we usually did at the market, but our jobs somehow seemed more tiring amid the fair setting. I blamed all the fried food, but that wasn't going to stop me from enjoying lunch.

"Having Monday off will be a nice break," Brenton said. "I can get my Internet orders packed and mailed, bake some more biscuits, and be back Tuesday easily. But don't go by what works for me. Henry, what do you think?"

Henry shrugged. "I'm almost sold out today. I'm easy. Business has been good, it would be good at Bailey's. Someone else choose."

"You know, we don't have to do this as a group. It would be great if we all agreed to be here or not, but if someone doesn't want to, it doesn't mean we all have to make the same choice," I said. "I'll be here." I would have to figure out how to come up with the inventory, but I could do it.

"Makes sense. Count me in too," Brenton said.

"Me too." Henry shrugged again.

"I'll be here with bells on and bread baked," Stella said.

I was on the side of the picnic table that faced the corn maze. I didn't have the courage to sit with my back to it; if that had been the only option, I probably would have stood. The temperature wasn't really cool, but it didn't feel warm either because of a continual light breeze, which was made evident by the stalks' gentle dance to and fro. The motion did not make the corn maze more appealing. But it was the shadow I saw move through the stalk-lined, serpentine twists that downgraded my assessment from unappealing to absolutely off-limits.

I didn't realize I'd gasped.

"What, Becca?" Stella asked.

"I thought . . ." I looked around the table. "Never mind."

"No, what? I want to know," Henry said.

I laughed. "Nothing. I just thought I saw something moving through the maze."

"Some gypsy magic?" Henry gently elbowed me.

I swallowed hard but tried to hide it. "What do you know about gypsy magic?"

"Nothing, just what I keep hearing around here. People talking about the Ferris wheel and how it killed its operator. People are saying that odd, unexplainable stuff happens all the time around Orderville, but usually it's good stuff. I've heard them talk about their 'gypsy protector.' " Henry bit into his roasted corn.

Stella, Brenton, and I looked at each other. When he didn't continue, Stella said,

"Who's their gypsy protector? Do you know her name?"

"Oh," Henry said with a full mouth. He chewed, swallowed, and then wiped his napkin over his chin. "No, they won't say her name. It's weird and kind of funny, but she lived in the house that was on this property. That billboard is a picture of the house. Ask me, though, I think they made it look scary just to fit with all the woo-woo magic stuff they like to talk about."

I knew I had seen a dark shadow move through the maze, just a few feet inside the perimeter. Or, I *thought* I had. Given that I wasn't fond of corn mazes in the first place, maybe I hadn't really seen anything more than what my overly active imagination had conjured.

"I'll check it out if you want," Henry said.

"No, that's okay. I'm okay."

"You're spooked," Stella said as she turned and looked at the dried stalks of corn.

"Not really." I wanted to change the subject. "Hey, my inventory is so low that I don't have much to sell this afternoon. I'm going to stick around because I said I'd do something with Scott later, so I thought I'd check out the animals and ride some of the rides. Anyone game?" I still might decide to leave and return at ten for tonight's poker

101

game, but I was beginning to think that the fair, outside the corn maze, of course, could use a closer look. If someone wanted to join me, all the better.

"Not me. I'm headed home and putting my feet up once all my stuff is gone," Stella said.

"You want someone to hang out with?" Brenton asked, but I could hear hesitation in his voice. If he sold out, too, he'd probably rather go home.

"Nah, just wondering if anyone wanted to. When we weren't busy, I didn't take the opportunity to experience the whole fair. I wish I had."

"Sounds fun. I'm up for it," Henry said sincerely.

"Good," I said as I smiled at Brenton. He'd be free to leave without feeling like he'd abandoned me. I turned to Henry. "You ready for that roller coaster?" I nodded to my left.

"Not sure I'm brave enough, but if you are, I'll fake it and make you think I'm not scared."

I wasn't sure I was brave enough either to venture onto something that made the screeching, clunking, and grinding noises the coaster cars made as they rolled over the tracks, but I'd think about it.

102

After lunch, Stella and Brenton told Henry and me to go enjoy the fair's offerings. They went back to the tents, promising that they could handle selling whatever products we still had.

For our first stop, Henry and I ventured into one of the barns. It was full of smaller animals, like tiny goats and cuddly rabbits, as well as shrieking children who wanted to hold or pet something soft and cute.

My initial impression had been correct: the people who manned the barns made sure the animals weren't mistreated and the kids had a good time. This could not have been easy, but the fair workers' patience and observational skills balanced the loud and youthful exuberance bouncing off the barn walls. It took compassion and talent to know when it was time to gently move an animal back from hands that might not know how best to pet a tired or overly taxed creature, and these workers had all the right skills.

"You have any animals?" Henry asked me. We admired a rabbit with fur so long that I wondered if there was really a body underneath.

"I do, a dog. You?"

"My wife has a parrot, but it doesn't like me and would be offended if I claimed part ownership of it."

I laughed. I had no idea he was married with a parrot, or that he had a sense of humor; it was nice to see him loosening up.

"What does your wife do?"

"She's a nurse. We moved to the farm from Charleston. She was a supervisor in a big hospital there. She's now a nurse at the small emergency clinic on Main Street."

"That change of pace okay with her?" I said as I scratched between the ears of a snow white rabbit.

"She's getting used to it. I gave her fair warning when we got married. I knew I would eventually inherit my uncle's farm. We talked about selling it when that became a reality, but thought we'd give it a go first."

"I inherited my farm from my aunt and uncle, too."

"Was it in good shape when you got it?" Henry asked as he reached down to pet a black and gray goat that was desperate for his attention.

"Perfect."

"Nice. Ours, not so much. I think that's been the hardest thing on my wife, all the work we've had to do on the house and the fields. Squash is great, but in his old age, my uncle kept decreasing the size of his crops. He neglected much of the land, and there's a lot involved in getting it back to good production quality. And the house is as close to a disaster as you can get without it being officially condemned. I was doing some construction recently and we ended up not having running water for a week. As I tell Mandy, my wife, she must love me, because she didn't leave even then."

"Where's your farm?"

"Just southeast of Monson."

"That's opposite of where I live, but Allison and her family live out your way. If you or your wife need . . . well, anything, I'm sure she'd be fine with you stopping by."

"I know. That's how we met. Opening a stall at Bailey's hadn't even occurred to me, but Mandy met Allison when she was at the hardware store picking up some mousetraps — yeah, that's a whole other story — and Allison told her about the market."

We'd come upon two miniature horses or ponies, I wasn't sure which, who were bright-eyed and willing to investigate our outstretched hands.

"Hey, there," I said to one.

"Ouch," Henry said. "Got me."

"She's a biter. Sorry about that," said the man sitting on a stool next to the small corral. He was tall and thin with a sharp-angled face. He wore a straw hat and jeans and a long-sleeved button-down shirt with an emblem over the heart that said "Grover Acres." "She doesn't bite kids, but adults bug her, probably because they're so tall. I should have warned you, but she's been pretty good lately. Again, sorry."

"No problem. She didn't hurt, just got my attention," Henry said. And to prove it, he reached for her again. This time she let him pet her and scratch behind her ears. Henry looked at me. "See, you just have to show them who's boss."

"Yeah, I see." I smiled at his gentle touch. I bet the parrot only pretended not to like him.

Situated in between the first and the second barns were the butter sculpture displays. They were set up in refrigerated containers and were much more impressive than I would have predicted. Each sculpture was a few feet high and/or a few feet wide. There was a cow, a pig, a collie-type dog, a chicken, and a creature that was either a beaver or a possum — I thought it might have been accidentally left out in the heat too long, but since you never knew if the artist was close by, Henry and I just shared looks of perplexed wonder and didn't comment.

The second barn housed the large animals. One corral held some of the biggest and pinkest pigs I'd ever seen. We petted some very vocal cows. Inside the last corral on our right, I saw two beautiful brown horses.

One of the horses seemed to be minding his own business as he chomped on feed from a bucket, but the other horse, clearly agitated, yanked at his reins, which were being held by a woman I thought I'd seen selling cotton candy. Scott was next to the woman, and they looked like they were trying to have a conversation but the horse's behavior kept interrupting them. Something about Scott's and the woman's evident impatience made me want to know what they were discussing. I put my hand on Henry's arm. He, somehow understanding I was curious, played along. We both stood still and silent as we observed.

The woman was trying to be gentle with the horse, but the animal was obviously stronger than her petite though fairly wide frame could handle. Scott leaned down slightly to talk to her and began gesturing with his right hand to emphasize his point. I'd seen the maneuver often enough. When he was trying to be adamant, he'd speak with that hand, punctuating his words by chopping the air.

Mostly, the woman focused on the horse, but once or twice she looked back and up over her shoulder at Scott. Each time she craned her neck, her expression conveyed annoyance and maybe even bitterness.

After the second look, Scott started shaking his head. He put both hands into his jeans' pockets and seemed to suddenly become resigned to having lost the argument. I didn't have a chance to interpret more because he saw me and Henry, and pasted a smile on his face before he signaled us toward him.

"Hey, Becca, Henry," he said. "This is Dianna Kivitt. She runs a bar in Orderville, but she does a bunch of other work around here, too. Tell 'em what you do, Dianna."

She looked at him with the same disdain I'd seen her direct at him a few moments earlier, and then she turned it toward me and Henry.

"I make sure there's plenty of popcorn and caramel corn around here, and I try to take care of the horses if they need some attention." Dianna turned back to the animal, who had calmed as we approached, or was it that Scott and Dianna had calmed down, and the horse sensed their the mellowing mood? I wondered.

"It's working," I said as I nodded at the horse.

"Dianna's amazing," Scott said blandly. Then he reached for the cell phone on his belt and excused himself to take a call. I watched him hurry out of the barn and realized I was seeing vintage Scott. He was avoiding something: me, Henry, Dianna, the horse? I had no idea what it was, but I'd seen him do it in one way or another hundreds of times before.

"How well do you know Scott?" I asked Dianna.

She shrugged and continued to pet the horse's nose.

I glanced at Henry, who was somewhat amused.

"You know Scott from outside the fair?" I rephrased the question to Dianna.

"We all get real friendly around here real quick like. It's the best way to survive," Dianna said.

My mouth fell open, and I was suddenly at a loss. Her words were ominous and unexpected, and I had no real response. I looked at Henry again, who was no longer amused. His eyebrows had come together and his mouth was set in a firm line

"Excuse me. I got someplace I have to be, too," Dianna said. She stepped out of the corral and back from the horse, who was no longer in any distress. In fact, he blew out an exclamation through his nose, turned calmly, and joined the other horse in eating whatever was in the bucket. Either Dianna had truly had a soothing way with the animal, or he was relieved that she finally let go of him. She followed the same path Scott had taken, and left me and Henry with matching perplexed looks.

"That was weird, right? That wasn't just me thinking it was weird?" I said.

"No, that was pretty weird, but Scott, and pardon me for saying this because I know the two of you were married, but he's kind of strange."

"He is? I mean, I'm not insulted in the least, but I never noticed that he was strange. Childish, impulsive, goofy, and bad with money, yes, but strange? No, never."

"Well," Henry began as we started to make our way out of the barn, "I didn't work with him for long, but he was so secretive."

"He was? I can't imagine. The Scott I knew would tell you about the scar on his behind that he got from falling on some broken glass, and then he'd offer to show it to you if you really wanted to see it. There wasn't much that he kept to himself when he and I were together."

After the two barns, there was only one more large building to tour, so as we exited the second barn I meandered purposefully in that direction.

"Well, maybe it's his wife," Henry suggested as we walked. "I didn't work with Scott all that long, but when he went from unmarried to married, he seemed to quiet down — no, not quiet down, just get more silent, I guess. I'm not sure I'm explaining it right."

"He grew up?"

Henry hesitated. "I don't know. I probably shouldn't have said anything in the first place. I didn't know him well enough to tell you much of anything. Sorry, though, if I said something I shouldn't."

"You didn't. No worries at all. I haven't seen him for years. We didn't stay in touch. I'm kind of enjoying seeing him again, and the fact that we aren't married only adds to that enjoyment."

Henry laughed. "Well, that's honest, I guess."

"Oh, he's a good guy, very loyal. It was just for the best that we got divorced. For both of us. It wasn't one-sided. We both drove each other crazy, I'm sure."

"That happens," he said.

Just by his tone I could tell it hadn't happened in his marriage. Just the way he'd spoken about his wife earlier made me think they only drove each other crazy in good ways. I looked forward to meeting Mandy.

"Ready to look at the pies and quilts?" he asked as we reached the entrance to the Ribbon House.

"I am, but if you'd rather not, I understand."

"Actually, I want to, especially the baked goods. I make amazing pies. I thought about entering one of mine, but since we're working here, I figured I might not be allowed."

Thinking he might be teasing me, I smiled as I looked at him. But he wasn't joking. "What's your specialty?"

"Strawberry rhubarb. Seriously, I'm good."

"Let's go check out who your competition might have been."

I'd been to a few fairs in my day, assessed a few pies and quilts, but the entries on exhibit in the Ribbon House were some of the best I'd ever seen. The intricate and precise detail on the quilts was stunning. I didn't have the patience for such exacting work, but the beautiful entries gave me an urge to pick up a needle and thread and give it a try.

The pies were beautiful, too, though I would have enjoyed the experience much more if we'd been able to sample them as we walked through. I knew two expert pie bakers: my Bailey's stall neighbor, Linda, and Mamma Maria at the Smithfield Market. They could probably both win prizes in pie competitions, but I wondered if either of them could have bested the apple pie that was currently decorated with a super-sized first place blue ribbon.

Some people have a gift for baking pies with what I call "flawed perfection." Their pies look both perfect and home-made at the same time. Linda and Mamma Maria had that gift, but so did Beth Jenkins.

Beth just happened to be standing next to her pie when Henry and I stopped to drool.

"Hi, how y'all doin'? I'm Beth," she said with a big smile and exuberant handshakes for us both. Beth was short and round with dimples, bright green eyes, and a smile that could rival Julia Roberts's.

"Congratulations on the blue ribbon," I said.

"Oh, shoot, I'm just so honored. I can't tell you how many years I've been baking pies. This was the first year I tried my grandmother's old standby apple, and whadda ya know, I won." She laughed.

"It looks great," Henry said.

"Thank you kindly. I wish I could bring a bunch of them and give everyone a slice, but after the two I baked for the contest, my oven up and quit on me. I'm chalking it up to that old gypsy magic at work again. I must have been supposed to win with Grammie's pie so Je— I mean, so that old gypsy must have worked her magic to stop me from baking anything else."

"Gypsy magic, huh? You were about to say her name."

Beth blushed. "I know, I know, I should never utter it aloud unless I want the hex and vex."

"I'm not superstitious and I'm not from around here, but I've heard about the gypsy magic. Would you mind telling me her name?" I nodded in the direction of the billboard that beckoned from the maze outside.

Beth looked around and then leaned toward my ear. "I'm not superstitious either. It's just that everyone around here is, so I try to be sensitive to all that silliness. Her name was" — Beth looked around again before she continued — "Jena Bellings."

"Tell me about her," I said.

Proving either that gypsy magic was, indeed, at work, or that I had terrible timing, Beth's phone jingled.

"Oooh, sorry, gotta take this, y'all. Forgive." She hurried away as she answered the phone. She glanced back briefly before disappearing behind a navy blue curtain. She wasn't coming back while we were still there, that much I knew. She might have said she wasn't superstitious, but I suspected that she'd only shared Jena's name because she was the type of person who liked to share a secret.

"Well, now I suppose we know the gypsy's name, but I don't think it's done us any good. You ever heard of her?" Henry said.

"Jena? No."

"Makes you kind of want to say the name to everyone, doesn't it? See what they do."

"Kind of."

After a long, thoughtful, and disappointing perusal of the roller coaster, we both decided that we weren't up for riding any rides. I told Henry good-bye and then searched for Scott but couldn't find him. I had lots of hours before I had to be back for the poker game. I briefly considered going home to my kitchen. I would need more inventory than I had prepared. That's what I should have done, but another plan sprung to mind.

Though I kept telling myself I wasn't the

jealous type, I hopped in my truck with a destination in mind that proved I was, in fact, more jealous than I wanted to admit.

I glanced once more at the quiet Ferris wheel and saw the top chair rock just a little.

"Silly gypsy magic," I muttered to myself as I steered my truck out of the parking lot.

SEVEN

Smithfield was about an hour from the fairgrounds, but I had the time, a full tank of gas, and the desire to know what a certain restaurant operator was up to.

Bistro, Betsy's restaurant, was on the outskirts of Smithfield and located in a building that resembled a low-walled warehouse store except for a long green awning spanning the length of the front walkway.

The restaurant had been around a long time and had a reputation for great service and excellent food at affordable prices. Since Betsy's takeover following the previous owner's untimely demise in my kitchen, that reputation had only continued to improve.

She'd found her passion and it showed.

It was long after lunch and a little too early for the dinner shift to be in full swing, but I knew I'd find Betsy at the restaurant. She was there all the time, except, of course, when she was at Ian's, and I was increasingly curious about just how many visits she'd made to his place.

As I entered the building, I blinked to adjust from the bright sun outside to the dark interior. I'd never been in Bistro during the late-afternoon lull. Normally, the restaurant reverberated with the steady hum of customers, waitstaff, and the occasional crash of a dropped glass or two. But at the moment only a couple customers were seated in the restaurant, and they were in booths far enough from the entrance that they didn't even look over as I walked in.

Betsy stood at the front podium and looked up as though expecting to greet a customer. Her smiled dimmed when she saw it was me. She was disappointed.

"Becca," she said. "I thought I'd run into you soon, but not quite this soon."

"I had the time, thought I'd visit."

"I see. Well, I'm kind of busy right now."

"No, you're not."

I truly thought Betsy and I had become friends, but, of course, now I wondered. Friends typically didn't attempt to steal friends' boyfriends. I'd been bothered and jealous, but as Betsy tried to avoid a face-to-face, a wave of hurt and betrayal also tightened in my chest.

She held my gaze a long moment and, employing what I now knew was one of her signature mannerisms, softened her stern glance and then said, "No, I suppose now might be a good time to talk after all, but I'm not going to apologize."

"Okay," I said.

"Okay. Follow me."

I followed Betsy to a booth well out of earshot of the other customers.

"What can we get for you?"

"Coffee?"

Betsy called over what looked to be the lone waiter currently on shift and requested two coffees.

"Okay, I changed my mind again," she said after the waiter had left. "I guess I am going to apologize. I guess it was pretty rotten of me to go over to Ian's and tell him he should break up with you."

"Yeah, as rotten as calling him a couple times and doing the same sort of thing."

Betsy didn't seem surprised. "See, I'm right about him, he's a good honest guy. He told you all of it."

"He *is* a good honest guy," I said. "And since we haven't broken up, you should know that he's going to tell me everything." I didn't have a moment's hesitation about that conviction.

Betsy crinkled her mouth and then sighed out of her nose. "Look, Becca, I'm not all that awful. I'm not trying to break you and Ian up. That would be impossible to do. Only the two of you — or specifically you — will . . . hang on, I should say 'can' do that. You're crazy for someone else, and though he hasn't said it to me — I want to be clear about that — I know Ian can see it, too."

My heart fell, but I hoped my flushing face didn't give away the despair I felt. It wasn't that I actually thought I was "crazy" for someone else, it was the fact that Ian might *think* I was. I really didn't care what Betsy thought.

"But we haven't broken up, Betsy. Isn't there some sort of decency etiquette that says you don't ask out someone who you know is in a relationship?"

Our coffees appeared and Betsy took a sip of hers. "You don't believe all's fair in love and war?" She smiled.

"No, and I'm surprised you do."

"Here's the thing. I don't. I'm right there with you. I believe that no one should butt into anyone else's serious relationship."

"Then I don't get it. Why are you doing what you're doing?"

Betsy hesitated, but only briefly. "Let this

be your wake-up call. You don't look like you're in a serious relationship; you don't really act like it. That's the view from out here. I think the only reason Ian is putting up with you is because he thinks that whatever the two of you had at one time might come back, but I'm almost certain he knows it won't."

It was my turn to sip the coffee.

I didn't think Betsy knew about Sam and the attack kiss, so she was basing her conclusions on incomplete information. I wasn't going to fill in the details, but I suddenly realized that though I didn't appreciate her behavior, hated the way my stomach was now turning, she might have a pretty good point or two.

"Maybe we're just in a lull," I said.

"It's a pretty deep lull."

Ouch.

"Nevertheless . . ." I said.

"I get it and I hear you. I'll stay away from Ian until . . . well, I'll just stay away from Ian." She stood. "We done here?"

I took one more sip of the coffee. "I suppose."

She took one step away but then turned around and put her hand on my shoulder. "The part of this that is crazier than everything else is that the person you don't even seem to know you're pining over is great; he's wonderful, Becca. Now, it's the two of you, when, in the rare moments that I've seen you talk to each other, when I've seen you look at each other, that sets my moral code on track. I wouldn't even dream of trying to come between you and Sam, because, let's face it, I think that there's something there that's . . . forgive the dramatics, but there's something there that's rare."

Suddenly, I needed to get out of Bistro. I needed air, and I needed for Betsy not to see she'd shaken me.

"Thanks for the coffee." I stood and as casually as I could muster, walked out of the restaurant.

When I finally got outside, I gulped in lots of fresh air before I climbed into the truck.

That hadn't gone as planned.

Or had it?

I didn't think I'd had much of a plan, though something made me want to see Betsy and talk to her. I hadn't attacked her; in fact, I thought as I drove back toward the highway, I'd let her talk first.

I didn't want to give much credence to the idea that was forming in my mind, but I knew I needed to face it. Maybe I hadn't gone out there to show Betsy I was angry with her. Maybe I'd just gone out on an information-gathering mission. If that was the case, then perhaps I could mark that mission as unexpected but accomplished, and move on.

I shook my head and turned up the radio. I still had plenty of time before the poker game. I didn't want to go to Bailey's, and I didn't want to see either Ian or Sam. I most definitely didn't want to see Allison; she'd sense my turmoil, and I didn't want to talk about it with her quite yet.

Fortunately, another idea came to mind, and I cheered up as I stepped a little harder on the accelerator and guided the truck toward the two most open-minded people I knew.

My parents had spent the last couple years traveling the country in an RV, but they'd returned home a few months earlier for a hiatus from the road. They had a number of rental properties in and around Monson that had given them a decent income, but Allison and I both knew they wouldn't stick around long. The itch would get to them; it always did.

They'd sent the RV in for a total mechanical overhaul and a little remodeling. Mom wanted to put in a convection oven, so Dad had redesigned the galley and found someone who could do the construction work. I thought they might head back out once the job was complete, but I hoped they'd stay at least through the holidays.

They were living in one of their rental homes, a cute, small (though larger than the RV) cottage in town. They weren't used to living so "in town," but they seemed to enjoy their current accessibility to Monson's small but well-equipped main drag. Mom said she could walk or ride her bike to the post office, bank, and grocery store and be home with dinner fixed all in about one hour's time.

Though when Allison and I were little, we lived in the country home down the road from Ian's farm, once we reached high school age, my parents moved us closer to town and closer to the high school. Still, this was the first time I knew of that they'd taken up residence amid so much civilization. Allison and I initially thought they wouldn't like it, but we'd been proven wrong.

By the time I reached their house, I'd calmed from my visit with Betsy. I decided not to give much credence to what she'd said. *Much* credence. Some of it did ring true, but I decided I would do as she said and consider her comments a wake-up call.

I needed to be a better girlfriend more than Ian needed to be a better boyfriend. I needed to be a better girlfriend to Ian than Betsy was a friend to me.

As I parked next to the curb, my dad descended a ladder propped up against the front of the house.

"Becca, what a great surprise! I thought you were in Swayton County," Dad said as I got out of the truck.

"I was, but I sold out for the day. We've been busy."

"Because of the murder?"

"I don't know for sure."

"Sad, sad story. You're being careful?"

"Always."

"Good. Well, come on in. Your mom is . . . well, I'm not sure exactly. I've been up there." He looked back at the house. "There's a leak. I think we're going to need a whole new roof."

"Not good. Sorry about that, but I'd love to come in."

Dad shrugged. "It happens."

Though they were still the old hippie parents I knew and loved, they'd changed over their last extended trip. Dad had come home with short, short hair and golf shirts, and Mom had tamed her wild frizzy hair and no longer wore long, usually beaded, earrings. I'd had to get used to seeing her in posts. But they were still easygoing, not quickly caught up in life's annoyances, things like needing a new roof. I wouldn't have been distraught over such a thing, but I'd have expressed my irritation with more than a shrug.

"Polly, Becca's here," Dad called as we entered directly into a tiny family room furnished with only a new couch, a coffee table, and a giant flat-screen television. My parents had never been much for watching television, but the previous renters had left the TV in trade for a couple months' rent they'd neglected to pay. Dad said he'd recently gotten back into watching baseball and was excited and ready for this year's World Series.

Until he told me about his renewed interest, I had no idea that he'd ever enjoyed baseball. It crossed my mind that he'd given it up because he had two girls who weren't athletically inclined, but Allison set me straight. She reminded me that Dad loved every second of having two little girls who liked to work in the garden or kitchen, and his not watching baseball during our childhood didn't mean he'd made a permanent sacrifice; it just meant he'd put that interest on hold for a while.

"Becca, how wonderful to see you," Mom said as she stepped out of the kitchen and into the family room. The kitchen was, oddly, a slightly bigger rectangular space than the family room and tended to be the gathering place for my parents and whatever company they might have.

Though the white appliances weren't brand new, they weren't old either. The countertops weren't granite, but the white-stained cabinets and the big window that looked out to a flower garden made the room cozy. Mom had found a vintage but well-maintained Formica table that had yellow glitter throughout the top. She'd also found shiny yellow cushioned chrome framed chairs that were comfortable and fit the table perfectly. Being in the kitchen was *almost* like stepping into the 1950s.

The house smelled like freshly baked bread.

"You baking?" I swooned.

Mom laughed. "As a matter of fact, I am. Would you like some fresh bread?"

"Maybe a whole loaf or so."

"Deal. Have a seat and I'll put on some coffee, too."

We gathered around the table, and I quickly devoured two pieces of bread, one with just butter and one with some of my

127

own strawberry jam.

"It's hard to believe they kept the fair open," Mom said. "But I guess the show must go on or some such thing."

"It's a strange community," I said.

"How so?" Dad asked.

I swallowed the first bite of my third slice, this one naked. "Well, I suppose the first reason is because Scott is working there, too. I haven't seen him for years."

"Scott? Which one?" Mom asked.

"Scott the second."

"That's a lovely surprise. I liked him the best of your husbands."

"Me, too, now that I have a little hindsight. Anyway, it's been good to see him. I'm playing poker with him tonight." I wouldn't tell them about his suspicious behavior or, rather, what I had interpreted as suspicious behavior. "He's remarried to someone named Susan, but she and her son are in Florida."

"I'd thought I'd heard he remarried," Dad said. "He seem happy?"

"As far as I can tell."

"Good. We wish him well," Dad said, and he meant it.

If Scott had done something during our marriage to hurt me, either physically or emotionally, neither of my parents would have wished him well, but fortunately, there was no reason for any bad feelings.

"So, uh . . ." On the way to their house, I decided I would ask them some questions I thought their somewhat metaphysical beliefs would help them answer. Discussions with my parents had always been easy and open. However, I suddenly felt uncomfortable and maybe a little silly.

"Becca, what is it, my girl?" Dad said.

I sighed. "What do the two of you know about . . . well, about gypsy magic?"

They both sat up and their eyes lit brightly. No one was laughing. I'd come to the right place.

"What do you want to know?" Mom said.

"Do you know anything about it in connection with someone from Orderville named Jena Bellings?"

Mom and Dad smiled at each other. Any sense of "silly" I'd had disappeared completely.

"That's a name I haven't heard in a good long while," Dad said.

Mom patted Dad's hand and looked at me. "You have to understand, dear, that your father and I were . . . well, when we were younger we were very open to just about everything."

Allison and I had heard that often, and it

was usually at that point in whatever conversation we were having that my sister and I would want to put our fingers in our ears and run away. Neither of us had gotten the hippie gene, and we both figured there were just things we didn't need to know. But today was different, today I was anxious for their experienced input.

"Now I know I've come to the right place," I said.

"Well, first of all, we don't put any stock into all that gypsy . . . I suppose we'd call it fantasy or make-believe now, but when we were younger it was fun, interesting," Dad said.

"As far as I know, Becca, gypsy magic is akin to any dark magic. Some people practice witchcraft, but 'practice' is about as far as they get. Dad and I don't have any strong beliefs in magic, though we're pretty strong believers in Karma, instant Karma at that," Mom said. "Anyway, you want me to get to the part about Jena Bellings, right?"

"Please."

"Okay. Well, 'gypsy' has a different meaning than 'witch,' and that's where the Jena Bellings story is interesting. There are still gypsies today, in fact. I've read stories about them, and they're given more of a bad rap than a mysterious rap. They're traveling people. I believe original gypsies came from northern India and they speak . . . Romany? Something like that. Anyway, Jena Bellings wasn't part of a traveling group, and she didn't speak anything but English, and Bellings was her married name. Her maiden name was Maloy, I think. Yes, Jena Maloy."

"How do you know?"

"My mom, Gramma, knew her. She was from right here in Monson."

"I don't understand. I still don't know the whole story, but from what I've heard Jena was mysterious and magical, and lived in a house right outside Orderville."

"Or she was very smart," Mom said. "I'll tell you her story, but I'm going to do to you what my mother did to me. You have to promise that you won't tell another soul outside this family. It's okay for us to talk about it, but we would betray an old vow if we share this with anyone else. And breaking vows isn't good for Karma."

"Pinkie swear." I held up my pinkie.

Dad laughed. "I don't suppose we need to make her offer a blood oath like your mother did."

"Really?" I said.

"No, your father's teasing you. Jason," Mom said sternly.

"I'll be good," Dad said.

"Sadly, your grandmother didn't know Jena more than as a high school acquaintance, and this isn't so much first-hand as it is passed around and passed down. Gramma told me about Jena when your father and I were first dating. Mom knew we were interested in . . . so many things. She was a great mother and never pooh-poohed anything, but she wanted to make sure that in our explorations we didn't tangle with the legend of Jena Bellings."

"Sounds serious."

"Sort of serious, mostly silly, I suppose, but Gramma didn't want to take any chances. Anyway, Jena grew up in Monson, like I said. Back in the day — this was a long time ago, remember — abused girls couldn't get the help they needed like they can nowadays. Even cruel parents were left alone to parent the ways they thought appropriate. Discipline was looked at differently, but I won't go into detail. Well, Jena's father was a plain old mean drunk. He beat up Jena's mother and Jena, and did worse, we're sure, though it wasn't spoken about in those days." Mom paused and sipped her coffee before she continued. "Jena was withdrawn in high school. Gramma said that she was a true beauty but had no interest in having friends. She rarely had clean clothes and could have used a bath and shampoo more than she got them, but people around here were sympathetic. Except for a few. There are always the bullies, of course. Whether it's fair or valid, back then gypsies weren't thought of as reputable. One day someone — Gramma said she never knew who specifically — derogatorily called Jena 'Gypsy' and the name stuck.

"But then something happened. It was as if labeling her with the moniker gave her a chance to have a whole new identity. She transformed. She cleaned up — rumor had it that someone offered her use of their bath — and she wore cleaner clothes. And then people started seeing her in new clothes. Everyone thought she must have been stealing them, but no one reported any thefts, and at the time there was only the general store in town, and no one dared steal fabric from there. More rumor had it that someone started sewing dresses and leaving them for her." Mom paused again, picked up her coffee, and took another sip. She looked at me over the rim. It took a second, but I got what I thought she was trying to communicate.

"Gramma! Gramma made the clothes?"

Mom shrugged. "She was an amazing

133

seamstress."

"Gramma was tied to Jena Bellings?"

"Like I said, they didn't really know each other, but Gramma felt sorry for her, so she did what she could to help, secretly. Even Jena didn't know. Gramma made very bohemian, very gypsylike dresses for her, which, of course, wasn't the style, but Jena wore them well. And, frankly, Gramma was pleased that she could help with the transformation."

"That's pretty terrific," I said.

"Yeah, well, maybe not," Mom continued.

"Uh-oh," I said.

"Shortly after this 'transformation' and the baths and the clothes, Jena's father was found dead, stabbed with a knife down by the creek that runs a ways behind where Bailey's is now."

"Jena killed him?"

"Don't know. His killer was never found. But Jena always claimed to be the killer." Mom sat forward and leaned her elbows on the table. "She said that she never even had to touch the knife, that she used gypsy magic to thrust it into his chest."

"Right."

"It was his murder, though, and her insistence that she did it that earned her her legendary status and forced everyone else to keep her secret."

"Secret?"

"I'm getting there. The authorities refused to arrest her simply because there was no evidence that she was the killer and the postmaster claimed to have seen her sitting on a bench almost the entire day that the murder was committed. Eventually, everyone began to think that Jena's mother killed him and Jena was just trying to keep her mother from going to jail. But, honestly, according to Gramma, no one cared much who killed him, they were just glad he was gone. It was the way things were back then. Not all crimes were prosecuted, but some innocent people were punished, too. It wasn't as lawless as the stories of the Old West, but things just weren't as clear-cut as we'd like to think they are now."

"How did Jena get to Orderville?"

"She just went. Well, not quite. She spread the word around Monson that she was leaving. She wasn't going far, but she made it clear that Monson citizens were never to claim her, never act like they knew her if they saw her or someone asked about her. She said she would use gypsy magic to curse anyone who gave her up and they would meet the same fate as her father. Of course, her threats were met with doubt and probably pity, but then she did something to prove she wasn't messing around. She called the town to a meeting in the downtown square, the one that's still there. She was manic, apparently, calling forth forces of nature and such. It was windy and rainy, but when she commanded lightning to 'fall from the sky and burn the boulder,' that's exactly what happened. A bolt of lightning came from the sky and burned a black mark into the big boulder on the edge of the square park."

"Nuh-uh," I said.

"Gramma said it happened, and it worked, too. No one gave up Jena's identity after she left for Orderville, found a husband, and, by all accounts, had a great life."

"Then what?"

"That's where my story ends. But it's said that she brought prosperity to the town of Orderville."

"Wow."

"Quite the story, isn't it?"

I nodded. "They don't like to utter her name. If I understand it correctly, they don't want to change whatever good fortune she brings to the town — it's like saying her name will jinx something. They're a superstitious group."

"And now there's been a murder," Dad said.

Mom looked at me. "Becca, we don't subscribe to all that nonsense, you know that don't you?"

"Sure."

"However, if there's any way for you to get out of the rest of your commitment to the fair . . . it might not be a bad idea," Mom said.

"Really?"

Dad laughed nervously. "Maybe. You know, just to be safe."

"I'm pretty committed at this point."

Mom thought second, but then her face relaxed. "We're being even sillier than we thought our own parents were, Jason. Becca will be fine."

Dad nodded. "Of course. We shouldn't become old fogies in our young age." Then he looked at me. "Be careful, though, you know, just be careful."

"Always," I said. And I grabbed one more piece of bread.

EIGHT

"Aw, go ahead and give me four," Jerry said to Scott, the dealer. The poker game was being held at a picnic table in a lit pavilion. The grounds were just as spooky now as they were when I pulled into the mostly dark parking lot, but Scott had met me at the entrance and I planned on asking him to walk me to my truck when the game was over.

"Four? You're not having the best night, are you, buddy?" Scott said.

"No, not my best," Jerry replied, not good at a poker face.

But none of us were. It was the most unusual poker game I'd ever played. Six players had joined the game. Along with me, Scott, and Jerry the corn-dog vendor, the woman who'd been handling the horse earlier, Dianna Kivitt, was playing. Her demeanor vacillated between friendly and extremely unfriendly, and it seemed her back-and-forth mood was deliberate. At first I took it personally, but then I noticed it was just her way with everyone.

I hadn't met the other two participants before. Ward Hicken was a local alfalfa farmer who also owned and operated the goldfish game at the fair. I hadn't known that he didn't use live goldfish but he proudly told me that he used plastic ones, instead, color coded to match other prizes, from candy all the way up to stuffed animals. He was a big, strappin' man, his shoulders still thick from farm work, but slumped a little from age. He reminded me of Barry the corn guy from Bailey's except that Ward walked with less effort than it took Barry, was a little quicker with a smile, and had a mischievous glimmer in his eyes. He claimed to have two big, strappin' sons, twenty-something versions of himself who worked with him at his farm, so he had plenty of time to do other things, like run the goldfish game at the fair.

Randy Knapp was a cute skinny guy with a baby face that made him look seventeen, though he said he was close to forty. He was in charge of all cotton-candy production — in the world, to hear him tell it. I thought I understood cotton candy's lofty status among fair concessions, but evidently

I didn't. Randy behaved as though he were the self-appointed South Carolina State Commissioner of Cotton Candy. He claimed that at a glance he could assess whether the proper sugar and the right spinning method were being used. I hoped my wide-eyed looks of dismay when he went on and on about the sweet treat weren't rude. I tried to control them, but it wasn't easy. How could anyone have so much to say about cotton candy?

And even when he was sitting, he seemed to be in constant motion; he tapped his fingers, he swung his legs, he snapped his neck, et cetera. I wondered if he was able to be still when he was asleep. He made me jittery and had already accidentally kicked my ankle three times. He'd apologized and I'd said it was no big deal, but I'd swung my legs over in the other direction and now they kept running into Scott's. I think he'd figured out the problem, though, and didn't seem to mind my effort to avoid being bruised.

I was again pleasantly surprised at how Scott and I could actually communicate and be in each other's company without a hint of animosity or attraction. It was as if we'd forgotten all the stuff that had brought us together and all the stuff that had torn us apart, and we could function as two people who were comfortable with one another.

I supposed that if we'd had kids it would be a different story, but the years since our marriage ended had matured and mellowed us both, and we were able to find a familiar civility.

"Dianna, any cards?" Scott asked.

Dianna bit at her lip as she looked over her cards. I'd already figured out that she did this when she had a good hand. She was either going to stay put or ask for one card, I was sure.

"Nah, I'm good," she said.

I smiled to myself, but I also knew I was no different than the others around the table. I couldn't maintain a poker face either; I sat up straighter and breathed out of my nose when I had a good hand and slouched and breathed out of my mouth when I had a bad one. Scott had informed me of this years ago, when we used to play five-card draw fairly regularly. I'd caught myself falling into the same habits this evening. I'd also caught him looking at me with a familiar grimace. I ignored it because, despite the complete and total lack of poker-playing ability we all seemed to have, I was having fun.

It had been a long time since I'd done

something unpredictable, like play poker on a Saturday night. I didn't have a big need to shake up my routine, but tonight was enjoyably different, and it would satisfy any wild urges I might have for quite a while. I did note to myself that my definition of "wild urges" had changed over the years. This was a mellow group, and I was grateful for that. Rowdy didn't work anymore, not that it ever had, but I used to have a little more patience for rowdy.

"Randy, cards?" Scott said.

"Oh, man, I'm just not sure," he said as he tapped at his high cheekbone with his finger. "Shoot, well, give me three."

"Three it is." Scott dealt the cards. "Becca?"

"I'm good," I said as I sat up straight and breathed deeply out of my nose.

Scott shook his head slightly. "Alrighty then, dealer takes one."

We all shifted somewhat as we looked at our cards. I had a full house with three kings and two aces. How could anyone possibly beat that?

"I'll raise by five licorice pieces," Ward said. Randy whistled an impressed tone.

We all "saw" his bet but didn't raise him. Yeah, I was not good at poker and didn't like to "raise" because I thought that gave

142

me away more than my straight posture and nose breathing. I know, I know.

But, to be honest, I wasn't necessarily there for the cards anyway. As fun as it was to do something spontaneous, I'd kept my commitment to play the game to try to find out more about Virgil Morrison, Orderville, South Carolina, Jena Bellings, and gypsy magic. I decided it wouldn't hurt if I could figure out what Scott was up to, too, but so far the only new information I'd gleaned was that he seemed to be more friendly with this group of strangers than I would expect for someone who'd only recently met them.

However, that might not mean much of anything. Scott had excellent "bonding" skills and could seem like your best friend only a few minutes after you met him. He was no longer shaken up about finding Virgil's body, but that might not mean anything either. "Resilient" was an understatement when describing Scott, though I used to think he was more about denial than resiliency.

And that experience of finding Virgil's body could be the reason he had bonded so quickly with these people. Perhaps he'd sought out shoulders to cry on, and perhaps this was a willing group of shoulders.

Virgil's death, his murder, was, by itself, a

horrible occurrence, but I felt more than just a general sadness. I felt robbed of a potential friendship. I never expected Virgil and I would become the best of buddies, but I was sure, for some reason that I'd never understand or now get to explore, we'd made a connection. He might never have moved beyond gruff, and I might never have found the courage to trust the Ferris wheel he manned, but that connection had been there, that click that you just sometimes feel but can't explain. I wanted to know more about him.

"Full house, aces high," I said as I put down my cards.

My gleeful tone was met with good-natured grumbles and Scott saying, "You didn't raise on that hand? You haven't changed a bit, Becs."

"Changed a bit? You two know each other?" Dianna asked, her voice friendly. For the moment.

"Yeah, we were married. I was her second marriage. We got along for a while, but it wasn't destined to last. I was immature and Becca was more of a grown-up."

I looked at Scott, and so did everyone else. He'd summed up our time together so succinctly, I wasn't sure if I was offended or proud. He looked at me, raised his eye-

144

brows, and laughed.

"Sorry, if that sounded . . . well, like it was no big deal," Scott said. "It was a long time ago. Becca's moved on and I'm remarried with a stepson."

"You've been divorced twice?" Dianna said. Her tone had swung to critical.

"Yes," I said. There'd been a time when I would have attempted to explain that I'd been young and had made poor choices, but I didn't do that any longer. What did it matter? Besides, if I'd said as much tonight, I'd offend both my exes, the second one in person. It just wasn't necessary.

"Kids?" Dianna asked.

"Nope."

I smiled at her. She smiled back, tentatively.

"Can I ask everyone a question?" I said.

No one said no, so I continued. "Did anyone know Virgil well?"

It was a good thing my eyes were on my companions and not on the hand of cards Scott had just dealt. Before anyone spoke, the group exchanged looks, looks I thought might be important to notice and remember.

Ward peered across the table at Randy, who was scratching at his elbow. At first, he didn't notice Ward's glance, but when he

145

did he stopped scratching and froze for an instant, his eyebrows high in question. He pulled his eyes away from Ward's a short second later and went back to scratching his elbow. I thought Ward rolled his own eyes, but I couldn't be sure.

Dianna, much less concerned about being obvious, rammed her elbow into Randy's side. He said, "Ow! What's that about?" Dianna shook her head as if to tell him to keep quiet.

"What's up, Randy?" Scott asked.

"Aw, hell, Dianna, I didn't kill him, you didn't kill him, what was that about?" Randy said.

"You just need to keep your mouth shut," she said.

"About what?" I said. "Something about Virgil?"

Scott reached under the table. It would probably have been weird for him to put his hand on my leg to keep me from pressing them for more information like Ian had done once or twice, but he did lightly tap my knee as if to relay the same sort of message.

It didn't work. "What's up?" I pressed forward.

"Dianna dated Virgil," Ward said. "She broke up with him two weeks ago. For some reason she thinks everyone will think that she's somehow connected to his murder because she broke his heart, which is not entirely true. As you can see, none of us are teenagers; they were friends who went out to dinner, but it never turned serious. She hasn't told the police yet, so she doesn't want anyone to know."

I suddenly felt sorry for Dianna. She wasn't young, that was true, but what did that matter? And maybe her moods were unpredictable, but one of her supposed "friends" just threw her under the bus. I'd liked Ward up until that moment.

"Breakups aren't easy," I said as I smiled at Dianna, who grimaced at me. "I'm sorry if it was painful."

"Shoot-fire, it wasn't painful. I'm just antsy about the whole thing is all. I should have told the police and I didn't. Now, it's eatin' at me," Dianna said.

Of course, the next logical response would have been something like, "Then maybe you should tell them." But it didn't feel like my place to say it. I hoped someone else would.

"And I shouldn't have said anything," Ward said. "Sorry about that, but everyone here, except our new friends Becca and Scott, knew already, Dianna. In fact, almost everyone else who works the fair knows, and someone might have already told the police. It'd be best if you told them, even if you are late with the information."

Dianna nodded.

Ward cleared his throat. "Dianna, Randy, and Virgil were our population explosion," he said as he looked at me. The others all looked at him.

"What do you mean?" I asked.

"Orderville is a small place — you probably already know that."

I did, though I'd never ventured into the town itself.

"Our population stays pretty close to the same number all the time. It seems like the second someone kicks the bucket, someone else has a baby to fill that space. Anyway, Virgil, Dianna, and Randy all came to town about twenty years ago, all within the same week, if I remember correctly."

"We didn't know each other. It was just coincidence," Dianna added.

Randy nodded as he scratched his elbow again.

"We called them the Outsiders. Even after a good long time passed, we still called them that: the Outsiders. I'd almost forgotten all about that," Ward continued.

"Since we are the three 'Outsiders,' the ones who aren't 'like the others' " — Randy rolled his eyes — "Dianna probably feels a little extra paranoid or guilty about Virgil. I had dinner at his house. Twice. I don't have any idea why he invited me, but he did and that was it," Randy said.

"Anyone else have dinner at Virgil's house?" Jerry asked. "Well, other than maybe you, Dianna?"

"I didn't. We had dinner out. I've been to his place but never for very long and never for dinner. Did he cook for you?" Dianna asked Randy.

"Yes, ma'am. Hamburgers on the grill, twice." Randy laughed. "He was funny. I think he was very against drinking. He joked that I didn't look old enough to have a beer. He knew me for years, but had me show him my driver's license before he let me drink."

"Where did he live?" Scott asked.

Dianna and Randy both pointed toward the north. "That way about a mile," Dianna said.

"Yeah," Randy said. "Nice little old country house. He was out in the middle of nowhere, but he didn't do any farming. You know, he told me that he'd been married once, which was something I'd never known before."

"I knew that," Dianna said almost defen-

149

sively. "I mean, I knew he was married, but that was a long time ago."

Randy nodded. "A long, long time ago apparently. His wife was killed in some sort of accident, but he wouldn't give me the details. I asked."

We all turned toward Dianna. She shrugged. "Never told me that much. I didn't know about an accident, just that he'd once been married. He said he didn't like to talk about it and it was another life."

Randy nodded.

"What else did you talk about?" I said to Randy.

"Gosh, I don't know if I can remember. Stuff, I guess. You know, sports and his time in the military. He was in the army for the full ticket, the full twenty years. Oh, the house was in his family, so he owned it outright. That's why he moved here, a free house. I asked him. I wondered how he was able to make any sort of living working the odd jobs that he worked. That's how I heard about the military retirement money he got and the fact that he didn't have any house payments. It was a pretty cushy life for a loner."

"What were some of his other odd jobs?" I asked.

Everyone laughed, but Ward said, "He did

everything, loved working at the fair, liked to paint houses, some construction, he was a waiter sometimes . . ."

"I heard he even walked dogs once," Randy added.

"Actually, Virgil's odd jobs seem to be a popular topic of local gossip," Jerry said. "At least that's what I've noticed."

"That's about right. Virgil was a loner, and the fact that Randy or Dianna knew him a little better is a big deal. Twenty years in town and I can't recall one conversation I had with him that lasted longer than about a minute," Ward said. "You just started at the fair this year, right, Jerry?"

"Yes, sir. I've only been in town for about six months."

"Huh, seems like longer," Ward said. "You already seem to fit in. Becca and Scott, you have to understand that we all work these two weeks at the fair, but most of us know each other outside of it as well. As I said, it's a small community."

"What are your regular jobs?" I said.

"Farmer," Ward answered. I knew that already.

"Corn dogs for now, but mostly in between," Jerry said sheepishly.

"I own a bar in town," Dianna said. "Bottoms Up." I about saluted with my soda but then realized she was stating the name of the bar, not offering a toast.

"I teach high school math," Randy said as he started scratching at his other elbow. I wondered if his ceaseless movement drove his students crazy, and then I wondered if his twitchiness was due to a medical condition. If that was the case, I felt bad about having moved my legs away.

I tried to picture them in their regular jobs. I'd already "seen" Ward as a farmer. I could imagine Dianna behind a bar. I could see Jerry being in between things; I sensed a sort of flakiness there I wasn't quite able to put my finger on. Baby-faced Randy as a math teacher didn't seem to fit, though. I couldn't envision him doing any particular job — other than cotton-candy overlord, of course — but not because he didn't seem smart.

"What did you do before you were in between? Where're you from?" I asked Jerry.

"I moved here from Los Angeles. I wanted to get away from the big city, and this is where I ended up. Other than the fair, I haven't had a real job or kept one, I suppose, but I have some savings. I'm still okay, but I need to start looking seriously."

I'd heard the story before. Sam had moved to Monson to get out of Chicago, and Ian had wanted to farm in South Carolina rather than in his home state of Iowa, but I had a sense that something other than the desire for a change of scene had lured Jerry this far away from home.

"What brought you two here?" I asked Dianna and Randy.

"Bar was for sale," Dianna said. "I wanted my own business."

"Wanted to teach in a small town, stay in South Carolina, and this was one of the jobs that came open."

"All right," Scott interrupted, "I need to know how many cards you all need."

We played a little longer, but it was nothing like the old days when Scott and I could play all night, which actually made this experience better. Somehow, we ended pretty even, all of us with similar amounts of peanuts and licorice. I enjoyed getting to know my fellow fair workers and tried to compare them with my farmers' market friends, but it was difficult. Most of my fellow market vendors worked at Bailey's full-time. It would be strange to think of one of them running a bar most of the time and their stall only part-time. But I knew we were a lucky and unique group at Bailey's. Not everyone gets to work their passion day in and day out.

I didn't ask about Jena Bellings and gypsy magic. The right moment never came, and I didn't want to ruin the good mood we all, even Dianna, fell into.

We said good-bye in the parking lot and planned on being back at the fair the next morning. It had been a long day, but as I drove my truck toward the exit, reveling a little in my wild ways of playing poker until the late hour of eleven forty-five at night, I happened to glance in my rear-view mirror. Scott had also gotten in his truck, but he let the rest of us leave before him. He and I were the last ones in the lot, so no one else witnessed him turning off his engine and climbing back out of his truck. The parking lot was lit well enough that I clearly saw what he was doing.

As I sat idling at the fairgrounds exit, I watched him disappear around Lucy's trailer. When he did not return even after a long two minutes, I decided I wasn't leaving without trying to figure out what he was up to.

NINE

I couldn't turn around and park in the lot again, unless I didn't care if Scott saw my truck. I did care. In fact, I suddenly really cared; if he was up to no good, he wouldn't play it out with me as an audience. However, I thought as I pulled my truck onto the road and then off to the side and into the gully, maybe he just forgot something and was retrieving it before heading home, or wherever he was staying. I'd seen him disappear around the trailer. That didn't mean he'd gone into it. He might have just gone back to the shooting gallery to gather something.

I stayed in the gully for another few long minutes. I turned off the truck, and the engine clicked a few times in rhythm with the crickets. The road was up the gully to my left, and a thickly treed patch of woods stretched out to my right. Those same trees bordered the parking lot and then one long side of the corn maze. I peered through the trees and was relieved to see that the meager glow from the few parking lot lights seeped between the branches enough to make the wooded area look only somewhat foreboding.

If Scott didn't leave soon, I would get out of the truck and walk to the trailer using the cover of the woods. I'd have enough light to see where I was walking.

What was I thinking? Was I really going to travel through a darkened wood next to a corn maze just to see if I could catch Scott in the act of . . . something?

No, I wasn't going to do that. I put my fingers around the keys.

But . . . I really wanted to know what he was up to. I took my fingers away again.

It might not be so bad. The dark was just the dark, after all, and I could stay well away from the corn maze.

And I'd stay close enough to the parking lot that if I needed to run away fast, I could.

But that was only if Scott didn't leave in the next few minutes.

He didn't leave — I watched five minutes click by on my phone's clock, and then five more. That was long enough.

I got out of the truck and tromped through weeds and gravel to get to the trees. Even if

I'd not had the parking lot lights to partially illuminate where I was going, my feet would have noticed the change in the terrain: it suddenly went from somewhat even and flat to uneven and bumpy. I'd have to be careful not to roll an ankle.

Despite the fact that I could see fairly well and that I knew someone was close enough to hear me if I screamed really loudly, walking through the woods, on the edge of them though I was, at night with the quiet rides ahead of me was more unsettling than I'd prepared myself for. As I'd noticed during the poker game, the fairgrounds were minimally lit with a few well-placed security lights, but the rides were mostly obscured in murky shadow. The Ferris wheel, of course, took on a murderous pose, its tall metal body appearing even more sinister and deadly in the sparse light. I shivered.

And then the parking lot lights went out. They went dark at the exact moment I blinked, which for a brief instant made me wonder if they'd actually gone out or if something had happened to my vision.

The only lights left in the entire world, it seemed, were the few and random security lights on the fairgrounds. For an instant I froze and blinked some more, hoping my eyes would quickly adjust. I was only about halfway to the trailer, and suddenly whatever bravery I had mustered for this excursion was replaced by a big dose of fear.

"It's not that far," I mumbled to myself. "There are no monsters in the dark." Of course, there might be snakes and other hazards, but I couldn't allow myself to think too much about those undesirable possibilities. If Virgil's killer was still in the vicinity of Orderville, I hoped he or she was smart enough to have already gone home for the night.

I could have used my phone as a makeshift flashlight, but I knew that would raise suspicion if someone happened to see its glow moving through the woods. I picked up the pace, hoping even harder that I didn't step on or into something that would harm me.

It was probably less than a minute later that I reached the trailer. I sat and leaned against the end of it, the side that faced the parking lot and not the fairgrounds. My heart was pounding in my ears, and I was out of breath.

"Calm down," I breathed.

I looked around as I attempted to regain my composure. There were no security gates keeping people out. I didn't see the security guards that I'd heard had been hired. After a murder, it seemed only logical to hire someone to patrol the grounds during the day and the night. But as far as I could tell, Scott and I were the only people on-site. His truck stood alone in the lot, so unless someone lived in the trailer and didn't keep transportation close by, it was just me and my second ex.

Surprisingly, that was a comforting thought. I had no doubt that Scott wouldn't hurt me. He wasn't capable of harming another human, was he?

I hoped not because when I heard the trailer door open, I peered around and saw that he was stepping out of it.

I was in almost complete darkness, but he was somewhat lit by one of the distant security lights. I couldn't see the details of his face, but his actions were clear. He stepped down the two short steps, looked around the fairgrounds, even glancing in my direction without noticing me in the shadows, and then locked the door. He looked around again and then put the key above the door, in a space between the frame and the trailer itself. Once that was accomplished, he hurried right past me and to his truck. A moment later, in a move that reminded me of the Scott I once knew and loved, he spun the tires and then peeled out of the parking lot.

"Guess you weren't trying to be quiet," I said to his taillights.

I sat at the end of the trailer a long time debating what I should do. I finally concluded that I should hurry through the lot, get in my truck, and get home to Hobbit.

But what I wanted to do was use the key and go into the trailer. It wasn't all that difficult to talk myself out of that maneuver, though. I didn't know what or who was inside it. I didn't know if Scott was supposed to have access to the key or not. I didn't know if a killer lurked within, just waiting for someone to enter and offer themselves up as the next victim. And the walls of a trailer could be confining. If I was going to happen upon someone with deadly intentions, I wanted it to be someplace where I'd at least have a shot at escape.

I was just about to pick the smart choice and sprint back to my truck when something else occurred to me. I'd snuck back to the fairgrounds to see what Scott was up to. I wasn't willing to go into the trailer, but I recalled that there was a storage space behind the shooting gallery. Maybe I could just look through it quickly.

Really, had anyone else been around, they couldn't possibly have missed me scurrying to the shooting gallery. I wasn't trying to be obvious, but I wasn't trying to hide well either. I didn't whistle or duck and hide as I moved past the empty food trailers that still smelled of sugar and grease. I decided that even the kiddie rides looked horrifying in the dark.

The shooting gallery target wall and the storage area were separated by a piece of flimsy black fabric. I pulled back the curtain, pushed the button on my phone, aimed it inside, looked around, and then stepped into the mess.

The space was about five feet deep and as wide as the target wall, about fifteen feet. I remembered Scott as being organized and neat, almost to the point of irritation. I wasn't messy, but though I kept my kitchen obsessively clean, I wasn't all that concerned about the preciseness of the silverware in the silverware drawer. Scott always stacked the spoons evenly or made sure the knives were laying in the same direction. If they weren't being used, his tools were always in the exact spot they belonged, and his closet was organized with his jeans together and his T-shirts grouped by sleeve length and color.

It had driven me crazy, but of course there was a point when we'd driven each other crazy no matter what we did.

I could think of only three explanations for the current state of the storage area: (1) Scott had been cured of his obsessive ways, (2) he'd been searching for something and hadn't had time to put everything back where it belonged, or (3) someone else had ransacked the place.

Cables, screws, nuts, bolts, tools were strewn everywhere. There were even a few broken-apart guns, their pieces spread throughout.

An old card table occupied the far end of the space. I high-stepped over the mess, intent on getting to the files I'd spied on the table. The mess didn't tell me much, but the files might provide some detailed information.

There were three of them, all old brown folders with worn edges. They were neatly stacked — surprising given the disarray around them. One held only a few pieces of paper, but the other two were fairly thick. One of the thick ones was full of documents about the Ferris wheel: schematics and blueprints of the machine, drawn with precision and detail. I thought the pictures might be interesting if I had the time to really look at them, but I only thumbed through, wondering why Scott had the folder. Toward the end of the papers, I came upon some engine drawings and realized he must have been using what was inside the folder to help him fix the motor.

The other thick folder contained papers similar to those in the Ferris wheel file, but these pertained to the roller coaster. The Mad Maniacal Machine was the shortest, probably slowest roller coaster I'd ever seen. But it was rickety, and I'd had no desire to try to work up the courage to ride it. I thumbed through those pages, too, and when I got to the end of the stack, I realized I'd seen a document that didn't quite fit with the rest. I moved slowly back through the papers. A few pages in, I found the sheet that had caught my attention: a drawing of only one part of the roller coaster track system. Like all the drawings in the folder, this one was black-and-white, but unlike the others, it had a big red arrow hand-scribbled on the paper and pointing at a spot on the tracks.

There were no labels or other markings to indicate what the arrow was meant to point out. I glanced at a few pieces to the front and to the back of the marked page, but nothing else seemed important. I closed the file.

The last folder, with the fewest pieces of

paper, was the most interesting one anyway.

Pasted on the inside of the front flap was the yellow sticky note I'd seen in Scott's wallet. It still read: "Virgil Morrison. Ferris wheel. One down!!!" The only other piece of paper in the folder listed what I surmised were the names of fair workers and vendors, with a dollar amount next to each name. I'd recently dealt with a mysterious list that ultimately lead to a killer. This list wasn't nearly as mysterious, and I doubted it would lead to anything, but I still thought it worth perusing. Above the column with the dollar amounts were the words "Still Owing."

The people listed must have owed the amount of money next to their names, though who they owed and for what wasn't clear. Jerry, who sold the corn dogs, had a zero next to his name, but my other card-playing buddies weren't so fortunate.

Ward Hicken was listed as owing two hundred dollars. Randy Knapp owed sixty-two. Scott owed one hundred and thirty-two dollars. And Dianna Kivitt was the big winner, owing seven hundred and fifty dollars. "Whatever that's for, that's a lot of money," I said quietly.

I wanted to take the list and give it to Sam so he could maybe give it to the police investigating the murder, but stealing it didn't seem wise. It occurred to me that I had an infrequently used camera on my phone. There wasn't enough light to guarantee a good shot, but the camera flashed in low light. I'd have to hope for the best.

I pushed the buttons needed to access the camera and aimed.

Just as I took the picture and the flash lit up the entire universe, I heard someone say, "Hey, who's there?"

I don't how I kept hold of the phone, because when I heard the voice, I reacted as if I'd heard a gunshot: I hit the ground and covered my head. I don't know how I managed to keep from screaming since the maneuver caused me to graze my chin on the edge of the table and then land hard, my leg hitting something that looked like a car's radiator. It rammed into the top of my thigh, sending pain in both directions so that I suddenly hurt all over and wondered if I was ever going to be able to stand again.

The pain was so intense that I considered yelling out for help, but I quickly rejected the thought. The good news was that I was on the ground, and the back wall of the storage area, made of thin metal, didn't really touch the ground. There was a good four inches of space I could look through and hopefully see who had called out.

Once I blinked away the pain-induced tears that had filled my eyes, I saw the person attached to the voice. I'd happened upon the security guard after all. A man I hadn't seen before was walking directly toward the shooting gallery. He'd come from the area near the Ferris wheel and moved slowly enough to make me think he was uncertain about which direction to go next. He must have seen the light but maybe only peripherally.

He was dressed in a dark uniform, and I thought I saw a gun on his belt, but I couldn't be sure. He wasn't young, but he wasn't old. He wasn't trim and in shape, but he wasn't heavy either. I hoped he was friendly and didn't have a quick trigger finger.

As he got closer, I continued to debate whether or not I should just call out and turn myself in, but something kept me from doing much more than clenching my jaw in silent defiance. I hated getting caught. And considering there had been a murder recently, I didn't want to draw suspicion upon myself.

The path the guard followed forked just before reaching the rear of the shooting gallery; one way led to a merry-go-round, the other to the roller coaster. I held my breath as I watched the guard approach, and let it out when he reached the fork, turned sharply, and hurried off toward the roller coaster. He'd pulled out a flashlight and flipped it on, aiming it in the direction opposite of where I lay, injured and scared.

I turned my head to look at whatever shone in the beam of his light, and I was almost certain I saw the shadow of a figure running away from him. A man or woman — I couldn't tell which — dressed in dark clothes, a head full of long, dark hair flowing down their back. Was someone else roaming around the grounds, too? Had they seen me?

There wasn't time to think about anything except getting out of there. I sat up, focusing more on my thigh than the fact that the tabletop was right above my head. I hit it with a nice, solid-melon thunk. I was in a hurry, but I had to hesitate a few seconds to let the stars clear from my eyes before I could test my leg.

Fortunately, standing wasn't as difficult as I thought it would be, and the leg held me up with only a little protest. I'm sure I made a banging, clanging racket as I trudged through all the junk to get out from the storage area, but I didn't turn around to see if I'd diverted the security guard from his mission. I galloped ungracefully away from the trailer.

I wasn't limping so much as dragging my leg to get it to go forward. Nothing was broken and I would be fine, but I was sure I'd have a few new bruises.

Once I reached the parking lot, I stopped briefly to debate whether to run through its darkness or the darkness in the woods. They both suddenly seemed a million miles long. I chose the parking lot, and once I'd made it about halfway, my leg began to move with a seminormal gait.

I reached my truck, relief finally overtaking fear, started it, and maneuvered up and out of the gully and down the empty highway.

It wasn't until I was almost home that I happened to glance in the rearview mirror and see the damage done to my chin. There was blood everywhere. I looked down at my lap and saw that my overalls were bloodstained in the exact spot where I was sure to have the bruise on my thigh. I hadn't realized I was bleeding. Had I left a trail from the shooting gallery to my truck?

There wasn't much I could do about it now.

TEN

I probably should have gotten stitches. But I didn't. In fact, the only one who knew about my injuries was Hobbit, who, in her own way, reprimanded me for not going to the hospital. Instead, I cleaned the inch-long cut on my chin thoroughly and managed to close up the gash using surgical tape. I thought I'd done a brilliant job, but I would probably end up with an ugly scar. Fortunately, it was under my chin and more on the right side than in the middle. The tape didn't add much character to my face, but the scar might.

I had my story ready. I would tell everyone that I was sitting at my dining table looking at some paperwork and I dropped a pen. When I bent over to retrieve it, my chin hit the edge of the table. I'd judge reactions to see if I needed to pad my fib or not.

The top of my head had a nice bump, but it wasn't noticeable, and the bruise on my thigh was covered well by my long overalls. The blood I'd seen on my lap had come from my chin. My leg was merely bruised, but it was a doozy of a bruise and I'd be sore for a few days at least. Fortunately, it wouldn't be too hot for long pants.

Between the pain and my concern over leaving a trail of blood, I didn't sleep well at all. Stella didn't need a ride, so when I was ready before sunrise — earlier than I normally rolled out of bed — I just got up and drove the truck to the fairgrounds. Ian was planning to pick up Hobbit and take her to George's about an hour after I left. I sent him a text apologizing that I wouldn't be there and saying we'd talk later. I would tell him the truth about my injuries, and though Ian wasn't one to lecture, he'd supportively point out that I probably shouldn't have done what I did. I knew that, and I wasn't quite ready to be honest with anyone yet.

"Becca?" said a voice from behind me as I got out of the truck. I'd parked where I thought I could search for blood drops. The voice startled me enough that I jumped.

"Oh, hey, Jerry, you're here early." I looked around. The sun was up, and there were plenty of other vehicles in the lot. It wasn't crowded yet, but at least I didn't feel alone.

"You, too — holy cow, Becca, what happened to your face?"

I told him my story, and he told me I probably should have gotten stitches.

"I'll be all right," I said as I unloaded the wagon that I used to transport inventory from the truck to the booth. Jerry jumped in and helped. If he were paying attention, he might have wondered why I kept looking at the ground.

The parking lot was just a big patch of dirt. I didn't know what blood would look like on dirt and hoped it would somehow disappear anyway. From what I could see, or couldn't see actually, if I had dripped, it *had* disappeared or gotten mixed in with the dirt or blown away. At first glance, the dirt just looked like dirt. A wave of relief helped me stop clenching my teeth so tightly.

"You sure you're okay?" Jerry asked doubtfully.

I veered the wagon in a right curve, hopefully still following the path I'd taken the night before. Still no sign of anything unusual.

"I'm fine." I smiled at him. "I'm sorry if I'm distracted. I didn't sleep much, but I'll shape up."

"No problem," Jerry said. "Here, let me

pull the wagon."

I let him. As we rolled and wove our way toward the temporary farmers' market stalls, I relaxed further. I didn't see anything anywhere that looked like blood and as we became surrounded by a few more people, I began to think that if the blood wasn't somehow gone by now, it would be soon. Except for anything that had dripped behind the shooting gallery, of course, but I couldn't dwell on that.

Though it was still early, I could tell the temperature would be perfect for attracting a good-sized crowd, and counter to my sentiments a few days ago, I hoped for a smaller, less exuberant one today.

"How busy will it be today?" I asked.

"Dunno." Jerry shrugged. "My first year, too."

"Of course. Sorry." It was just last night that Jerry had shared he was fairly new to the area. "You're from California, right?"

"Yep. Different world."

"Do you like here?"

"Sure," he said hesitantly. "Oh, sorry, I should say 'Sure!' "

"You were in LA?"

"Yep."

"Well, no wonder you don't know if you like it here or not. A different world is an understatement. I bet if you give it long enough, you'll get used to it, and maybe even come to love it. If not, there are some pretty big cities around."

"We'll see," he said.

I looked at him. Any other day, perhaps a day that I didn't hurt from having beaten myself up, I might have asked more questions and wanted to get to know him better. But not today.

"Looks like you've already got a crowd," he said.

I stepped around him and looked up. A small group of people had gathered by the farmers' market stalls, but it didn't look as though they were waiting for me. They seemed to be lined up in front of Stella's space, Stella's empty space.

"I guess I'd better see what's going on," I said. "Thanks for the help. I can get it from here."

"Sure. Hey, stop by my trailer later. Lunch on me." He held out the wagon handle.

"Oh, that's . . ." I looked at him. He wasn't asking me to lunch, he wasn't flirting, he was just being friendly. "That'd be great. Thanks, Jerry."

"Sure. Bring your ex-husband. He's a funny guy."

"Okay," I said. "Funny" meant as a compliment to Scott wasn't something I was accustomed to. "Funny" as in "goofy," well, I'd heard that plenty of times.

"See ya later." Jerry turned and hurried back to his trailer as I hurried over to the stalls.

"Becca, hi," Henry said as he stepped around part of the crowd. "We're having a run on Stella's cinnamon bread. I hope she's on her way."

"I'm sure she is," I said as I surveyed the crowd. About twenty people were milling around, semi-patiently waiting for Stella's delicious bread. It seemed that it was just as popular in Swayton County as it was at Bailey's.

"What happened to your chin?" Henry asked.

I told him my story, and he said I probably should have gotten stitches.

"What's this?" Stella said as she came up behind me.

"Your cinnamon bread," I said.

"Wow, really? Well, I'm glad I brought plenty." Stella and her husband each pulled a wagon.

Henry and I helped them unload the wagons. We jumped in and assisted with the constant flow of transactions, Stella's and our own. Brenton arrived a short time later, and the line to his stall suddenly grew, too.

As we were in the middle of the crazy rush, I saw Lucy walk by in the background. She smiled and sent me a thumbs-up and then pointed at her chin as if to ask me what I'd done to mine. I only had time to shrug and wave it off as if it were no big deal. She imitated pulling a needle and thread. Even at twenty feet, she thought I needed stitches.

Truthfully, the fair wasn't as busy today as it had been on Friday and Saturday, but we four Bailey's vendors seemed busier than ever, at least in the morning.

"See, the word spread and you all did well today, didn't you?" Lucy said when she stopped by my stall around noon. "I knew it would. I just knew it."

I smiled. "We've all almost sold out of everything. You were right."

She smiled bigger. "I do predict, however, that this afternoon will be less busy for y'all, but busier for the rides and other attractions. I think we've benefitted each other."

"We'll have Monday off, but all of us will come back next week."

"Oh! I was so hoping you'd say that. That thrills me, just thrills me. I'll leave you to it, but I'll stop by later. You probably will want to leave early today, particularly Stella. It looks likes she sold every single item she brought."

Stella was sitting on one of the folding chairs behind her display table. She sat back with her legs straight in front of her as she fanned her face with a piece of paper that had been folded into an accordion shape. Her cheeks were bright red. She'd worked hard today.

"I'll probably suggest she go ahead and take off. She looks exhausted," I said.

"That is so much better than aggravated because she didn't have good business." Lucy patted my arm and seemed to jump in the air a little before she turned and, carrying her ever-present clipboard, walked away.

I was about to encourage poor Stella to go home when another voice sounded from behind me.

"Becs, hey, what's up?"

"Hey, Scott," I said as I turned.

"Yikes, what happened to your chin?"

The conversation played out like the others I'd already had except that Scott looked at the tape and the cut even closer than everyone else. He told me to stay put and he'd be back to put it together better. I didn't know what that meant, but if I saw him coming at me with a needle and thread, I'd run.

I turned back to talk to Stella and was again interrupted by someone else greeting me.

"Becca, hi."

"Sam!" Trying to mellow my enthusiasm, I cleared my throat and said in a calmer, more normal voice, "Hi."

"What in the world did you do to yourself?" he asked.

By that time I really wished I'd just gone to get stitches.

ELEVEN

As Sam waited patiently, I managed to talk to my fellow farmers' market vendors before Scott returned with a black bag that looked like a cross between a briefcase and an old-fashioned doctor's bag, the kind you saw in old movies set in the days when house calls were common practice.

I sent Stella home and told the other vendors they could leave whenever they sold out. Stella was cheerfully exhausted and didn't know if she could possibly bake enough cinnamon bread to keep up with the demand next week. She'd be back Tuesday, but I thought she was ready to be back at Bailey's, where cinnamon bread was popular but not quite *that* popular. Brenton wasn't sure how long he'd stick around, and Henry was interested in perusing the baked-goods ribbons again. He said that even if he sold out, he'd probably stay awhile.

Scott instructed me to come with him. He

asked Sam to accompany us and assist him with whatever he was going to do. Sam and I dutifully followed my ex to a covered pavilion that was similar to the one where we'd played poker except that it held four picnic tables instead of only two.

"Sit up here," Scott said as he pointed to one of the picnic tables. I obliged. "Officer Brion, Sam, can you hold this light? Aim it at Becca's chin."

"Sure."

"Scott, what's going on? What are you doing?" I asked as I tried to keep the light out of my eyes.

"I'm an EMT, Becca," Scott said. "You should have had someone look at this, but I could have stitched it up for you. It's too late for stitches now, but I can clean it out and tape it up better."

Scott couldn't have surprised me more if he'd said he was the president of the United States.

"You're a what?" I said.

"EMT. I also own the shooting gallery, but that's not a full-time gig, neither is my medical work. Now, I'm going to take this amateurish tape off, but it might hurt. I want you to take this bottle of soap and this washcloth and go clean it out. The fairground bathrooms aren't the most ideal,

179

but they'll have to do." Scott reached for my chin.

"Hang on, you're an EMT? A medical professional?"

Scott looked at Sam. "Clearly, she doesn't believe I'm capable of bettering myself."

"Clearly." Sam smiled.

I wanted to say more, but the only words that came to mind were less than complimentary to Scott. Even if I'd said something like "Good job!" or "That's great!" I would have sounded patronizing. I was shocked and impressed, but I'd have to keep that to myself.

I closed my mouth and lifted my chin.

"Damn, Becca, you got a little tape happy, didn't you? Uh — don't answer that, just let me get this stuff off."

"How long were the two of you married?" Sam asked.

"Three years. We had a good time, but we were young. Becca was in college, I was pretty immature, but I was very cute," Scott said.

"I bet," Sam said.

I literally could not speak. Scott held my chin and pulled on the tape so that I knew that if I spoke I could make the injury worse.

"Becca was married once before we were," Scott said. "I don't think I was a rebound thing, but we never really talked about it."

I tried to communicate with my eyes, but I doubted they held as much impact as my words would have.

"I knew she was married twice. Maybe third time's the charm for her," Sam said.

The tape removal hurt, and my eyes watered a little.

"She says her personal life's a little complicated right now. Maybe she'll get it together," Scott said.

"Complicated? Hmm, interesting."

Scott stopped pulling on the tape and looked at Sam. "Oh, I, uh. Oh."

Sam just smiled at Scott and then looked at me. "Almost done, Becca."

Scott finished pulling off the tape and then tilted my chin. "Not bad, actually. Here, go wash up. No! No talking until we get this done. Don't want to rip the cut further."

I wanted to talk, I really did, but vanity won out. In the light of day, I realized I really didn't mind a scar under my chin, but I hoped it wouldn't be too disfiguring. I marched to the bathroom, which was surprisingly clean and empty for a public space, and washed my hands with the foamy antiseptic-smelling soap Scott had given me. Then, using the washcloth and more soap, I gently washed the cut. It wasn't pretty, but it looked as if whatever scar I'd end up with would at least be straight.

I still didn't think I should talk until Scott somehow secured the injury. He'd said it was too late to stitch it, but I hoped he was better with tape than I was. I also hoped that the two of them would stop talking about me as if I weren't there. I put on a steely glare and, armed with the wet washcloth and the soap bottle, made my way back to the pavilion.

The steely look wasn't going to do much of anything. Both Scott and Sam sat on the table and watched me walk toward them. They had almost identical smug smiles on their faces, and I thought Scott was trying not to laugh. I rolled my eyes.

"Hop on back up there," Scott said. "Good. Sam, can you hand me that tube of cream and then put on some gloves. After I put the cream on, I'm going to pinch the two sides of the cut together. You can either put the butterfly bandages on or keep the cut together. Which would you prefer?"

"I think I'd rather put the bandages on. You pinch."

As they went to work, they fell into another discussion, one I was certain had been rehearsed while I was in the restroom.

"So, Sam, about Becca's personal life,"

Scott began.

"Yes," Sam said.

"If it's currently complicated . . ."

"I think it is."

"Well, I think she just needs to listen to her gut. I think she needs to follow her heart. She needs to do all that stuff they tell you to do in poetry."

"I couldn't agree more."

"But she's probably a little wary. She's made some rough decisions in the past regarding who she wanted to be with."

"Well . . ." Sam said.

"No need to be polite. She did, or she *thinks* she did. She made one bad decision. Scott, the first, was a bad move, but I wasn't."

"I see."

"Well, maybe I was at the time, but I turned out pretty awesome, don't you think?"

"I do."

"See, Becca, you're not all that wrong when it comes to choosing a guy. You were just a little premature with me. In fact, let's call it insightful. Maybe you've grown into yourself. There, you're all taped."

"May I talk?" I said without moving my lips much.

"Sure."

"First of all, thank you for putting me back together." I opened and closed my mouth. Everything seemed to work much better with the butterfly bandages than the surgical tape I'd used. "Second, way to go, Scott, on becoming an EMT. And third —"

But I was interrupted by a snap and rumble that sounded like the trunk of a huge tree breaking in half.

"What the?" Scott said.

I hopped off the table and joined Sam and Scott on the edge of the pavilion. We looked in the direction of the noise and tried to find the event attached to it.

It had been loud, too loud, almost like a violent lightning strike, but there wasn't a cloud to be seen; the sky was clear blue. I turned toward the woods on the edge of the parking lot, but nothing appeared out of place there. The corn maze wasn't open yet, and nothing seemed to be on fire from lightning. Everyone had heard the sound, and the hum and buzz of people quieted, leaving only background organ music, dinging prize bells, and a few crying babies.

Just when it seemed the moment had passed and the noise would remain a mystery, a scream sounded from somewhere in front of us. The words that followed the scream were the stuff of pure nightmares.

"The roller coaster! It's breaking! Help!"

The three of us broke into a run.

In fact, the roller coaster was breaking, or more specifically the track was breaking. You could see the exact spot; it was in a small valley on the side of the coaster that faced in toward the rest of the fair.

The coaster had three small cars, each of them with eight seats. One of the cars had cleared the break cleanly — maybe it was that car that had caused the break — but the other two cars, each of them full of people, were careening toward it.

"We've got to stop those cars," Sam said.

"I'll try to help get the electrical shut off," Scott said as he broke into another run toward the coaster operations.

Sam turned on his professional mode and started telling the gathering crowd to step away, step back.

"Call 9-1-1, Becca," he said, and suddenly I remembered the last time he'd said that to me. Someone had been killed. So far, we were okay, but if the track broke all the way or even a little more, the cars would derail and, though the drop to the ground from the small valley was only about twenty feet, I was pretty sure we'd have another tragedy on our hands.

I called 9-1-1, and as soon as the dispatcher confirmed that emergency crews were on their way, I hung up so I could help. If only I could figure out *what* to do to help.

The good news was that the coaster was definitely smaller and slower than modern coasters. It had one big hill about three-quarters of the way through the ride. The car that had traveled over the break was almost to the big hill. It was suddenly the least of my worries. I was freaking out, however, about the other two cars that were still making their way to the broken area.

"Sam! What are we going to do?" I didn't remember finding him again.

"Scott needs to get that electrical shut down."

"He will. He knows all about that stuff." *Come on, Scott, get it shut down.*

I could tell Sam was debating whether he should stay put or go find Scott and see what was taking so long.

"Damn," Sam said.

The first of the second two cars was about to go up the slope that led to the down slope that led to the valley with the broken track.

"Sam! What do we do?"

"At this point, I don't know," he said painfully.

By this time the eight riders in the car had figured out that something was wrong, but I didn't think they knew exactly what. The noise level from the crowd had risen, and we were all watching in horror as the car rolled up the slope and then started down. I didn't even know I was clenching my fists until a shot of pain ran up my arm. I was squeezing so hard that I had popped my knuckles like they'd never been popped before.

As the car hit the valley, the entire world gasped. The car rode over the break and up the next slope, but not without creating another loud snap and pop. It was then that all the riders on the coaster figured out what was happening. Two of the three cars had cleared the break, but all twenty-four riders were panicking. Though the roller coaster was old and, apparently, about to collapse, the security bars that kept the riders in place worked perfectly. If they hadn't, the riders might have thrown themselves out of the ride.

Of course, even though two cars had cleared the break, that didn't mean the entire track system wasn't at risk of falling apart.

"Scott!" I said aloud, but I still didn't see him. I had no idea where he'd gone.

"I'll find him." Sam ran away. I was left alone with the frightened crowd.

The last car was approaching the up slope, and we all stepped forward. We forgot Sam's words of warning and commands that we stay back. Somehow, irrationally, we must have thought that if the people or the car fell, we could be there to catch them.

And then as the car reached the top of the slope, it stopped. It froze in place for a long, long time, still putting weight and pressure on the break. The track sagged and I thought we were about to hear another loud crack and snap, perhaps the final one before everything fell apart.

And then the car rolled backward, away from the valley with the break. I could see the track relax back into place. If we could get the riders off the roller coaster quickly, everyone would be okay.

Suddenly, we were all cheering, some of us were crying, but mostly we were all happy that someone had saved the day. I didn't know if it was Scott or Sam or someone else, but I forgot about their teasing and I wanted nothing more than to hug them both and tell them thank you.

TWELVE

The emergency crews arrived only a few moments later, but it was Lucy who seemed to do the most good. She calmed the coaster riders so they stopped trying to climb out of the cars before it was safe to do so. She took over the controls of the machine, too, and before long brought in the two cars that had passed the break. Then she backed up the other car so that the riders who hadn't hit the break yet could also disembark. She was amazing.

No one was hurt. No one was even scratched. Some had to be treated for mild shock, but no one seemed to have sustained any long-term injury. I think everyone was surprised at how lucky we'd been.

If the death by Ferris wheel hadn't been enough, the faulty roller coaster tracks were the final straw. The fair was officially shut down, not to reopen for the rest of this year or probably ever, or at least that's what I heard. The corn maze could open, but if the authorities had their way, no one would ever again ride a ride on those grounds. The police asked everyone to exit the park, after they were briefly questioned, and to stay or come back only if they worked at the fair and had to gather their things.

In a hurried, haphazard way, we were questioned, in groups mostly. It wasn't as thorough an investigation as Sam would have liked, I suspected, but I could tell the police wanted to get everyone out of there as quickly as possible.

The main rides weren't the pack-and-go kind, and though the game and food trailers were only temporary installations, some of them required more than a quick hookup to a truck to leave the premises.

As I walked around to see if anyone needed my help, I suddenly remembered something I wished I hadn't remembered.

There was a time that I might not have minded turning Scott in to the authorities if I thought he'd done something illegal. In fact, there were times I was so angry at his immature behavior, I wished I hadn't met him at all; this attitude had probably contributed to the divorce.

I wasn't sure if my sense of loyalty to him had grown in the years since we'd parted or if the changes in his behavior made me more sympathetic to him, or maybe it was because he was now a family man, but I hesitated strongly when I thought about telling Sam what I'd seen in the files at the shooting gallery.

As I watched a cotton-candy vendor clean out her bin of sugar, it occurred to me that the sketches I'd seen hadn't been merely interesting, they might also have been more telling than I wanted them to be. I couldn't be sure, but I thought the big arrow drawn on the roller coaster schematic had pointed to the exact spot where the track had broken.

It was a damning piece of evidence, if I was remembering it correctly. I had no doubt it would lead the cops to suspect Scott of attempted murder.

I turned away from the cotton-candy trailer and ran back to the shooting gallery.

"Hey, Becca, you doing all right?" Scott asked as I halted.

"Fine, fine."

The back of the gallery, the place I'd snuck into, was fully exposed. Scott had removed the flimsy metal walls and stacked them to the side. The storage area no longer existed. What had he done with all the junk that had been there just last night?

191

"This is quite the setup. How long will it take you to tear it down?" I asked breathlessly.

"Almost a full day. I'll have to either stay late tonight or come back tomorrow. I've already carted a load out to my truck. Your tent stalls are much easier to disassemble."

"Can I take a stack of something out for you?" I said.

Scott had been leaning over the front counter of the gallery. He held a screwdriver in his hand as he straightened. "You in the mood to be helpful?" Suspicion lined his words.

"Sure, why not?"

Scott looked around. "There's not much more you could carry. I took all the small stuff out. I'll need to bring my truck in for everything else, but there's no need to do that until I'm ready to load. Thanks, though."

I nodded. Why had he taken out the small stuff? Why hadn't he just waited to load everything at once? Were there things he didn't want anyone else to see? The sketches? I hadn't examined any of them closely enough to know with certainty whether the arrow had pointed to the broken part of the roller coaster or if the Ferris wheel sketches contained anything suspicious. I suddenly wished I'd reviewed them more carefully or memorized them. Or had had time to take more pictures. The one I'd managed was just a blur of white light.

"Scott . . ." I began.

"Yeah?"

I thought way too long about what I wanted to say next. Should I just confront him, admit that I'd rummaged though his stuff? He'd be mad, but he'd probably also forgive me quickly. Unless he was hiding something big. Despite how things looked, I didn't want to believe he was capable of some murderous act.

But just in case he was, it probably wasn't a good idea to let him know I knew things that might point to his guilt. I decided to take the safer route for the time being.

"Nothing . . . no, wait, where do you live? Are you still in Charleston?"

"Yep, but I'll stick around Orderville for a few days. Susan and Brady won't be home for a week or so, and I just want to make sure everything gets taken care of . . ." He paused. "Well, I need to make sure all my stuff gets taken care of." The last sentence seemed forced, as though he were correcting himself.

"Give me your number," I said. "Maybe

193

we can get together. I'd love to meet Susan and Brady if that's not too weird."

"No, not weird at all," Scott said unconvincingly. "Sure."

I had Scott dial my number so that we had each other's.

"You still here?" Sam said from behind me.

"Hey, yeah, just saying good-bye to Scott. Want to walk me out to my truck?"

"Sure." Sam nodded at Scott, who turned his attention back to the screwdriver and some fixture on the other side of the shooting gallery counter.

My fellow farmers' market vendors were gone, as were the temporary tents and stalls that had been set up for us. Only two folding tables remained in the space where our booths had been, but they'd probably be loaded up in a few minutes, too.

"That was something," I said as we stepped over an electrical cord that snaked across the ground from some hidden location.

"That was almost as bad as it gets," Sam said.

I looked at him; he sounded angry, unusually so.

I stopped walking and put my hand on his arm. "What's up?"

He stopped, too, and looked around. "Not here. Let's talk in my car or in your truck."

I looked for Lucy as we passed the trailer, but didn't see her or anyone else. The door was closed, and all the blinds were shut tight.

We got in my truck, but I left the windows up. It was just warm enough to be stuffy in the cab but not miserable. It would have to be okay. We needed the privacy.

"What?" I said when we were not only shut but also locked inside.

"I'm angry that the roller coaster incident even happened, Becca. That place should have been shut down after Mr. Morrison's death. I told the local officers they should really take a closer look, but they assured me that they had things under control."

"How did they have things under control?"

"They said they had a security company patrolling the place for them, night and day."

"But a security company can't do much about faulty rides and equipment. Maybe they didn't expect the track to fail." I was parked facing the fairgrounds. I could see the Ferris wheel and the topmost hill of the roller coaster track. Though it was a bright, clear day, the dark clouds I'd imagined

195

above the Ferris wheel now hovered over the roller coaster, too.

"No, but one look at those rides and the entire operation should have been shut down before it even opened. I was going to call the Swayton County officials tomorrow and beg them to come out and inspect the rides. If the officials are any good at all, they would have condemned the entire place."

"Looks like someone beat them to it," I said.

Sam paused and then said, "You think the tracks were sabotaged?"

Again, I found myself debating what I should say. Well, I knew I *should* tell Sam, the police officer, what I'd found in the back of the shooting gallery. But I couldn't bring myself to do it. I wasn't sure what those drawings meant, but whatever it was, Scott was involved. I tasted the bitter wash of guilt at the back of my tongue. If I ever sought psychotherapy, I'd have to explore deeply why, despite that my feelings about him had once soured enough that I'd wanted to divorce him, I could neither turn in my second ex-husband nor believe him capable of murder or attempted murder.

I hoped my hesitation didn't have something to do with my own ego, that it wasn't the result of my not wanting to shine the bright light of truth on the bad decisions I'd made when it came to men. Maybe I didn't want to find out, even all these years later, that I'd once chosen to be with someone who'd ultimately become so evil — if Scott was, in fact, the culprit.

I'd begun to believe my judgment was improving. Ian was more than amazing, and Sam, well, if Sam and I ever became a couple, he was spectacular, too.

Finally, I said, "Should be looked into, don't you think?"

"Yeah. What a mess." Sam stared out at the grounds and then turned back to me. "I'm glad you and the other vendors . . . I guess I'm glad that everyone's okay after today. Hopefully the only casualty from this situation will be Mr. Morrison."

"Did you find out anything else about him? Did he have a long list of enemies?"

"I haven't learned much. He lived and worked around Orderville for about twenty years. Can't find any information on where he came from. Believe it or not, I'm trying to figure it out based on the tattoo. Maybe some organization or group he belonged to is into spider tattoos on their necks. I came here today to snoop around."

"He was retired military. Maybe it was something his regiment did," I said.

Sam blinked. "I don't think he was ever in the military, Becca. I searched, couldn't find anything to indicate that. If he had been, he'd be much easier to trace."

I thought back to the poker game the night before. Had it only been the night before?

"He inherited his house, a place out in the country, from his aunt. He didn't have a house payment," I said.

Sam shook his head. "That's not what I found. He paid cash for the house twenty years ago, so yeah, it was paid for, but it wasn't free."

"Do you know who owned the house before he did?"

"Not offhand. I'll check it out, though."

Why did my poker friends think he was retired military and that he'd inherited the house? I thought back harder. They'd all been in agreement about Virgil, where he'd come from and what he'd done for a living. "He did lots of odd jobs," I said.

"That I know. I'm looking more closely at all of them."

"Hang on. Why are *you* looking so closely at Virgil's death? It's not in your jurisdiction. What's your interest?"

"It's a murder, and fortunately, Monson's a little quiet in the murder department at the moment. I have faith in the local authorities, but I can't get over the fact that this fair was allowed to open its gates at all. It's bothered me since I was here a couple days ago. There's something else going on. I have no idea what it is, but if I'm not too busy in Monson, it won't hurt to poke around here a bit."

I bit my tongue. I had information that would help him. But I just couldn't tell him. Yet.

I did have something I was willing to contribute, though. "I hope the case is solved, and quickly. I know a lot of people who have enjoyed working at and attending this event, Sam. Closing it will hurt the owners financially, probably, but my sense of it is that the vendors weren't here for the money. From what I can tell, most everyone is local and they look at the fair as something fun."

I suddenly wondered, though, how many of the vendors were local? Were me and my fellow market vendors and Scott the only ones who weren't? That was something I wanted to know. I peered toward the trailer and pondered how difficult it would be to track down Lucy and how willing she might be to answer some of my questions.

"That's my sense of it, too," Sam said, but

his thoughts were churning. His eyes scanned the fairgrounds, but he turned back to me a moment later. "Hey, I gotta go. Thanks, Becca, for the information. I'm going to look a little closer . . . at everything. I'm glad this one's not around home. You might be more willing to stay out of it, huh?"

I waved away his question. "Yeah, I've got work to do. Can't be getting in the middle of this mess."

Sam got out of the truck, held the door open, and shook his head. "Don't think you're kidding me for a second. I know this is all too much for you to resist. Be careful. Call me if . . . *when* you need me. But getting back to work really would be the best idea. Keep it in mind." Sam smiled before he shut the door.

"Damn," I said, but I got over it quickly, particularly when just as Sam passed through the gates again, I saw Lucy walking purposefully toward the trailer.

If I ran fast enough, I'd reach her before she managed to shut herself inside it.

I turned off the truck and propelled my sore self out of it.

THIRTEEN

"Lucy!" I ran at breakneck speed — well, breakneck speed for someone who wasn't all that fast anyway and who had a big bruise on the top of her thigh and a cut on her chin that was extra painful with every footfall.

Lucy held her clipboard under her arm and kept her eyes to the ground as her legs took her directly to the trailer.

"Lucy!" I yelled again just as she put her foot on the first metal stair. Everyone else in the vicinity heard my screechy yowl and sent me questioning looks, but it took her a second to turn in my direction. When she did, my heart fell. She looked emotionally beaten: sad, tired, distraught. Of course she did. From all indications, Lucy loved and lived her job. The tragic events would be painful. As far as I knew, she wasn't an owner or an investor in the fair, but I could tell she took ownership of every job she was given. My sister was like that, and I recognized the type. They threw their whole selves into their tasks, always striving to exceed expectations.

Lucy was devastated.

"Hi," I said as I stopped in front of her. "Sorry to bug you." Past experience told me that if she'd gone into the trailer, she wouldn't have answered my knock, but I was sorry to have interrupted.

"Becca, you're still here. Do you need help with anything?" she asked wearily.

"No, no, I'm packed. I was just hanging around . . . anyway, Lucy, I'm sorry about the turn of events. It's great news, though, that no one was hurt as a result of the coaster tracks."

"Yes, it is." She stared at me expectantly. I wasn't quite sure how to drop some questions on her, but she saved me. "Your chin looks better. You had someone here patch it up?"

I smiled. "Yeah, my . . . did you know that one of my . . . well, my ex-husband works here. Scott, the guy with the shooting gallery. We were married, but for a short time."

"I knew that," she said. "He rebandaged it? That makes sense. Him being an EMT and all."

She knew that he and I had been married?

I wondered how, but that wasn't the most important question I had.

"Yeah. He did a good job. I was wondering, well, I've gotten to know some of the people working here and I'd like to keep in touch. I know that Scott doesn't live in Orderville." I laughed; I wasn't smooth, but Lucy didn't seem to care much. "Is everyone here from Orderville?"

"No, but most of them are. Some of the vendors, like your ex, Scott, travel with their games or food trailers from fair to fair or event to event. However, off the top of my head, besides you, your fellow market people, and Scott, I can think of only a couple others. The funnel-cake lady, Carolyn, is always on the move. There's a big need for funnel cakes apparently. And, there's a guy who's . . . who's supposed to have been here, but he didn't show up after the first couple days. He has a chocolate-dipped-pretzel trailer." She looked out toward the grounds a moment. "He's from your neck of the woods, Monson, or maybe Smithfield. He was excited about being part of the fair, but he never even got his trailer all the way set up and then he left altogether after a couple days. His name is Walter Logan. You know him by chance?"

"Never heard of him." I didn't even think

I knew of a Logan family.

"Well, if you run into him, tell him he doesn't get his space deposit back."

"I will." I nodded. "Lucy, I want you to know how much we appreciate how you tried to make us feel welcome. I'm sorry if we were cranky."

Lucy waved away my apology. "That's my job, and I understand why you were cranky. Business was pretty bad at first, and now . . . this."

"You couldn't have controlled this."

Her eyes flashed big and wide for an instant as if maybe there was some aspect of the unfortunate events that she could have controlled, but she didn't say as much. I was probably just reading into it, hoping for some substantial reaction or clue.

"We're going to move forward with the opening of the corn maze. Are you still willing to donate some pumpkins?" she said.

"Of course. I'm planning on it."

"Great. I'll have my guys there Tuesday night to help."

"Thank you." I paused. "So, how are the owners?" I continued.

"In bad shape, though they're eternally grateful that no one else was hurt. Virgil's death was hard enough. If someone else had been killed or hurt, I'm not sure they could have coped." She glanced toward the shut trailer door.

"Is that where they keep their office?" I nodded at the trailer.

"What? Oh, no, they're never out here. This is just my office."

"Who are the owners?"

Lucy shrugged, then put her hand on the door handle. "A couple brothers."

"What are their names?"

Lucy looked at the phone on her hip. "Excuse me, Becca, I've got to take this."

I hadn't heard the phone ring or buzz or jingle or give any indication that a call had come in.

"Sure."

"Let me know if you or the other Bailey's vendors need anything." Lucy held the phone to her ear as she pushed down the handle and hurried into the trailer. I tried to peer in behind her, but I didn't see anything. Once the door was closed, I didn't think twice as I reached for the handle myself and pushed. It didn't budge; in the flash of time it took her to shut the door and me to reach for the handle, she'd locked the door.

What was in that trailer?

"Becca," said a voice behind me.

"Jerry, hi." I turned to see the corn-dog

vendor standing behind me, his hands in his pockets.

"You need to get in the office?" he asked.

Actually, yes I did, but it was only to feed my ever-growing curiosity about what was so important that it was kept locked up and hidden from everyone except Lucy and Scott.

"No, I was just going to thank Lucy again."

"I've never been able to get in there, never gotten any answer when I knocked," he said. "It's weird."

"Huh." At least it wasn't just me.

"Yeah, you outta here?"

"Soon. How about you?"

"I'm packed and ready. It looks like my entrepreneurial venture wasn't as successful as I'd hoped."

"I'm sorry about that, but there are other fairs, other events that need corn dogs, surely."

Jerry shrugged. "Dunno. No big deal. I rented the trailer. I'll find a place to park it for the next week or so. I'll look for something else in Orderville, or maybe I'll check out Monson. It's a little bigger."

And there's a farmers' market in Monson. A farmers' market that doesn't sell corn dogs. Yet. I wasn't in any position to offer Jerry a space, but I knew the boss.

"Give me your number; I'll let you know if I come across anything."

"Great."

We exchanged numbers before Jerry hurried to answer someone's plea of "Hey, can I get a hand here?"

I assisted a couple people with light lifting, tried to help with some packing but found that my efforts weren't as precise as the vendor liked, and then looked around for either Sam or Scott. I found neither.

The only thing left for me to do was go home. Just a few days earlier, I couldn't wait to escape the fair, but suddenly I didn't feel ready to leave. There was more to know about the Swayton County Fall Fair and Festival, but it kept its secrets well hidden, probably under years of history that I'd never understand and wasn't meant to understand anyway. I'd be back on Wednesday with the pumpkins, but I doubted I'd learn much more than I already knew.

I did one more search for Scott and Sam but came up empty even though both of their vehicles were in the parking lot and Scott's shooting gallery wasn't yet fully disassembled.

More reluctantly than I would have imagined, I steered my old orange truck out of the parking lot and toward home.

FOURTEEN

But I didn't go home, or at least I didn't stay there. I stopped by to drop off the few supplies I'd originally taken to the fair: a small display rack, a folding chair, and what was left from a stack of my business cards. Since the day had been cut short, I still had inventory, so I deposited the unsold jars of product into one of my oversized refrigerators. I could have used the time to make more product, but my official return to Bailey's wasn't scheduled until the next week. I could wait a couple days before heading back into the kitchen. Hobbit was with George, so I took advantage of the time to make an unofficial visit to my sister and fellow vendors.

I'd mostly recovered from the horrifying near-disaster on the roller coaster. In fact, I was so relieved that no one else had been hurt, I was almost buoyant. I was sure that once the adrenaline wore off I'd be exhausted, but for the time being I was infused with energy.

My sister wasn't in the small building that housed her office, so I joined the medium-sized crowd in the market aisles and searched for her or for someone else I could talk to without bothering them too much.

The first available vendor I happened upon was Abner, the wildflower man. His science-fiction-like greenhouse kept his wildflowers growing all year long, so he never took time off from the market.

"Becca, what're you doing here? What happened to your face?" he asked as I approached. Though his gruff tone made him sound like he didn't want to see me, I knew better. It was just his way. Abner's crankiness was his strongest personality trait, but we were pretty good friends.

I told him my injury story and about the day's earlier events, finding that talking about them was almost as disturbing as living them.

When I finished, Abner whistled and said, "Holy moly, little girl. You should have high-tailed it outta there sooner."

"I'm taking in some pumpkins on Wednesday, but that'll be easy."

"Golly, I haven't been into Orderville in a number of years, can't remember why I had to go last time. It's as small a town as you can get."

"Believe it or not, I haven't seen the town yet. Haven't made it that far."

"You're not missing much," Abner said. "S'cuse me." A customer had come up on the other side of the stall.

As I waved good-bye, I wondered, though. Maybe I had missed something by not driving into Orderville. Maybe I could learn more about Virgil if I asked around the town. I wished I'd thought of it earlier, but at that point I wasn't in the mood to backtrack.

I sauntered up and down the aisles, stopping to get some eggs from Jeanine the egg lady and chatting with my stall neighbor and best friend, Linda.

"He's coming home for sure?" I asked, referring to the return of her husband, Drew, who was off on some convert Navy SEAL mission. He'd been gone a long time, and a number of worldwide happenings, such as rescues of kidnapped political prisoners and assassinations of some very bad men, had occurred in his absence. Drew wasn't allowed to have much contact with his wife while on assignment, and he was strictly forbidden from sharing the details of his missions, but she and I had speculated a number of times as to whether or not he was involved in the things we heard about in the news.

"He'll be home next week," she said. "Understand that he's not the one who told me this. Someone else called me, claimed to be one of his commanding officers, and told me the good news."

"That is more than good, that might be some of the best news I've heard in a long time."

"Ian finished the sculpture I had made for him. You'll have to stop by and see it. It's perfect."

"Ian's great at what he does."

Linda blinked, then crinkled her forehead.

"What?" I said.

"You sounded funny."

"I didn't mean to."

"Okay," she said doubtfully.

"Really, I didn't."

She laughed. "Sorry. So tell me about the fair. And your chin."

I described the day's terrifying events, and she seconded Abner's suggestion that I should have "hightailed it out of there" sooner, with no plans to return.

I waved at Bo in his onion stall and at Herb and Don in their herb stall, but they were all too busy to chat.

"Little sister, what are you doing here?" Allison said as she came up behind me.

We were fraternal twins, but she'd come into the world a full minute before I had; she often noted this fact.

We looked as different as two sisters could possibly look. She was the spitting image of our tall, dark, and handsome father, and I favored our short, blonde mother. She was the most put-together, well-organized person I knew, and most of the time, I just tried to keep up with her.

"Looking for you," I said.

"Right here."

"Your office?"

"Sure."

She was stopped for questions only twice as we made our way back to her small office, which was located in the only real building on the property.

Once the door was shut, I again relayed the events of the day.

"How in the world did they even get the permits to open the fair?" she asked when I was done.

"Apparently, Orderville isn't well regulated from outside authorities; at least that's the impression I'm getting."

"Still."

"That's what Sam said. He was going to

try to get the county authorities to shut it down, but the breaking coaster tracks took care of it for him."

Allison blinked. "Sam?"

I told her about the call he'd received when Virgil's body had been found and then about his continuing curiosity, and then I told her about Scott.

"Well, that's . . . interesting. And Scott and Sam . . . I guess there would be no reason for them not to get along, but you certainly do attract a crowd." She smiled.

"Their being at the fair had absolutely nothing to do with me."

"No, I know but . . . holy cow, Becca, you leave an interesting history in your wake."

I waved away wherever she was going to take that thread of the conversation.

"Hey, I wonder if you might be interested in having a corn-dog vendor here, at least for a little while, maybe just for a week, maybe longer."

"Hmm, not a bad idea, especially considering the cooling weather. The baked potato cart is really picking up business. I'd probably rather have hot dogs, but we could see how corn dogs went over. I need some references, though."

"I'll call him and have him call you."

"Great."

"And do you by chance know someone named Walter Logan? He was going to set up a chocolate-covered pretzel stand at the fair, but he flaked. Since you know everyone, I thought I'd ask."

"Name's familiar," she said as she pulled open a drawer to the side of her desk. "Logan, Logan, oh here it is." She pulled out a file.

"Tell me he's got a record, and I can call Sam and tell him that he's our killer."

"Hmm, no, sorry to say, I don't think so. In fact, he's a very reputable guy who has a shop in Smithfield, not in Monson. It's a chocolate and candy shop. He knows his way around chocolate. I tried to get him to consider setting up a stall at Bailey's, but he wasn't interested in anything long term. He does attend fairs and the like. I imagine he got a close look at the Swayton County event and decided it wasn't for him."

"That's it, that's all you've got?"

"That's it. Sorry, but I don't think he's your guy."

"No, probably not."

We chatted a little longer about our parents and how good it was to have them back in town for a while, and I left to pick up Hobbit and go home.

When I'd left my parents' house the night

215

before, it had been dark, so I'd been unable to clearly see the boulder on the town square park. Now, as I headed out of Bailey's, I decided that rather than going directly to George's, I would detour to downtown and inspect Jena Bellings's alleged handiwork personally.

Ten minutes later, I stood in front of the boulder, staring at the charred black mark on its top side. I didn't know if it was from lightning or just some natural pigment of rock. My mother hadn't seen Jena pull lightning from the sky, but her mother had told her she'd seen it. And Gramma hadn't been a liar.

I inspected the rock closely but could see nothing that told me much more than that there was a big black mark on a mostly gray boulder.

Disappointed, I picked up Hobbit, made sure George was set for dinner, and went home. By the time I pulled into the driveway, the adrenaline had subsided and just as I'd expected, I was totally exhausted.

I took care of Hobbit, made myself a sandwich, and headed to bed. Thankfully, I was so tired that images of gypsies and breaking roller coaster tracks stayed far away from my subconscious dreamworld.

FIFTEEN

"I tried to call him but got no answer. I'll keep trying," I said to Allison.

"Sounds good. If he gets me his references, I'll check them quickly, and he can probably be frying corn dogs by Wednesday or Thursday. The more I think about it, the more it sounds like fun."

"Good. Thanks," I said. Hobbit and I were on a morning walk, and my cell phone reception was best on the small slope of land that abutted one of my fields.

"You're welcome. And if you see Scott again, tell him to stop by Bailey's and say hello. Hope this doesn't bother you, but I wouldn't mind seeing him. I don't think a shooting gallery would work here, but I'd still like the chance to say hi."

"I'll let him know."

"Gotta go. Good to see you yesterday. See you someday soon?"

"Yeah, Ian and I are spending the day

together today, but I plan to get back to Bailey's next week."

"Well, I'm glad you're spending the day with Ian." Allison's voice was appropriately cool. She was the unhappiest of all my friends and family with me regarding my kissing Sam. She'd made it clear, both directly with words of tough love and indirectly with disapproving tones of voice and critical glances, that I needed to get my poop in a group and not lead anyone on.

I'd posted notice that I would be away from Bailey's for the entire two weeks. Though I'd thought about an early return, I had a few more ideas how to spend at least a couple more days away from the market.

"We'll have a good time," I said, though it sounded forced and not completely true. I cleared my throat.

"All right. See you later."

"I'm sure I'm a disappointment to her," I said to Hobbit after I hit the end button.

Ever on my side, no matter how oddly tilted my side might be, Hobbit nosed my knee, telling me that she thought I was perfect. I *knew* she was perfect, so we were good.

Ian's truck rolled down the driveway just as Hobbit and I exited my pumpkin patch.

"I brought donuts," he called out of his

open driver's side window. "Are we really going to Orderville?"

"If that's still okay," I said.

During my drive home with Hobbit the night before, I'd formed a plan for Ian and me to spend today traveling to and exploring Orderville. Though the town was close to Monson, I'd never been there; I was curious about it, and I thought it might be a fun way for us to pass the day, away from the distractions of work and home.

I knew Ian had a million and one more important things to do than visit a small South Carolina town, but I'd called him first thing this morning and told him everything that had happened at the fairgrounds yesterday, and then I invited him to go to Orderville with me. I didn't tell him about my visit with Betsy. I thought I'd see how the day went first. I almost told him the Jena Bellings story that my mother had told me, but she'd said it could only be shared with family, and Ian wasn't technically family.

"I'd like to know more about the community, maybe more about Scott. So, want to come help me look around and be nosy?" I'd asked.

I was pleased when he said yes, but something about that moment, about the tone of his laugh and his quick acquiescence had set off a warning bell in my head. I knew we'd have to talk about it. Eventually.

That *thing* was that Ian was a great friend. We got along and always had a good time together. We had the physical attraction that went along with a romance, too, but more than anything, we were buddies.

I'd told him a number of times that he should dump me. I'd even thought that Sam should never talk to me again. But Ian wouldn't dump me. And Sam and I were again speaking to one another. Of course, if we were destined to run into each other in our small corner of the world, it was probably a good thing that we figure out how to get along.

For now and for the first time in a long time, I was thrilled at the idea of spending the day with my friend.

"It's more than okay," Ian said as Hobbit and I reached his truck. "It'll be great to get out of town for a while. We've both been working hard. Even if we only road trip to Orderville, I think it'll be good to take a break."

"Great!" I was thrilled that he saw it the same way I did.

I didn't want to be put in the position of having to leave Hobbit alone in the truck in a town she wasn't familiar with, so we told her she didn't get to join us but that we'd bring her back something and promised her another day with George.

Ian would soon be moving out of the apartment above George's garage, and George would then sell his old French Tudor, but the twist that none of us had seen coming was that Ian had redesigned the house he was building so that George could move in with him. George would have his own space: a bedroom, bathroom, small kitchen, family room, and another room that would be furnished with bookshelves, his own leather chairs, and a fireplace just like the library in his home. Ian said he was even going to scent it with some pipe tobacco. George's current library still held remnants of the days when he would read gruesome mysteries, in his hand a magnifying glass or a pipe just like Sherlock Holmes's.

It had taken Ian about six attempts to convince George to move to the farm with him. George loved company but had recently been thinking he was a burden. That was definitely not the case, but convincing him of as much had been work, though well-rewarded work. Ian was just as excited to have George at the farm as George now seemed to be that he was going.

"It looks like Scott and Sam got you put back together fairly well," Ian said as we rolled down the state highway toward Orderville. "You're pretty bruised. Does it hurt?"

"Not all the time," I said. "I'll be okay."

"I hope I get to meet your ex-husband," Ian added.

"Actually, I do, too. We might have to drive by the fairgrounds just to see if we can find him," I said before taking a big bite out of a giant chocolate-covered donut. Biting and chewing food hurt my chin, but the donut was worth a little pain. "Running into him was a surprise, but not a bad one really. Unless he's a killer or something."

"I doubt he is, Becca, although I think what you found behind the shooting gallery is off-putting at best."

"I wish I'd just asked him about it, but I would have had to admit that I'd snuck in there."

"Well, I don't think you should have told him, not without letting the police know first, or maybe having someone come along with you. Be careful."

"I will be."

"We'll see how it goes today. I'll be there, so if we find him, maybe you can ask him about it today."

I looked at Ian. "You're enjoying this, aren't you?"

Ian smiled. "Kind of. I like that you felt like you could talk to me about what you've been up to before you got shot at or a knife thrown at you."

My stomach sunk. Suddenly, the donut didn't taste so good. "Do you think I don't share because I don't trust you?"

"No, not really, not completely at least. I guess I'm just glad you trust me enough now."

"It's because I don't want you or Allison or Sam to try to stop me. Does that make sense?" *Which is a form of distrust, but still.*

"I wouldn't even dream of it," Ian said.

I was such a horrible girlfriend. I should have known that even though Ian would always try to be my voice of reason, he'd be as supportive as possible and not stand in my way.

I bit into the donut again but didn't taste anything.

"Let's change the subject," Ian said, clearly noticing my discomfort.

"Good idea," I said with a full mouth.

Though I'd told Ian about the fair events and about Scott, I hadn't given him the details regarding my poker buddies. As he drove, I filled him in on as much as I could remember. I also mentioned Virgil's house and asked him to drive by it before we went all the way into Orderville. I'd found the address easily with an Internet search. I didn't think Virgil's killer would be lurking in the bushes or breaking through a window, and I wanted to see the house that everyone thought Virgil had inherited but that Sam said he'd paid for. Maybe it was the connection I thought we'd had, the potential friendship, but something about Virgil drew me to him, something more than his spider tattoo and the fact that he manned the crippled Ferris wheel. Again, the lost potential and his unsolved murder haunted me enough to want to see where he'd lived.

The country surrounding Virgil's home was packed with trees and flowers. Even if he hadn't inherited the house from an aunt, it was an easy story to believe. The house and the grounds were nothing if not fit for an old Southern lady.

The bungalow that sat amidst nature's abundance was equipped with a full, wide front porch where three rocking chairs held court along with several wicker side tables that had surely seen many glasses of iced tea. I couldn't picture Virgil sitting on the porch, rocking and sipping. The setup felt funny. If he *had* inherited the house, it had happened twenty years ago, yet this furniture looked fairly new. But maybe he'd thought that leaving feminine white rocking chairs on the front porch would honor his aunt.

Or maybe I was just wrong. Maybe Virgil had liked whitewashed rocking chairs, wicker side tables, rosebushes by the dozens, and bougainvillea with its sweet-smelling flowers. The house reminded me of my own grandmother's home, not that of a man who did odd jobs to support himself and had a tattoo on his neck.

"What do you know about spider tattoos?" I asked as Ian came to a stop in front of the house.

"Not a lot. I don't think I've ever known anyone with a spider tattoo. No, wait, I have seen one before. On a college friend's arm. It was a spider coming down from a string of web. It was kind of cool, kind of creepy, but mostly interesting. I can't remember if I even knew what it meant. I'll think about it."

"Thanks." I looked at the grounds. "Don't worry, I don't want to break in or anything, but I really want to look through those windows. You want to come?"

"Sure. It's not a crime scene, and you did say you wouldn't be trying to break in."

I smiled.

"Come on," Ian said as he got out of the truck.

There wasn't another person or house or car in sight. Sooner or later, someone would drive in one direction or the other down the road in front of the house, but it was unquestionably an out-of-the-way place. That fit with the Virgil I'd started to get to know. Maybe he had purchased the house twenty years earlier and just never had the energy to make it less feminine. Maybe he'd made up the story about inheriting it from an aunt because he didn't want people to know he had money.

This was a small community, though. Someone usually caught on to a lie like that in a small community. Eventually. If he had been less than honest, perhaps his lies had never caught up with him. Or maybe they had and he'd been killed for them, but telling people you'd inherited your house seemed like a pretty innocuous lie.

There had to be more to him, more to the story than just how he'd acquired the house.

A cobblestone path led to the front door. I followed Ian as we wove our way through the strongly scented yard. Again, the grounds and the scents reminded me of my grandmother's house. Since the conversation with my parents Friday evening, Gramma had been on my mind. The setting only brought out more good memories. I liked thinking about her.

"Should we knock on the door before we start looking in windows, just in case?" Ian asked.

"Not a bad idea."

No one answered, and still a car hadn't passed by in either direction. It wasn't scary or uncomfortable — probably because Ian was with me. It was peaceful, and though the grounds had no open fields for farming, I liked peaceful.

Two big picture windows, one on each side of the front door, afforded a clear view inside. I stepped to the one on the left, put my hand up to shade the glare, and peered in. The inside of the house was as masculine as the outside was feminine. I saw a decidedly neutral and utilitarian front room. There was a brown couch and a nonmatching brown recliner, a brown coffee table with two matching end tables, and a couple lamps with bases that must have been covered with brown cork. The television against the wall next to the window wasn't a modern flat-screen but the older, boxy type, topped with rabbit ears.

The room was well-kept, no messes anywhere; no piles of paperwork cluttering the tabletops, as was usually the case in some parts of my own house. Everything seemed neat and clean, but slight indentations in the cushions of both the chair and the couch told me it was probably also a much-used room.

I crossed to the other widow, and Ian and I both put our foreheads to it. We could see the dining room and the kitchen beyond it. Nothing looked new, but nothing looked messy, and everything appeared to be well taken care of.

"Tell you anything?" Ian asked.

"I used to have a stove that color green. I got rid of it to get something a little less 1970s. But the green one had the best oven I've ever owned. The only unusual thought that comes to my mind is I wonder if that oven cooks as good as mine did."

Ian looked at me with raised eyebrows.

"I don't see anything out of place. Everything is tidy and doesn't look dirty."

"What about the front porch?" Ian said. "The . . . furnishings?"

"They seem strange for a single guy, is that what you mean?"

"Yes, that's exactly what I mean. I'm probably as far from macho as anyone you know, right?"

"Yes."

"Even I don't think I'd have these sorts of things on my front porch by choice. If you wanted them, or . . . well, the woman in my life wanted them, then sure, but not of my own choice. Did you know him well enough to know if he was dating someone?"

"He and a bartender in town dated but broke up a couple weeks ago. Dianna Kivitt. She said she never came out here, though, and it wasn't a long relationship."

"Well, I don't know. I don't want to read into something that's not really there, but you said he was a tough, gruff, silent-but-strong type of guy with a spider tattoo on his neck. I can only think of a couple reasons his front porch would have rocking chairs and wicker furniture. He was either dating someone, or he had another, secret life. Either way, down either path, there could be a killer, his killer."

"Or it could mean nothing at all. Nothing," I said.

"It could," Ian replied doubtfully. "But I just don't think so. Let's go into town and see what we can find out."

"First stop, the bar? Drinks on me."

Ian laughed, and I realized how much fun it was just to be having fun with him.

SIXTEEN

If my hometown of Monson, South Carolina, was small, Orderville, South Carolina, was downright miniscule. And Monson had weathered the ticks of time better than Orderville. We'd maintained some of our old, small-town values and architecture, but lots of the buildings had been updated since World War II. That didn't seem to be the case in Orderville.

It wasn't the speed limit sign as much as it was the road conditions that caused Ian to slow down as we reached the edge of town. The road was paved, but suddenly and almost without warning, it became less than ideal, with ruts and cracks that wouldn't have been kind to even new shocks and struts; Ian's old truck would have protested loudly.

"Look at that guy," Ian said as he nodded to our left. "Is he real or a mannequin?"

The gentleman he spoke about was on a

stool, leaning back against the blue chipped-paint wall of one of the smallest gas stations I'd ever seen. His face was mostly hidden by a brimmed hat, but a long piece of straw came out from his mouth. He wore a red and blue plaid shirt and long overalls that seemed much more authentic than mine. His were heavily faded, worn thin in spots, and latched over only one shoulder. It was the movement of the piece of straw from one side of his mouth to the other that made me realize he was, indeed, real. Other than that, he was stone still.

The station building was a cube that seemed just big enough to accommodate its overalled keeper and maybe a counter with a cash register. A single gas pump sat outside, but there was nothing modern about it. There was no evident way to pay at the pump, unless of course, the gentle-man leaning against the wall came to you and took your money. The pump was red and white with a clear globelike ball on the top, the writing on which had long ago worn away. I wondered if the machine made din-ging noises as it pumped gas.

"He's real. I thought those types of pumps were outlawed for safety reasons or some-thing," I said.

"I thought so, too, but did you see how

the road changed when we reached the border of the town? Maybe the laws are different in Orderville." Ian shrugged.

Following the station were five old boarded-up shacks, but a much less dilapidated building occupied a plot on the other side of the road. It wasn't a well-put-together structure, but it didn't look like it was going to crumble soon either. It was wide and deep and the hand-painted sign out front said, "Plant Starts. Get'em Here."

"A nursery," I said.

"Just the starts of one." Ian smiled.

"Right."

Dianna Kivitt's bar, Bottoms Up, was located in a non-shack-like building down the road a bit from the nursery. The two buildings were separated by a small expanse of weeds and grasses; had deep tire ruts not marred the grassy area, it might have made a picturesque setting.

Bottoms Up appeared to be part of an improvised mini strip mall. Next to the bar was a hat store, cowboy hats specifically, and then an upholstery shop. The three establishments, though right next to each other, weren't connected, and each had its own distinct look: the bar was all blacked-out windows; the hat store had no windows at all, its flat façade painted with illustrations of hats instead; and the upholstery shop sported two big windows in which several chairs were displayed. The ample parking lot in front of the three businesses was currently occupied by only a couple trucks, all directly in front of the bar. It wasn't quite noon, and I smelled the distinct scent of hamburgers and French fries.

"There, Ian, let's stop at that bar."

"That the one?"

"Yep. That's the one Dianna said she owned. She's the one who supposedly dated Virgil. And I smell the opportunity for a yummy hidden dive burger and fries."

"Sounds good."

Ian parked next to a truck that was older than mine and though also orange, was much more faded.

Inside, Bottoms Up was dark and cold, and smelled more like cigarette smoke than hamburgers and fries. It didn't look like anyone was drinking yet, but toward the back wall a pinball machine bell dinged as an older gentleman played and cursed it at the same time. A string of Christmas lights decorated the front of the long wooden counter, the area behind which was the only well-lit space in the bar. There, Dianna Kivitt was at work, her attention focused on something she was either cleaning or organizing.

"Welcome to Bottoms Up," she said without looking up. "Sit anywhere, or make it easy on me and come up to the bar. Either way, a tip is always appreciated."

We wove around the few tables and chairs and then found a couple comfortable stools at the bar.

"Hi, Dianna," I said.

She finally glanced up. It took her a second, but she soon said, "Becca, right? The one with no poker face at all?"

"That's me."

"Well, welcome to Bottoms Up, I guess. Couldn't get enough of Swayton County? Had to come find us today?"

"Something like that. This is Ian."

The smile she beamed at him was much friendlier than the one she'd had for me.

"What can I get for you?" she asked suspiciously.

"I'd like a diet soda," I said.

"I'll have the same," Ian said.

"Sure."

She had the sodas, with cherries, in front of us quickly. "So, really, what are you doing in Orderville? Nobody comes here just to visit me. Well, that's not totally true. Lots of people come from around town to visit the bar, but that's only because there's no other one closer to where they live."

"I was curious," I said.

"About?"

"Virgil."

"Oh." Dianna nodded and then looked away. She picked up a towel and started drying some shot glasses that clearly didn't need to be dried. "I told the police. This morning, I told them I'd dated Virgil. They didn't seem to care."

"Bet that made you feel better, though," I said as I chewed the cherry stem. I was going to order my diet soda with a cherry from now on.

"It did. But like I said, they didn't care a bit. They . . ."

"They what?"

"All they did was ask me if Virgil ever acted funny around me. They wanted to know if he and I had ever been followed or some such nonsense."

Ian and I shared a questioning glance. "Had you? Had he, acted funny, I mean?" I said.

"I dunno." Dianna shrugged. "Virgil was a funny guy. I'd known him some twenty years, and I still didn't know him all that well. What was supposed to be funny? And if someone had followed us, I wouldn't have known. Why would I pay attention anyway? We're a small town; we all see each other everywhere and all the time. I could have mistaken being followed for someone doing the same errands as I was. And we didn't date all that long either. We weren't in love, you know."

"Did he go on to date anyone else?" I asked.

"Not that I saw, but he never invited me for dinner at his house like he had Randy, so what do I know?"

"Do you know where he lived? Had you ever seen, driven by, his house?"

"Sure, I already told you I did, at the poker game. It's one of the ways to get to the main highway."

"So you know about his big porch?"

"I guess."

"White rocking chairs and wicker furniture?"

Dianna blinked. "No, not on Virgil's porch."

"He owned the bungalow right outside town? The one with all the rosebushes and bougainvillea?" I said.

"Yeah."

"Ian and I drove by there today, and there were white rocking chairs and wicker furniture on the porch."

Dianna shrugged. "Well, maybe he'd put them there just recently. From what I remember, there was only one chair on the front porch, a lawn chair. Virgil chewed, too. I remember you could see his spittoon from the road."

I'd seen no lawn chair and no spittoon.

Honestly, none of this meant much of anything. Virgil's taste in furniture might have changed recently, or maybe he'd wanted to stop chewing tobacco, so he got rid of the spittoon. Maybe the house was being put up for sale and the real estate agent thought a slight porch redecoration would up its curb appeal, but I couldn't help but think that Ian was right: there'd been some sort of female influence in his life. It clearly wasn't Dianna, though, so who would it have been?

Orderville was small enough that if someone sneezed, surely they'd hear a "bless you" from the other side of town. And who would know more about the citizens than the local bartender? *Maybe the local hairstylist,* I thought.

I felt kind of like we'd hit a dead end, but something else occurred to me. "Dianna, do you know anything about the two brothers who started the fair?"

"No, not a thing." She was lying. A flicker

of surprise had crossed her face when I asked the question, and then she'd looked away so quickly, I had no doubt she knew exactly who I was talking about.

Ian nudged my knee with his. He knew she was lying, too.

"Excuse me a minute," she said. She didn't put down the towel or the shot glass she was drying as she scurried down the bar and around a curtain.

"That was interesting," Ian said. "Even you're better at lying than she is."

"Why wouldn't she want to tell us?"

Ian shrugged.

I didn't know what else to ask Dianna, but Ian and I didn't want to leave. We'd been there only a few minutes, and though burgers and fries didn't sound as appealing as they had before we walked in, there might be more to learn at Bottoms Up. Besides, I didn't know Orderville well enough to know where we should go next anyway.

Dianna would have to come out eventually. I assumed the kitchen was behind the curtain, along with whatever other places were needed to run a bar — an office, maybe?

My instincts about wanting to stay put paid off a few minutes later. The door opened, letting in a figure silhouetted by the block of sunny light behind it. Once the door closed, my eyes quickly readjusted and I saw that the new customer was Jerry.

I waved him over.

Like Dianna, he took a beat or two to realize that he knew me, but he was much quicker with his smile.

"Becca, the jam lady and Scott's ex-wife. Hey, what're you doing here?" He bounded up onto the stool next to me.

I shrugged and introduced Ian.

"I tried to call you, but it rang twice and then went silent," I said.

"Really? Huh. I don't know why. I'm here now, though. What'd'ya need?"

"What are your plans since the fair is done?" I asked.

"Sad, huh? It was a big deal around here. Oh, I don't know what I'm going to do. Thought I'd stop by and see if Dianna had any good ideas."

"I might have something. My sister manages the farmers' market where I sell my jams and preserves. She said a corn-dog trailer would be a welcome addition. You just have call her. She'll check your references and you can jump right in."

He seemed to freeze for an instant, and then he blinked. "Really?"

"Yeah."

"I . . . that's super great of you. Thank you."

"You're welcome. You know where Monson is? Bailey's?"

"I'll find it. I won't call. I'll go out there this afternoon."

"Good. You'll like it there."

"Awesome. Hey, can I buy you two a drink, lunch?" Jerry said.

"No, thanks" — I took a sip of my soda — "but do you have a second? I have some questions about . . . Orderville."

"You thinkin' of putting a farmers' market here? Hey, that's not a bad idea." Jerry scratched the side of his head in thought.

"Not really, but someone did mention the idea was being considered. I tried to answer their questions, but I think I need to know more about the town to give an opinion about whether a market would work here."

"Sure. I haven't been in town long, but there's not that much to know, I suppose. It's so small."

"Maybe the fact that you're still kind of an outsider will help. You won't have any strong prejudices yet."

"Go ahead."

"First of all, why was the fair such an important event?" I asked. "I think I can say this to you since you're new to the area.

240

I don't want to insult anyone, but really, what was the big deal? It took a murder to get people even interested in coming out to it. And the rides, well, they were in pretty bad shape."

Jerry rubbed at his chin. He looked like he was putting real thought into his answer. There was an intelligence to his eyes that I hadn't noticed before. That assessment probably wasn't fair because we'd only known each other briefly, but the difference was so stark, I couldn't help but wonder about it. Then, just as quickly, his eyes went back to the Jerry I thought I knew: a little less intelligent and a little confused.

"Good question," he finally said. "All I know is that it was the talk of the town. It was all I heard for a while — who's going to work at the fair? What's so-and-so going to do at the fair? You know, that kind of thing. But there was also something else. There was a sense of . . . well, people were worried, too. I think the fair's always been a challenge, always been hard to get people to come out to it. I noticed the rides, too, but I didn't think anyone was worried about them as much as they were about attendance." He looked around the bar. The man playing pinball was still the only other customer in the place. "I just think no one has anything else much better to do. I think it's a good diversion. People get pretty bored doing the same thing all the time. It just gave everyone another option. Maybe. Or . . ."

"Or?" Something told me he actually knew the real answer but had mumbled through all the other stuff first.

"Aw, shoot, I guess I can tell you, but I don't put much stock in it, you gotta know."

Both Ian and I nodded.

"It's that silly gypsy magic."

"What do you mean?"

"The festival is a tradition, put in place to honor Jena Bellings — people don't like to say her name, though; it's weird — but I don't know the details about her. Anyway, it's said that the years they don't have the festival are the years everyone suffers. Crops fail, people get sick and die, bad things happen, so they just keep having the festival so as not to be cursed by gypsy magic." Jerry laughed.

I didn't laugh. It took a minute to get my mind around the idea that an entire town could be held hostage by something like "gypsy magic." But if my mother's story about Jena was true, then Jena had held Monson hostage, too, in a way.

"Who's Jena?" Ian asked.

"Oh, yeah, you weren't at the fair," Jerry said. "Have Becca tell you about the billboard painted with the creepy house sticking up from the middle of the corn maze. That was apparently Jena's house. I wish I could get the whole story, but she was some sort of 'gypsy' I guess. People around here whisper about her; something about good and bad luck."

Ian nodded. "Interesting."

"They're a superstitious and secretive bunch." Jerry had transformed again, sounding somehow different, perhaps more serious. "Guess we all have our secrets though, huh?"

I blinked at his tone, but he smiled again and his eyes dimmed back to normal. It was a curious trick.

He leaned close to me, though Ian could hear him when he said, "Some crazy people even get spider tattoos on their necks."

I blinked again. "You knew Virgil better than you mentioned when we were playing poker?"

"Nope, it's just something I noticed is all."

A thread of defensiveness ran through me. I felt protective of my "almost friend" Virgil. Was Jerry making fun of him? I shook it off.

"Who are the brothers, the ones who apparently own the fair?" I asked just as Dianna came out from behind the curtain.

Jerry looked at her and then said, "I don't know. I've asked the same question. I have no idea. Hey, Dianna, how about a cold one — oh, no, I'm driving to Monson. Just a Coke, then?"

"Sure thing," she said.

"Hey, I might have a job," Jerry said. "At Becca's farmers' market."

"That right?" Dianna avoided looking at anyone as she pulled out a can, popped it open, poured it, and put the glass in front of Jerry. "Good luck with that."

"Thank you."

What an odd woman, I thought.

Dianna must have had more to do behind the curtain because she disappeared again. I asked Jerry what he knew about Virgil's personal life, if he knew whether Virgil had been dating anyone, but he didn't have any answers. No other customers came in to motivate Dianna to show herself, so once Jerry excused himself to the now available pinball machine, Ian and I decided it was time to explore more of the town.

The bright glare of the sun blinded us momentarily as we made our way over the gravel lot to Ian's truck.

The sound that came from the side of the

building, the skinny slot between the bar and the hat store, was a distinct "psssst."

Ian and I turned toward the sound.

Dianna was wedged into the small space. "Hurry. Come here," she whispered loudly.

Ian and I looked at each other and then did as she'd asked.

"You don't want Jerry at the farmers' market," she said.

"I don't understand. Why not?" I asked.

"Trust me. Now go away and don't tell anyone what I told you. You need to just get out of Orderville. And mind your own business."

I thought about following her as she turned, sidestepped her way back down the narrow alley, and then reentered her building through a back door, but I quickly dismissed the idea. She'd wanted to make sure she talked to us secretly. If I betrayed that trust, I might put her in some sort of jeopardy.

"You're not going down there, are you?" Ian asked.

"No." I shook my head. "But that got my attention."

"We're not going to leave town and mind our own business either, are we?"

I shook my head again. "I don't think so. Not yet."

SEVENTEEN

There wasn't much more of Orderville to explore. Down the road from the bar was the "downtown," if you could even call it that. I'd traveled through my share of small towns, but Orderville put a new spin on the whole idea.

Only five buildings occupied the strip: a post office, a diner, a VFW post, a yarn shop, and finally a drugstore — the sign said "Drugstore," not "Pharmacy."

I didn't see a police station — or any other government buildings, for that matter, aside from the post office — or a library or a bookstore. I didn't even see a grocery store. As I looked around, I wished I'd noticed earlier whether the sign on the way into town listed the population.

"I don't know why people live here," I said.

"I don't even see neighborhoods. It just looks like a lot of farm country," Ian commented.

"Where do people go for their groceries?"

"Maybe Monson, I don't know," Ian said. "Should we grab lunch from the diner? Could be kind of fun, and since you're not ready to mind your own business, it'll give us something to do."

"Good plan."

Combined with Dianna's strange behavior, the old town's desertedness made me uneasy; even in the bright sun of the middle of the day, the place felt spooky. When Ian turned off his truck, I expected to hear a suspicious quiet, interrupted perhaps by the distant sound of wind whistling through some mysterious chasm somewhere, or maybe even a scream.

But that's not what we heard. Instead, there was the far-off rumble of an engine, probably a tractor working a field, and the laughter of a group of kids who had just rounded the corner and were hurrying down the street, though I didn't know to what. They passed the buildings and then turned out of view.

"Are we in the twilight zone?" I asked Ian as we watched the kids.

"I don't know," he said, far too honestly.

The diner wasn't spooky, though. In fact, it was cheery.

"Hey, hey," said a round woman from behind the long counter. "Y'all find a seat anywhere there's one to be found."

The diner had only about twenty tables, half of them already occupied by customers who didn't pay us much attention.

We took a couple seats at the counter and had our sandwiches ordered in record time.

As she was filling our waters, Liz, the waitress and hostess, asked, "Y'all traveling through?"

"We were hoping to visit the fair, but it looks like it got shut down," Ian said. "Too bad."

I was suddenly very proud of him. Good answer.

"Shoot, that was a scary moment. The roller coaster about went flying off the track and nearly killed everyone. There was already someone who died a couple days ago. Ask me, the place should have never been opened in the first place. Death trap."

"Really?" I said. "Then why was it opened?"

"It was tradition. It's what we did. Swayton County comes together for the fair. The fair brings . . . brought us together. It's a shame, though, a sad shame."

At least she didn't mention the gypsy magic. I said, "I bet the owners are upset about losing the income."

"Nah, those boys couldn't care less. They've got money up the wazoo, they don't need more. I think they're probably more worried about being sued at this point." Liz's eyes suddenly got big. "Dang, I shouldn't be talking like that. I've got to learn to keep my mouth shut."

"What boys, who?" I asked, hopefully before she took her own advice.

"The Bellings boys. Everyone knows them, don't they?" She laughed. "I know, I know, people not from around these parts wouldn't know the Bellings boys from Adam and Evan, but we all know them. Oh, excuse me, I've got to get some coffee out to the thirsty throng."

Bellings boys. Jena Bellings. Well, at least those parts of the puzzle were beginning to come together.

"She answered that easily," Ian said quietly. "She didn't think a thing of it. Gave you another link to the gypsy woman Jerry talked about, too. She must have been something."

I nodded. I had to bite my tongue to keep from sharing the story I'd heard from my mother. "I bet they really are afraid of being sued. Maybe they told everyone not to give out their name. I don't know. We need to find out who they are."

"At least we have a place to start now."

My grilled ham and cheese was perfect, buttery and melty but with nice crispy bread. The fries were skinny and crunchy on the outside, soft on the inside, just the way I liked them. I tried to enjoy the meal, but I couldn't help myself from looking around and wondering who else I could talk to or who I could ask about the Bellings brothers.

It was because of my constant and less-than-furtive glances that I happened to be looking out the front window just as Scott walked — no, sauntered — by. He had his hands in his pockets, and though I couldn't hear him, it was obvious he was whistling.

"Uhm, pay en go," I said around my mouth full of food. What I'd meant was, "Put some money on the counter and let's go."

"Excuse me?"

"Scott!" I said after I swallowed. "Scott just walked by. Let's go see what he's doing."

"Your second ex-husband?"

"Yep."

"I'm game."

Ian left money on the counter and we hurried out of the diner, probably looking like we were dining and dashing, but no one stopped us.

The door closed behind us just as Scott turned the corner, the same corner the kids had turned. I still couldn't hear him whistling.

We scurried behind. If anyone was watching us, they'd surely think we were up to no good, but still no one questioned or stopped us.

We both slowed as we reached the corner, then peered around it together, Ian's dark ponytail hitting the top of my blonde head, and spied a whole new world.

Just behind the tired small strip of downtown, was life and civilization.

We saw another service station, this one a little more modern, with a couple gas pumps and a building big enough to sell staples like bread and milk, and snacks and soft drinks. It was set back from where we stood about half a football field; two other roads, unnoticeable from where we'd come into town, led up to it. Next to the first building was a four-bay garage, each bay occupied by either a car or a truck. I counted five guys, including Scott, who were inside the bays, presumably working on the vehicles. Perhaps there were even more people hidden behind lifted hoods, but we couldn't be sure.

"He told me he's an EMT," I said aloud, though I was talking to myself more than to Ian. "Why is he still in town, this town, and at a garage?"

"He might not be working there. He might just be visiting people. Maybe one of the vehicles is his."

"Why? What's he doing in Orderville, South Carolina, Ian? Who does he know? Why did he set up a shooting gallery at the fair? He told me he was just here for the fair, but that doesn't make sense. He's up to something, and I want to know what it is," I said. "Let's go."

We stepped out from behind the building and walked purposefully toward the bay that Scott was in. He stood next to a brown pickup talking to a guy in a work jumpsuit who was leaning against the front of it. They looked comfortable with each other, as if they knew each other well.

"He's blond. I never would have pegged you for liking blonds," Ian joked quietly as we marched forward.

"Well, both he and the other Scott were blond. I must have learned my lesson," I joked back. Ian's dark coloring was a sharp contrast to the fair complexions and near tow-headedness of both of my ex-husbands.

I didn't have time to dwell on it, but I enjoyed the light-hearted joking with him. It wasn't as if we'd suddenly and magically fixed our relationship; but we *were* having a good time together, without the shadows of whatever I'd done to create a strain between us. As strange as Orderville might be, the change of scenery felt good.

"I see." Ian smiled. "Oops, looks like he saw us."

Scott had casually glanced in our direction, but it took a second, neck-jerking look before he realized who we were, or who I was, at least.

When the flash of recognition hit his eyes, it mixed with something else. It was as if he was surprised, then concerned, but he quickly covered it all with a forced smile.

"Becca," he said too exuberantly as he came out of the bay. "What're you doing here?"

"Lunch," I said. "At the diner. What are you doing here? Why are you still in town?"

Scott wasn't a liar. He was always and sometimes annoyingly honest, so when he attempted to lie at that moment, even Ian could see through it, and they hadn't even met yet.

"I, uh — just helping people get packed up. I told you yesterday that I was going to stick around."

He had, but still.

"Hey, how ya doin'? I'm Scott," Scott said as he extended his hand to Ian.

"Ian Cartwright."

"Nice to meet you. You know, Becca and I used to be married." Scott was working too hard at changing the subject.

"She mentioned that." Ian smiled.

"I was the good Scott. The other one, not so much." Even when he was being annoying, Scott could still be kind of charming.

Ian smiled again. "Well, she hasn't gone into those details, but good to know."

"Hey, lookee here, it's a party," Scott said as he peered over my shoulder.

Ian and I turned at once.

If I hadn't kissed him a few months earlier, I might have been thrilled to see Sam Brion walking toward us. However, since I had thrown myself at him and that one act had tipped every personal relationship I had in a wonky direction, and because Ian was with me, I wasn't all that excited to see Sam give me a semiapologetic glance as he stepped surely up to us.

I didn't know if Ian and Sam had seen each other recently, but I knew they hadn't done so with me present. I wanted to kick my stupid self.

It didn't register with me that I'd made any sort of noise until a few seconds after I'd made it, at which point I realized I'd just let loose what sounded like a cross between a groan of pain and a gasp of panic.

Ian cleared his throat.

"Sam, thanks for meeting me," Scott said. "You must have come in on the main road. To get to the garage back here, you have to take a few side streets. Come on, I'll help you."

"Thanks, I appreciate it. Ian, Becca," Sam said as he shook Ian's hand.

"Good to see you, Sam," Ian replied sincerely.

"A guy here does amazing things with old Mustang engines," Scott said to me. "I told Sam he should bring his car here."

By the way Scott seemed to want to explain Sam's arrival, I suspected that the two of them had discussed more than car engines. He had been lying, and he had been uncomfortable because he knew that Sam was about to show up. I didn't know how much Scott knew about me and Ian and Sam, or how much Sam had shared — or why he would share anything at all — but the moment was most definitely awkward.

"We'll be right back," Scott said as he

escorted Sam back in between the buildings and presumably to his car.

I looked at Ian. I had no idea what to say.

"It's okay, Becca. Sam and I were . . . are friends. We're going to get along just fine. We needed to get this moment over with, don't you think?"

I still didn't know what to say.

"Hey, did you see the sign?" Ian said as he nodded toward the pumps.

Glad for the diversion, I turned again. "Oh, that's a good discovery. Come on, let's see what we can find out before they get back."

The sign said "Bellings Bros. Tires and Service."

As we hurried toward the store part of the station, I decided I'd have to think about running away if my other Scott showed up. And if my dance date from junior high school also appeared, I'd probably have to just commit to a life of being single so I wouldn't ever have to face one these embarrassing moments again.

EIGHTEEN

Hal wasn't as friendly as Liz. The kids we'd watched earlier were still in the station's larger-than-I'd-thought shopping area, noisily deciding on which kind of candy and soda they wanted, or at least had enough money to purchase. From his spot behind the counter, Hal, according to the name embroidered on his bright blue shirt, kept one suspicious eye on the kids and the other, equally suspicious eye on us.

We were strangers in town, and we were asking about the name on the sign. Who were the Bellings brothers? I was sure Hal wondered why we cared and why we wanted to make our curiosity his problem.

Finally, after he rang up two customers and we saw Sam's Mustang roll into one of the bays, Hal said, "They're the owners."

"Of the service station and the fair?" I asked.

Hal nodded.

"Do they ever come in here?"

"No."

"Do they have offices anywhere? I'd like to meet them," I said.

"Why?"

The question kind of stumped me. I wanted to meet them just because I wanted to meet them. I wanted to better understand this small Stephen King–ish town. I wanted to know why they'd let their fair gates open with the rides in the condition they'd been in. I had a bunch of questions.

"I'd like to talk to them about a farmers' market idea. I hear they are thinking of putting one in town." At least it rang somewhat true.

Hal shifted his weight from one foot to the other, a move that seemed to reposition him a good three feet to his right.

"A farmers' market, huh?"

"Yeah. A few fellow market vendors and I set up temporary stalls at the fair. We got some decent business. Maybe there's a good spot for a market in Orderville, maybe not, but I think the Bellings brothers would like to hear my take on it."

"If anyone would, I suppose they would," Hal seemed to tell himself.

The group of kids had decided on their treats, and they crowded up to the counter, forcing Ian and me to step back or be trampled by little feet. As Hal rang them up, we waited, attempting to look like we were being patient. Our new position gave me a clear view of the bays and the pumps. At first I didn't notice Scott and Sam, because they'd moved away from the bays and were standing on the edge of the station's property. They seemed to be deep in discussion, but not about a car. Scott was doing most of the talking, and Sam was doing most of the listening, his hands on his hips and his face ever-serious.

"Yeah, yeah, see you tomorrow. Can't wait," Hal mumbled as the kids gathered their booty and left the station. We stepped forward again.

"You know, a farmers' market sounds like a good plan. I guess I could call the Bellings brothers and tell them you'd like to talk to them."

I'd noticed that the Bellings brothers were always mentioned together, as one. No one had given up either of their first names, and no one seemed to want to talk about just one of them.

I'd hoped for more information, but it would have to do. I wasn't a hundred percent sure Hal would do what he'd said, but I knew that if I continued to bug him, he'd for sure do nothing at all. I glanced at Ian, who confirmed my thoughts with a quick nod.

I wrote my name and phone number on a piece of receipt roll that Hal pulled from the cash register, and we moved outside to rejoin two of the other men I'd kissed.

I took a deep breath. I was about to do something that would test even the most patient of people, but I thought it would be better to do it with Ian present. "You okay if I ask Sam to come have coffee with us?" I asked Ian.

"Sure," he said after only the slightest hesitation.

"I think it's time to tell him what I found behind the shooting gallery, don't you?"

"Actually, yes, I do, Becca. I think that's a very good plan."

I had no idea what Sam and Scott had been talking about when I spied them on the other side of the bays, but whatever it was, I thought that Sam should be armed with the knowledge I had. It was unusual that I wanted to share, but I also didn't have much motivation to spend any more time in Orderville, South Carolina. I didn't want Scott to be involved in the tragic events that had happened at the fair. He'd been right when he'd mentioned that he was the better of the two Scotts. He was, but keeping what I knew from Sam was just some misplaced and long-expired loyalty. If it had been the other Scott, I might have called a meeting of all law enforcement in South Carolina. But it wasn't, it was the better Scott, not one I ever wanted to be married to again, but better nonetheless. And he had a step-son, a family.

Still, if he was involved in a murder or even an attempted murder, the police needed to know, and Sam was the officer I wanted to tell. If Scott wasn't involved, all the better, but Sam should still know what I'd found.

Fortunately, as we approached Sam and Scott, Scott announced that he had some-thing else to do. He gave us a hurried good-bye, his eyes locking with Sam's an instant too long. I was even more certain they hadn't been discussing cars, but I didn't think Sam would give me the details.

"Sam, you want to join Ian and me for coffee, dessert, something at the diner?" I asked.

"Oh, well, I need to get back to Monson," he said in a tone that didn't sound quite like him.

I peered into the bay. The hood was up on his Mustang. "How were you planning on getting home?"

"My car should be ready any minute."

"Sam," Ian interrupted. "We knew this moment was bound to happen. I'm okay, and you and I were pretty good friends before . . ."

"I ruined it," I offered. That made Sam cringe briefly, but then he forced a smile.

"Anyway, Becca wants to tell you some things. If you're uncomfortable around me, I'd be happy to wait in my truck," Ian said.

"No, no," Sam said too quickly. "I'm fine. Sure, let's go. Let's talk."

I couldn't remember one other time that Sam had acted rattled. His professional demeanor was so unflappable that there were times I tried too hard to make him crack a smile.

"Don't suppose we could all laugh about this soon. Like today?" I said.

Ian smiled.

And then a beat later Sam smiled.

Then they smiled at each other.

"We are adults, I suppose," Sam said.

"Well, you and Becca are. I'll get there someday," Ian said.

Then we laughed. It was only a small laugh from each of us, but it was genuine and real. I felt the weight of my inappropriate kiss lift just a little bit.

The diner was still busy, but it looked like a different group this time, except for the waitress, Liz.

"Well, hello again. Y'all rushed outta here like the devil himself was chasin' ya. But you left a nice big tip. Welcome back. Same rules apply: sit wherever you want."

This time we took the booth closest to the front windows. The nearest customers were three booths away. As we drank coffee and ate chocolate pie that rivaled not only the fruit pies of my friend Linda and the cream pies of Smithfield Market's Mamma Maria but also surely the blue-ribbon winners I'd admired just a few days ago, I told Sam everything about my time at the fair.

I looked to Ian to help me fill in spots that I'd told him about earlier. Ian described our visit to Virgil's house and the porch furniture that might mean nothing at all but that had struck us as odd.

Sam listened, sipped his coffee, and finished his pie, and when Ian and I were done, he surprised us both.

"Well, I don't think you've come upon anything that implicates your ex-husband in any crime, Becca. I think your imagination might be in overdrive, though."

"Wait. I'm not looking to send Scott up the river, and I guess I can understand why you might think some of it is my imagination, but what about the pictures behind the shooting gallery? What about the arrow pointing at the spot in the coaster tracks that almost gave way and killed a bunch of people?"

"I question that memory, but only a little bit."

"I don't understand," I said. A combination of hurt and anger simmered in my chest. It wasn't that Sam was acting condescending, but he was questioning what I had seen. For the first time ever, I was putting everything out there, laying it on the table. I was being one hundred percent honest and forthcoming. No matter how little I'd told him in the past, he'd never questioned the information I gave him. His reaction was unexpected to say the least.

He shrugged and looked into his coffee cup before he looked back at me. "Becca, while I don't know your ex-husband all that well, I know that he was working on some of the rides at the fairgrounds, fixing them. Maybe that's what the sketches were about. As for the location of the arrow, I think that might truly be your memory getting a little shaky. You beat yourself up, literally, when you ran out of the fairgrounds. You were bound to misremember some of the details."

"Sam," Ian said, "I hear what you're saying, but I really don't think Becca is misremembering. I agree that the sketches might mean nothing, but you know Becca's not one to exaggerate or make something of nothing."

Sam shrugged again. "Well, I'll look into it, but I really do think your ex is a pretty good guy. He wouldn't kill or plot to kill anyone."

I blinked. His icy blue eyes were steady on my own. I didn't think he was trying to get under my skin. He didn't seem angry or vindictive about anything, including the kiss.

"Listen, Becca, this might be one of the craziest situations you've gotten yourself into, and you've had your fair share of crazy situations. I'm going to look into what you've said, I promise, but really, Scott didn't kill anyone, that I'm certain of."

Sam rubbed his hand over his late-day stubble.

And I suddenly realized: that was new.

Sam Brion didn't allow late-day stubble on his face. Even on his days off, he was barely able to set his hair free from the thick gel that kept it combed back and neat when he was on duty. What had he been doing all day that he had stubble on his face? He was in his civilian clothes. What had he been up to?

"Sam, what were you doing before you brought your car to the service station?"

He blinked. "I was on my way into town."

"What about before that? What were you doing in Monson?"

Ian tapped his knee on mine. He probably wondered why I cared and why I sounded kind of snotty when asking the questions.

"Working in my yard. Why, Becca?"

"Even when you just work in your yard, you shave," I said.

Sam's unshaven face was even more curious than the feminine furniture on Virgil's porch. I knew Sam. I knew him so well that . . . I just knew that stubble meant something.

Sam laughed. "I got up a little late today. It happens, even to me." He stood. "Thanks for the information, Becca. I don't think I've been as appreciative as I should be. This is a big step — you telling me what you know. Thank you. You, too, Ian. Really."

Ian and I watched him put some money beside the cash register on the front counter and then leave the diner.

"What do you make of all that?" Ian said.

"I have no idea."

"I've never seen Sam act like that, but I

266

don't think it was because . . ."

"Because?"

"I don't think that had anything to do with what happened, what happened between you two. Becs, you're more uncomfortable than Sam and I are about . . . what happened. Sam rushing out of here was something else, though. He was either in a hurry or didn't want us to know about something that he knows about."

"That's likely."

"What were you getting at with all those comments about him not shaving?"

"He never doesn't shave. He's anal, he's OCD, he's annoyingly predictable when it comes to personal grooming. You've noticed how he looks when he's in his uniform, right? You've noticed how wrinkles are afraid of him? They stay away. Something happened — not that he overslept — something happened to keep him from shaving. It might have absolutely nothing to do with murders or attempted murders at fairs in Swayton County, but something pushed him off his normal routine this morning. I'd like to know what it was."

Ian looked at me for a long moment. He smiled with only half his mouth and said, "No, I didn't notice those things, but you have some good points. Come on, I think

267

we've seen enough of Orderville, South Carolina, for one day. Let's go home."

I had an urge to tell him I was sorry. Ian didn't say anything more about my observations of Sam's grooming, but I realized what I'd said sounded too personal, too knowing of someone I wasn't supposed to pay that close attention to.

As Ian drove us back to Monson, I silently made some decisions.

Ian was right; I'd been more concerned and worried than both he and Sam had been about . . . everything. And we were bound to all run into each other. If today's inadvertent rendezvous between me and the men in my life, past and present, didn't highlight how truly small a world it was, then nothing would. Time to grow up and get over past mistakes. I'd been trying not to hurt anyone's feelings further, which might be a noble idea, but in the process I'd been less than fully honest with myself and with the people I cared about.

If my hippie parents had raised me to be anything at all, it was to be honest. I decided I wouldn't intentionally hurt anyone's feelings, but I was going to have to stop worrying about what I said and how I behaved as long as I was being true to myself.

I was just going to have to be me, and me

was going to have to be good enough, no matter what.

Nineteen

Of course, me being me meant that Hobbit and I slept alone that night. The solitude was the unexpected outcome of yet another kiss. One that occurred when Ian dropped me off after our adventure in Orderville. I suspected it would probably prove to be pretty significant, but other events soon pushed it from my immediate thoughts.

I was awakened at six by my cell phone buzzing on the nightstand. Actually, I was awakened by Hobbit's insistent nose nudge. *She* was awakened by the phone buzzing on the nightstand.

Probably because of all the recent craziness, I was wide awake quickly, my heart pounding hard as I tried to remember what day it was and what I'd missed to warrant such an early call.

"Becca Robins?" said the stern female voice on the other end of the call.

"Uh, yeah."

"I'm calling for Renard Bellings. You would like to speak to him regarding the possibility of a farmers' market in Orderville?"

"Yes."

"He can meet with you today, this morning at seven thirty. Otherwise, he won't be available again until next week, but we can schedule for that time if that works better for you."

"No, no, I'll be there today. Where should I go?"

"There's a diner on Main Street. You can't miss it. He looks forward to meeting you."

"Excellent, I'll —" I began, but she'd clicked off on her end.

"Who are these people?" I said to Hobbit, who would have preferred to still be sleeping.

I got ready quickly and left a message for Allison regarding my plans. I was just irritated enough at Sam not to want to let him know what I was doing. And I knew Ian was busy today, and . . . well, after last night, I wasn't quite ready to face him again.

After a slice of buttered toast and with a travel cup of coffee in hand, I was ready to roll.

I'd slipped on some jeans instead of overalls today, and they covered well the continually transforming bruise on the top of my thigh. I'd applied a fresh butterfly bandage to my chin and was pleased to see that the cut was coming together evenly, though I would still have a scar. The bruise around the cut had taken on an interesting hue, which I tried to cover with a little makeup, but it was still visible.

The drive to Orderville was as uneventful as it had been the day before, until I got to Virgil Morrison's house. I had no intention of stopping again, but nonetheless I pulled the truck to the side of the road. Something was different, and it only took a few seconds to realize what it was: the porch furniture was gone. The white rocking chairs and wicker tables were missing, and there was no sign of a lawn chair or spittoon either. The porch was now completely empty. I was beginning to think a real estate agent was responsible for the two transformations.

Of course I realized that since Virgil was gone, his house would have to be emptied at some point, but for an instant it sat funny with me that the porch had been cleared the day after Ian and I noticed it and mentioned it to others. Who had we talked to about it? Dianna Kivitt and Sam, I recalled. I didn't think we'd brought it up with anyone else. I hurried down the front walkway and peered inside the windows. The interior of the house seemed undisturbed.

The porch had been cleared but nothing else?

Strange. Or maybe not.

I hurried back to the truck and filed the discovery to the back of my mind. If an opportunity to ask someone about it presented itself, I would — even if I did not know yet who that someone would be.

Oderville's main drag had a bit more foot traffic this morning. Mostly, kids with backpacks darted here and there. I hadn't seen a school, but there must have been one somewhere close by. Still, I was able to park my truck right in front of the diner.

It was crowded, much more crowded than the two times I'd been there the day before. I looked around at the many customers, none of whom struck me as someone who could be named Renard Bellings.

"Ms. Robins," said a man from the end stool at the counter.

"Yes?"

"Hi, I'm Renard. I got us a couple of stools. That's the best I could do. Sorry. If a table opens up, Liz will grab it for us."

Renard Bellings wasn't anything like I'd expected. I wasn't exactly sure what I'd expected, just definitely not the man who greeted me.

Renard was close to my age, maybe a little older, and handsome in that dark-haired, fit, friendly looking way that men were handsome. He was probably six feet tall and dressed perfectly in slacks and a long-sleeved button-down reddish shirt, the color of which brought out the amazing green of his eyes; in fact, the red-green combination reminded me of Christmas. He kind of took my breath away, but I could tell he was somewhat accustomed to such a reaction. He smiled and waited a patient beat while I composed myself.

It was rare that my head was turned by a pretty . . . everything, but Renard was difficult not to just stare at.

"Please, pull up a stool," he said as he guided the way.

"Thanks," I finally uttered. I scooted up to the stool and swung it a little so that we were facing each other.

"Thanks for coming here so early. I have to leave town later this morning and won't have time to meet again until next week. Hal called me and told me you wanted to talk about putting a farmers' market in town. I'd like to know more. In fact, Lucy told me that she told you what we were considering."

I didn't feel bad that I was there under false pretenses, but I wasn't sure how to lead into the questions that I really wanted to ask. Finally, I just said, "Who are you and why are you so mysterious?"

Renard laughed. "I am kind of, huh? Both my brother and I are. Please understand that many people want our attention. We have to pick and choose who we spend time with, which might seem rotten and mean and arrogant, but we'd never get anything done if we didn't."

"Okay, but still, who are you?"

"Fair enough. My brother and I . . . well, we own the town. My grandfather started a tobacco farm right over that way" — he pointed toward the front window — "and my brother and I continue to run the family business. We own pretty much every business in Orderville. We're a small community that would have faded away a couple decades ago if someone hadn't invested in it to create a viable economy. Gramps put up the money so he could keep the community together and employed."

"Wow."

Renard laughed again. "Well, Gramps was the good guy. Sebastian and I just show up and get to work every day."

"Sebastian and Renard," I murmured, visualizing the brothers next to d'Artagnan in a ferocious sword fight.

"Family names. Gramps was Sebastian Renard Bellings. They split it for the grandsons."

"And your grandmother was Jena Bellings?" I said quietly.

"Yes."

I had a million questions about her, but most of them came from the information my mother had shared with me, and though I hadn't had to offer a blood oath, I'd promised not to reveal Monson's secrets about Jena. I decided I'd have to just see if Renard offered anything more.

Finally, I shook my head a little and said, "Boy, you just never know what's going on down the road until travel down it and ask."

"I like that. True. Now, tell me about the farmers' market idea."

I wasn't totally unprepared.

"Well, yes, I talked to Lucy briefly. So sorry for everything that happened at the fair."

"Yes. Dreadful set of circumstances this year. I'm the one who's sorry, though."

I nodded. I had more questions along those lines, too, but I didn't want to rush into them.

Renard ordered us coffee and sweet rolls as I told him about the eventual success we Bailey's vendors had had at the fair and how he should consider opening a market. I lied and told him that Allison would be happy to meet with him and give him some direction. Actually, she would, but I hadn't asked her yet. I told him I was a self-appointed advocate for buying local products. I was, but that wasn't exactly my true motivation today.

He listened intently and then asked intelligent questions about location, electrical needs, potential profits for the market owners, et cetera. I answered most of the questions fairly well but had no problem suggesting he talk to Allison for those I was unsure about.

"Well, I think it's a great idea and might offer more employment for this area, too. I'm sure I'll contact your sister. Thank you for bringing this to me," Renard said when we'd covered most of the pertinent details.

"You're welcome." I paused politely. "Uh, do you mind if I ask you some questions about your community?"

"Shoot."

"The fair. Gosh, Renard, I don't know how to ask this without insulting you."

"You're wondering why we allowed it to

even open, right?" Suddenly Renard's dashing and gorgeous green eyes weren't smiling.

"Yes, I am," I said.

He took a sip of his coffee and pushed a sweet roll crumb around on his plate with his fork.

"It was a mistake to open it, but there was a reason, a good reason," he finally said.

"What was that?"

Renard sighed. "I can't tell you."

A chill zipped up my spine. Renard's good looks and stunning eyes suddenly seemed a little more good-looking and stunning, but in an exaggerated and wicked way. The transformation from pleasant to alarming had happened in a blink. What was going on in this town?

"Gypsy magic?" I said, but I swallowed quickly after I said the words.

Renard glanced up from his crumb-covered plate. After what seemed like forever, he simply said, "No."

"Tell me about Lucy," I said with far too much forced cheer. I sensed I was going to lose him if I continued down the gypsy-magic path.

His smile returned, but the dimness stayed in his eyes. "Lucy's amazing. She's a godsend to me and my family."

"Did you work out of the trailer on the fairgrounds?"

"No, never. That's Lucy's domain. Honestly, I didn't even like to travel out there. The entire thing made me nervous."

I shook my head. "You're so powerful. I really don't understand why you allowed it to open."

"Again, there was a very good reason. Let me restate that: we thought there was a very good reason. Hindsight tells us it wasn't such a good reason after all. If only hindsight could change things."

"There was a good reason to open an event with rides that seemed dangerous?"

"Yes. Well, we didn't think they were as dangerous as they turned out to be. There's . . . well, I suppose I can tell you this. There's an investigation into the rides. Sabotage is suspected. What I'm trying to say is that when we agreed to open the fair, the rides might not have been perfect, but they weren't dangerous. We think someone messed with them."

"Would that person have killed Virgil?"

"Makes sense, doesn't it?"

"It does, except . . . why?" I said.

"I do believe that's the question everyone is asking themselves."

"Why do I think that the answer has

something to do with why you opened the fair in the first place?"

Renard's eyes flashed. "You're a smart woman, Becca. You might be right. Might be."

"Do you know Scott Triplett?"

"Of course," he said, but he cleared his throat as though he'd answered too quickly. "Yes, he had the shooting gallery at the fair."

"He and I used to be married."

"You're *that* Becca?"

"So you *do* know him better than just as the shooting gallery owner." I smiled this time. It was fun to catch people trying to hide something.

But Renard didn't answer. He took a sip of his coffee and looked at his watch. He pulled some bills out of his wallet and set them on the counter, then he turned on the stool and stood.

"Ms. Robins, it's been nice meeting you. I'm now fully aware that you didn't want to talk to me about setting up a farmers' market, but I'm not sure I understand your curiosity. I suppose . . . well, no matter what, I've enjoyed talking to you."

"Thanks for your time."

Renard bit at his lip for a moment and then said, "Becca, we're a very small community and we're very much out in the boondocks, so to speak. We're far away from what a lot of people consider civilization. Things might happen here that only happen in those sorts of out-of-the-way places. You might want to keep that in mind."

Was I being threatened? I didn't like that idea at all. I sat up straighter and squinted at Renard, but I didn't have anything else to say, for the moment at least.

I watched him leave and then swiveled my stool back to the counter. I'd been in some scary situations, but never had I been told to leave town or else. I wasn't totally sure that's what had happened, but it certainly felt like it.

I should have gotten in my truck and high-tailed it out of Orderville, South Carolina. I should have gone home. In fact, I should have gone to Bailey's and sold some jams, preserves, and syrups. I had plenty to do other than stick around a place that had been proven dangerous and where I wasn't welcome.

But, of course, I didn't.

TWENTY

Ward Hicken's alfalfa farm was easy to find. I drove out the other end of town and came upon a huge farm with a convenient sign hung above a long gravel driveway: "Hicken & Sons Alfalfa."

I hadn't planned on finding Ward Hicken; I'd hoped to just drive around a little more, see if I could better understand Orderville or uncover where Stephen King was hiding. But Ward's farm was a lucky discovery, and visiting it gave me something substantial to do.

Farming was a big part of my life, and I had a solid grasp on what it took to grow strawberries and pumpkins, but I wasn't quite so familiar with other crops. Alfalfa, in particular, was one I knew very little about. It always seemed like a whole bunch of purple-flowered groundcover. I had learned that alfalfa was a feed crop and not directly a part of our dinner tables, but that was about it.

Ward's farm was enormous, stretching out on one side of the road as far as the eye could see. But his house was surprisingly small for such expansive surroundings. This farm deserved a huge mansion with pillars and perhaps a carriage or two out front, but disappointingly, there was only a one-story clapboard with chipped paint and a shutter missing from one of its two front windows. A huge and much more well-maintained whitewashed barn loomed behind the house, further dwarfing the smaller structure.

I pulled into the long gravel driveway, planning to park at the end right next to the house, but something flashed in my vision and caused me to step on the brakes.

At first, I thought a black ball had rolled across the driveway. I waited, foot still on the brake, expecting a child to come chasing after it.

No child appeared, so I put the truck in Park, got out, and walked around to the front. On the ground, directly in front of one of the tires, was a small black kitten. It looked up at me, all big green eyes and wobbly legs, and gave one short "meow."

"Hello, there," I said as I reached for it. "Where is your mama? You shouldn't be roaming around out here all alone."

It had been some time since I'd picked up a kitten. I'd held a few in my day, but I was more experienced with the full-grown variety. And I hadn't had a cat myself in a long time.

As I put my hand around the creature that was as small as stick of butter with legs, it ferociously dug its tiny lethal claws into my skin.

"Uh, oh, that hurts," I said, but I didn't dare let go. I didn't remember if kittens could move quickly, and I didn't want it to run away.

"Put her to your chest," someone called from the open front door.

"Excuse me?" I said.

"Hold her to your chest, up by your neck where it's warm. You're scaring her the way you're holding her. She thinks you're going to drop her. She'll feel secure up close to you."

"I won't drop her."

"That doesn't change the fact that that's what she thinks is going to happen. Put her to your chest." Ward had come out of the house now and stood with his hands on his hips.

I pulled the mewing kitten to my chest and said, "There, is that better? Ouch."

The creature had turned and dug the claws from all four of its miniscule feet into my chest. Fortunately, my shirt helped mute the pain from her back claws, but her front claws had landed on exposed skin, piercing me like two little knives.

I tried to pull her away, but using some magic I didn't know existed, the kitten dug in more. She was close to becoming a permanent fixture.

"Uh," I said.

"There, that's better," Ward said.

"For her maybe," I said quietly.

"Now, just keep her there and come on in."

With the black furry alien clinging to my chest and neck, I made my way into Ward's small house.

The inside was nice, not elegant or modern, but clean and kind of sparse. The TV room was off the small entryway, and to my right, a door, slightly ajar, led to a bedroom. Ward pulled the door closed after I walked by, but I'd already noticed that the bed was made.

"Though you're always welcome, can't say I don't wonder what you're doing here, Becca," Ward said as he signaled that I should sit on a clean but vintage 1970s beige couch. After the kitten and I took a seat, Ward found one in the matching chair with wide armrests.

"Well," I began as I grabbed the kitten and pulled, to no avail. I looked at Ward for help, but he clearly didn't think he needed to assist me. Shrugging internally, I soldiered on. "I'm not totally sure. I was just driving by and thought I'd stop and see if you'd be willing to tell me why your town is kind of creepy." The claws in my chest had given me the desire to be blunt, to not beat around any bush or lie. That, plus the veiled threat from Renard Bellings had set me off and the rebel in me wanted to tell the truth just to see what reaction I'd get.

"Creepy?" Ward said after a moment, though he didn't sound offended.

"Yeah, what's going on around here?"

"I don't know what you mean. You seem upset. Can I get you some lemonade or something?"

"No thanks," I said just as the kitten seemed to relax into the spot right above the collar of my shirt. She still had her claws in me, but at least she'd withdrawn them from the middle of my lungs.

"Could you take the kitten?" I asked.

Ward thought a moment. "I think it's best if she stays there. She's been dumped by her mama. I've been taking care of her, but she keeps finding a way to escape. She's calm and not trying to run away. She seems pretty happy. If you don't mind, just keep holding her. She'll start purring any second."

"Her mother abandoned her?" I said.

"Yeah, it happens. She'll be fine. I'm taking good care of her, but she's definitely an escape artist, one of the best I've ever seen. My guess is that Mama didn't have the patience to keep rounding her up, so she let her go on her way."

The kitten suddenly relaxed a little more. She wasn't purring yet, but she was becoming more tolerable.

"What'd you do to yourself?" Ward pointed to his own chin.

I realized then that I hadn't seen him at the fair on Sunday, when everyone else had commented about me needing stitches.

"I fell and hit a table. Where were you on Sunday? I looked for you." I was counting on the fact that he, indeed, hadn't been at the fair.

He shrugged. "Too much to do around here."

"What do you make of the breaking roller coaster tracks?"

He shrugged yet again. "It happens."

"Not really, not much in fact."

"But it does. Look, Becca, I'm sorry if the events at our fair seem creepy to you — I guess they are to me, too. But I've got the history." He tapped at the side of his head. "I've got the memories of what the Swayton County Fair used to be. They're good memories."

"I don't get it, then. Why was it allowed to fall apart?"

"It wasn't."

"But it did."

"It wasn't *allowed* to, though. It just happened." He rubbed his chin and squinted at me. "The fair wasn't huge. We haven't had big crowds in years. Virgil's death brought a new wave of interest, but if that hadn't happened, the fair might have gone on and finished without a hitch."

"The tracks were in bad shape."

"Maybe that was because there was such a crowd. The coaster got a workout like it hadn't gotten in a long time. It was bad, but it was bad because of circumstances that weren't necessarily foreseeable. And now it's shut down."

I wanted to point out that I didn't think the circumstances had been that unforeseeable, but I could tell Ward wasn't buying into whatever conspiracy I was trying to vocalize. If I continued to press him on the topic, we'd only end up talking in circles.

I didn't realize that I'd started to pet the kitten. I noticed it when her tiny tail swung up and grazed my chin, the side without the butterfly bandage. The creature had started to purr, but just as I was beginning to enjoy the sensation, she started kneading into my chest. I was certain she was drawing blood.

"The night of the poker game you all mentioned how important the fair was because it brought the community together."

"That's right."

"And that's really true?"

"Yes, completely true. It's a way to see our closest and yet geographically distant neighbors."

"Did the Bellingses make all the money from the fair?"

Ward laughed. "Oh, sorry, but that is funny. No one really made any money. I know the Bellingses liked to let people come in with food trailers and such and those people made money, but most of us were volunteers."

"Wait, Virgil was a volunteer?"

"Yes ma'am."

"How did that man pay his bills? He had odd jobs and then worked as a volunteer at the fair?"

"I suppose, but he did fine with his military retirement pay. His house was paid for. He inherited it from his aunt some twenty years ago, remember."

"Did you know his aunt?"

"Sure. Ethel Jackson."

"Did she mention Virgil?"

"Well, before she died I didn't know much about her, and then Virgil just showed up one day."

"What about the rest of her family?"

Ward rubbed at his chin again. "She didn't have any that I recall."

"Hmm," I said, now afraid to move even a little bit. The stiller I stayed, the less kneading occurred.

"I see where you're going. You want to know if anyone knew of Virgil before he came and claimed that Ethel was his aunt. I don't know. But he couldn't have just taken over her house. Someone would have stopped that from happening."

"I suppose," I said, but I wondered. "Do you know where Virgil lived before he came to Orderville?"

"Of course . . . he moved here from . . . well, I'll be, I don't remember offhand."

I looked at him, and when he looked back at me, I felt like I might have actually said something that made him begin to wonder,

290

too. It was strange that he didn't know where Virgil came from, or so I thought.

"You know, Virgil did move here twenty years ago. He might have told me way back when and I've just forgotten."

So much for getting him to think deeper. I'd probably overdone it when I mentioned that I thought Orderville was creepy. Most people didn't like to hear their hometown described in such a way. But since I didn't have anything to lose really, I tried another route.

"What about Jerry, the guy who sold the corn dogs?"

"He came from California, that I know." Ward was pleased with himself. "He hasn't been here all that long. He only moved here six months or so ago."

"Right, but what do you think of him?"

"I guess I don't think of him at all. He's nice enough, I suppose. He's never asked me for a job, but I know he's asked plenty of other people."

"I'm trying to get him a spot at the farmers' market where I work. We could use a corn-dog trailer, at least for a little while to see if there's a market or not."

"That makes sense."

"Why would Dianna Kivitt tell me to stay

away from him? She seems afraid of him," I said.

I hadn't thought much about sharing what Dianna had said and done. If she knew I'd just told Ward about her warning, she might be angry, but again, I didn't feel like I had anything to lose.

For a moment, Ward seemed perplexed by the question, but then a wave of understanding crossed his face.

"Jerry seems pretty harmless to me," he said. "I don't know why Dianna said what she said except that she's a little paranoid and even more so when it comes to strangers. You might have picked up on her paranoia during the poker game."

"She seemed concerned that the police might investigate her because of her involvement with Virgil, but she didn't seem paranoid about anyone else."

"That's because you were only around her a short while. Given more time, you'd see more of it. She's a nice person, but that's just Dianna." He said it so sincerely that I couldn't find one thing that rang false, no matter how much I wanted to.

"What about the Bellingses?"

"What about them?"

"I met Renard this morning," I said.

"You did? That's interesting. Where?

They're not all that available."

"I noticed that, but I'd heard they might be interested in opening a farmers' market here. I asked one of the guys at the service station to help with the communication. He did and we met."

"How'd that go?" Ward sat forward in the chair. It must have been the most interesting thing I'd brought up.

"Okay."

He circled the air with his hand as if to prompt me on.

"Renard liked the idea of a farmers' market, but I don't think he liked me very much."

"What makes you say that?"

It was my turn to shrug. I realized that the kitten had fallen asleep on my chest and the kneading had softened so that I barely felt the ends of the sharp claws. I was reclined almost all the way back on the couch and it was the perfect time to remove the kitten, but now I didn't want to.

"So, the Bellings family made their money from tobacco farming?" I asked. Ward nodded. "Does their seeming 'rule' over the town bother people?"

"No, not at all." Ward sat back. "They are beloved. We all . . . well, we all owe them a lot."

"Jena Bellings was Renard and Sebastian's grandmother, right?"

"That's right."

"What's with all the gypsy magic that's associated with her?"

"Ah, s'nothing."

"Ward, I've got to be honest with you, that's part of what's creepy. The Bellingses sound like a combination of royalty and deity, which makes me wonder if they aren't more like godfather and dictator. And everyone is weird about Jena. Some people don't even want to say her name."

Ward laughed nervously. "It's just old gypsy lore."

"*Just* old gypsy lore?"

"Yeah." He paused.

And there it was again: gypsy lore, gypsy magic. This was the point where everyone except my mother stopped talking about it. So, I tried a different approach. I didn't say anything but merely stared at Ward over the kitten on my chest and hoped the silence would gain more than my questions had.

I played it right.

"Shoot, there've always been stories about the old Mrs. Bellings. She was the woman who married Sebastian Renard Bellings, the patriarch of the family. She was something else, that much I can tell you. I remember her scaring the silliness right out of me when I was a teenager. So you met Renard, you know what he looks like?"

I nodded.

"Well, he's the one who got his grandmother's exotic dark hair and unusual-colored eyes. Anyway, she was beautiful and wild, always had big funny hair and wore long funny dresses."

"My mom was a hippie. She still wears some of that stuff," I said, but I kept to myself that my own grandmother had made some of Jena's first dresses.

"This would have been before your mom's time even, I'm sure. And as stories have it, Jena Bellings just showed up in town one day. This was a long time ago, back when we were a thriving farming community. She showed up on a wagon, with a band full of gypsies, and put a spell on Sebastian."

"Really?" I said, wondering how she'd managed to get a seat on that wagon. "Sounds kind of spooky and kind of romantic."

"I suppose. But this spell she put on him was a good one. Their tobacco crops thrived, and Jena made sure that Sebastian spread the wealth and took care of the community."

"So, she was a good witch?"

"We like to think so." He smiled. "She

295

died tragically, though, and you know how legends can grow when someone dies tragically."

"How did she die?" I asked.

Ward hesitated again. "He was acquitted."

"Who?"

"Sebastian Renard Bellings himself."

"Oh."

"Yes. Jena was found hanging from a tree, a belt from one of her exotic dresses as the noose. For a good long time, everyone thought Sebastian killed his wife, but no evidence was found. It was just difficult to believe that Jena would kill herself. She was so full of life."

"Hanging. Just like Virgil Morrison," I said.

"No gun wound," Ward said.

"No."

"Anyway, each year the fair begins on the anniversary of her death. It was originally a festival put in place to celebrate her . . . her . . . well, magic, I guess. She was just one of those people who everyone else was drawn to. You know the type?"

"I think so," I said, though I knew she hadn't been that type of person in Monson. She'd changed more than just her clothes and bathing habits; her entire persona, it seemed, had transformed when someone had, probably offhandedly, called her a gypsy. I didn't share that part of the story. "Renard was cagey, but he told me there was a good reason they opened the fair this year. Was it simply the superstition? Something to honor his grandmother?"

"Maybe. I guess. I don't know."

"See what I mean, Ward, your town is kind of creepy." I lifted the kitten off my chest.

He laughed but didn't reach for the creature I was holding out to him.

"We like our stories."

"I think some of you like to make up your stories," I said.

Again, he wasn't offended.

"Hey, you have a farm, right?" he asked.

"I do," I said.

"You have a cat?"

"No, a dog . . . no, hang on, I don't have time to take care of a kitten."

"Sure you do. They're easy. You'll have to dropper feed this one for a while, but not for long."

"I can't," I said.

"Aw, her mama turned her away."

"And you're doing fine with her."

"She needs a home. I've got plenty of cats and now kittens. I'm going to have to find homes for some of them. This would work. She's attached to you already."

"She was literally attached to me. She just wants a place to put her claws. That place can't be my place." I didn't know how Hobbit would react to my adding another animal to her world, but I didn't want to risk it.

"Shoot, well, it was worth a try. I'll just have to take them to the shelter, see if they can find them some homes."

I wanted to punch Ward for such manipulation. And I wanted to cry when he finally took the kitten from my hands.

As he pulled the evil creature to his own chest, she reached her lethal front paws to me and mewed.

It was no big surprise to find myself driving home with a small black furry creature attached to my chest.

TWENTY-ONE

And I drove right past my own farm. I actually saw Hobbit sitting on the porch waiting for me, but I lost the heart to introduce her to a new family member unless I absolutely had to, or had prepared her first. I'd fallen in love with Hobbit so quickly, I barely even knew what hit me. My feelings for the kitten were beginning to get there, but I had another idea, hopefully a better one.

I'd called Ian, who responded favorably to the idea of a kitten and future cat in his life, but he wasn't sure he had the time to devote to caring for it either. He had yet another idea. He called George, who was going to be joining him at the farm, and asked if he'd be interested in taking care of the kitten at his house until they could both move to the lavender farm.

If it had been to anyone other than George, asking the question would have been both rude and just plain wrong. But

George would either welcome the idea or not, and he wouldn't dance around the answer with the hope of sparing anyone's feelings. If he said no, my next stop would be Allison — well, her son, Mathis, first. I could be just as manipulative as Ward had been.

But George wasn't only agreeable, he was enthused.

"Oh, yes, of course I was meant to take care of you." He took the kitten from my hands. She willingly let go of the grip she had on me and happily curled into George's neck. "See, she feels secure right here. She feels my body heat and my heartbeat."

"She's not weaned, not really, George," I said. "Her mother rejected her, so feeding her could be a challenge."

"Oh, pshaw, I've dealt with such a thing before. Ian will be here shortly with all the accoutrements she and I will need." He petted her back and tried to twist his neck so that he could look at her.

George's vision, though aided by thick-lensed glasses, was very poor. When Ian suggested that we ask George if he'd want to take on the task, his vision was my biggest concern. If George couldn't see the kitten well, he might not be able to find her if she got away. But Ian said that George wasn't worried in the least.

George loved Hobbit so much that Ian and I had discussed getting him a dog of his own, but truthfully this might work out better. Cats didn't need to be attended to quite as much. A litter box, some good food, lots of love (on their terms, of course), and a nice lap could please a cat forever. I could see that this kitten was pleasing George. As I watched the two of them, I wondered why we hadn't thought of it before.

But things happened when they happened.

"What will you name her?" I asked.

"Oh, I'm not sure. I'll have to get to know her better. It's almost Halloween, and she's as black as slick oil. I'll have to come up with something appropriate."

I inspected the kitten. She wasn't kneading, she wasn't fussing, she was curled in the hollow at the base of George's neck. I thought I caught her looking at me with an attitude of "See, this is how you do it."

I raised one eyebrow at her but was truly thrilled to have made a love match.

Ian arrived moments later with an entire pet store — well, at least the cat care portion.

We set up the litter box in the utility room off the back porch and figured out how to feed the kitten with a dropper and some appropriate food. Before long, she seemed to own the place, or at least she quickly became master of George. And it was a position he relished.

We left them to themselves, promising to stop by later and make sure everyone was okay. George thought we were being silly to worry.

As Ian walked me to my truck parked out front, he broached the subject I was so hoping I'd never have to broach.

"Becs, we need to talk, don't you think?" he said.

"About?" But I knew the second I looked into those dark and wonderful eyes what he wanted to talk about.

"That kiss, last night."

"Yeah. Maybe my heart wasn't in it," I said. "Care to give me another chance?"

Ian smiled.

So right there, in front of George's house on Harvard Avenue in Monson, South Carolina, I stepped up to my toes and kissed my much younger, much wiser, and awesome boyfriend.

"Hang on," I said as I lowered back down to my flat feet. "That wasn't just me, was it?"

For the first time I could remember, Ian

looked sheepish. He was intelligent, confident, and funny. Sheepish wasn't his thing.

"Ian, you felt the exact same thing I felt, didn't you?" I said.

"Becca . . ."

"No, no, just tell me. It wasn't there for you either, was it?"

"Let me answer my way, please."

I nodded.

"Becca, I had so much fun with you yesterday. Our 'investigation' and time in Orderville was something I wish we'd done a long time ago . . ."

"But?"

"But I think it made me realize something, something you've already realized. We are really great friends."

"But not meant to be more than that," I said quietly and almost involuntarily.

"I'm beginning to think so."

I thought I might feel the stab of rejection or that hollow sense of being dumped, but he was right. Ian and I were very good friends, and though a good friendship is the basis for a successful relationship, I suddenly realized that ours wasn't meant to become that.

"Oh, Ian."

"Do you suppose there's any way we can continue to be friends? I don't want this to be the last time I see you. In fact, I'd like to be very good friends. I'd like to be able . . . well, to hang out with you. Do you think that's possible?"

"I do," I said.

"Good, now get home to Hobbit. Do me a favor, keep yourself safe. And, if you need someone to be a sidekick again, give me a call."

I peered deeply into those beautiful eyes. Was this something he'd concocted because he knew that my heart wasn't as into this relationship as it should have been? I truly didn't think so. I knew that Ian was honest to a fault. I knew that he had been hurt by my betrayal, but I also knew he'd forgiven me. He wasn't releasing *me,* he was releasing *us.*

"That's it, then?" I said weakly. I wasn't devastated, but I suddenly couldn't help but feel that terrible abyss of something ending.

"Not even close. I think we should both stop by and visit George and that kitten over the next couple of days. Hopefully, we'll stop by around the same time, maybe even call each other when we're on our way. I think that's a great way to continue our friendship."

Ian got in his truck and I got in mine. As I drove toward home and Hobbit, I couldn't help but wonder whether I, or Ian and I, had been touched by a little gypsy magic.

Twenty-Two

The evening was cool enough that I needed a sweater as I walked through what was left of my pumpkin crop. The boys Lucy sent to help me harvest them had come and gone. They'd been quick and efficient, loading the pumpkins into the back of my truck like pros.

Something about the vines and wide leaves without the big orange gourds seemed to fit my mood. As Hobbit and I walked through the picked-over field, the sense of "ending" was magnified by the breakup, but only slightly.

I'd been relieved to get rid of my two ex-husbands and hadn't really felt any major loss — other than the welcome loss of an unwanted, grudging weight. Though I wasn't relieved to be out of my relationship with Ian and I certainly felt a little sad, it also felt right, in that torturous do-what's-best-not-what's-easy way.

"What do you think, girl?" I said to Hobbit. "You believe in gypsy magic?"

I was pretty sure she nodded.

The night was clear with a bright and brilliant half moon.

Another year of farming and, despite the recent turn of events, I couldn't have been happier about the life I had. I'd clear out the vines this weekend and then till some nutrients through the soil. I'd soon be spending all of my work time either in my kitchen preparing preserves, jams, and now syrups, or at the market, selling the items I made. The market was always busy but would slow down to a steady hum once Halloween was over. Though many vendors left their stalls after the solstice, Halloween somehow had become the marker for the transitioning seasons.

"You know, we won't be seeing Ian as much," I said to Hobbit.

Her eyes glimmered in the moonlight, but she seemed to nod again, as though she understood that it was for the best.

"Good girl. Let's get inside."

I made myself some hot chocolate and carried it to my desk, where I sat down and flipped on my infrequently used laptop. *Just about everyone out there leaves a mark in Cyberland,* I thought.

First I looked up "Ethel Jackson, Orderville, South Carolina." I immediately found her obituary as well as the location of her grave. There was even a picture of the simple carved stone with her name and her birth and death dates. The stone bore no other details about her life, no engraving like "Loving mother, sister, aunt, friend," which wasn't all that strange, I supposed. But the obituary didn't mention family either. She was the "only child" of her parents, who had predeceased her. I could find no reference to her having had a husband ever. How had she been an aunt? Unless the title had been a courtesy extended by family friends, Virgil could not possibly have been her nephew, at least biologically.

Certainly, other people in Orderville knew this. Was Virgil not thoroughly questioned when he moved into her house? Someone must have thought it odd. But since it had happened twenty years ago and since Virgil was now dead, too, anyone who might have cared probably didn't care any longer.

That was the sum total I could find about Ethel Jackson.

My next search brought a bunch of links. I typed in "Jena Bellings, Orderville, South Carolina."

The first link took me to a blog called

"Real Gypsy Witches." I laughed as I read the title. The post was from last year, last October, in fact, and read:

Many years ago, it was said that a real gypsy witch ruled the land in and around Orderville, South Carolina. She charmed the land into bringing forth a hardy and bountiful tobacco crop so that her husband could become rich. She charmed herself so that she would give birth to a beautiful son, Wallace, who would grow to become wealthy and just as powerful as his father had become with his tobacco crops.

Jena Bellings arrived in Orderville on the back of a gypsy wagon. She saw her future husband as he walked down the street. She immediately took herself off the wagon and walked beside him, telling him she could see their future. It was said that she told him about his success, their marriage, and their son.

They married within the week.

Now, yearly, right outside Orderville, Wallace Bellings's three children, two sons and a daughter, began and continue to hold a fair and festival devoted to the good fortune the town has seen, good fortune that is said to have come to the community because Jena Bellings jumped off that gypsy wagon.

Though I was disappointed the blog post didn't mention Monson, I was intrigued. It was fun to attach good fortune to a legend and all, but the town wasn't quite as well off as the blogger seemed to think. Orderville was getting by just fine, and from what I could see no one seemed to be struggling, but fortunes weren't abounding — well, at least not for anyone who wasn't a Bellings, perhaps. The only new building I'd seen that was in good condition was the service station. Everything else had seemed somewhat worn down. And the rides at the fair had been in bad shape. Renard had mentioned that it was his family that kept the town's economy up and running, so either their fortune wasn't that large, or the Bellingses were a little stingy. I didn't have the whole story so it probably wasn't fair to speculate.

The rest of Jena's links led to similar items. I found some black-and-white pictures of the mysterious woman, too; she looked just as she'd been described to me: long, wild hair, and a beautiful angular face. I couldn't make out her eye color, but I could easily see how Renard favored his grandmother. I was sure her eyes had been just as spectacular as his.

There wasn't much that was substantial, though. One post talked about her death but didn't mention that her husband had been accused of the crime, or that it had been a crime at all, or a suicide. It simply said that she died by hanging. Her death had occurred a long time ago, but I thought it odd that I couldn't find anything more about it.

I typed "Orderville, South Carolina" in to the search engine.

Apparently, the town had been established in the early 1700s and was all but a ghost town when Sebastian Renard Bellings planted and harvested his tobacco crop in the 1920s, bringing the town back from its near death. The most current information stated that the town was a small farming community with a rarely changing population of about twelve hundred.

Nothing about Jena had been included in the few articles about Orderville.

I plugged in "Virgil Morrison, Orderville, South Carolina."

I found three mentions of Virgil Morrison, but only one of them lived in South Carolina. One link was an article from Friday's paper describing his horrific murder and how the authorities thought the killing was random. They thought that perhaps the killer had already left the area. I hadn't known either of those things.

One Virgil was located in Florida and had won a horseshoe championship, and the third one had been a cattle driver in California some forty years earlier.

My phone suddenly buzzed.

I wasn't in the mood to talk to Allison about the breakup, so I hoped that wasn't why she was calling.

"Hey, sis," I said as I answered.

"Hey, what's going on?"

"Not much. You?"

"Well, I'm calling about your corn-dog friend, Jerry."

"Did he come by today?"

"Yep and I checked his references."

"Uh-oh. You calling because they were bad?"

"No, they're perfect, immaculate. He's a well-liked guy back in California. He managed a couple grocery stores, made them money, too. His personal references glow as well. Thanks for sending him over. He'll be a good addition to Bailey's."

"You're welcome," I said hesitantly.

"What?"

"Nothing."

My reaction to what she'd found had been

wary. Really? I wanted to say. Then why couldn't he find a real job in Orderville? The economy?

"What's up, Becca?"

"I don't know. I'm glad his references came back so great, but did he strike you as that kind of guy? The kind that makes a business money?"

"We didn't talk for all that long. He's young, though. Maybe he doesn't know how to come off as polished yet. He must be a hard worker."

I shook off the funny feeling. "I'm sure he is. I hope to get to know him better."

"He'll do well at the market. I'll come get Hobbit tomorrow about two, okay?"

"Thanks, she'll love spending the afternoon with Mathis."

"He's so excited. Oh — gotta go! Talk to you soon."

After she clicked off, I typed "Jerry Walton" into the search engine and hit pay dirt, but just for men with that name. I clicked on at least twenty links, but nothing seemed to lead to Jerry the corn-dog guy.

Last but not least, I typed in "spider tattoo." I got a lot of information about spider symbolism and some amazing pictures of wicked-looking spiders and impressive tattoos. I didn't find one thing to indicate spider tattoos were inked on to the skin of Russian mobsters like I'd hoped I would.

Finally, when I was tired enough to think my wonky feelings about Orderville, Virgil, Jerry, and everything else didn't matter, I shut off the laptop and the light and fell asleep with Hobbit keeping me warm.

It was no surprise that I dreamed of black kittens, gypsy magic, and wonderful men with exotic brown eyes and long, dark hair.

TWENTY-THREE

When I woke up, I called Lucy to make sure the pumpkin-decorating contest was still on. I could deliver the pumpkins to Bailey's if plans had changed, but she assured me that plenty of people would show up excited to decorate a pumpkin and visit the corn maze for the first time of the season. I didn't have to set out for the maze until after lunch, so Hobbit and I went for a run and then I raked up the pumpkin vines. It was Wednesday, my normal day for deep cleaning my kitchen, so once the field was cleared, I pulled out the cleaning supplies and got to work. I exhausted my body and tried to halt my overly active mind just a little. Or at least give it something to do other than think about Ian and the strange town of Orderville, South Carolina. I'd found that sometimes, when I quit trying or thinking so hard, that thing that I didn't realize I was looking for could become suddenly clear.

So as I scrubbed and mopped and scrubbed some more, I forced myself to focus on the songs coming from my iPod. I sang along to "Midnight Train to Georgia," "Piano Man," "Dancing Queen," and whatever else came up on the "shuffle songs" setting.

While the entire experience was exhilarating, by the time I was done, nothing new had popped into my mind. All the questions I'd had before I started, I still had, and all the oddities of Orderville and its citizens seemed no less odd.

But my kitchen was spotless.

On the drive to the corn maze, I came to a few more conclusions about myself and the way I'd behaved. Though I was sad about Ian and me, I still wasn't devastated. We were both going to be okay. I actually thought we might be able to handle being only friends. I hoped so, at least. I also decided that though I was sad about Virgil, and curious, too, I wasn't going to be able to find his killer. I'd done my part. I'd told Sam about the documents I'd found behind the shooting gallery. If Scott was somehow involved, then the police would have to figure it out. Scott wasn't my problem anymore. I was going to just leave things alone, let them be.

I hoped Scott wasn't guilty, though.

The food trailers and the other temporary setups like the shooting gallery were gone, leaving only the bigger rides and Lucy's trailer. Extra measures had been taken to make sure the world knew the rides were off-limits. Yellow tape was strung everywhere. The vacant machines, empty fairgrounds, and yellow tape added to the corn maze atmosphere, and though the day was warm and sunny, it felt just as it should: a little creepy and a lot of fun.

Lucy was standing outside the fairgrounds and to the side of the corn maze as I steered the truck down the lot. She held her clipboard at the ready and seemed to be relieved to see me. She waved and guided me forward.

"Look at all those pumpkins! How wonderful, Becca. Pull over there and back into that small corralled area. I've got some boys who will help unload."

I did as she'd instructed, guiding the truck down a path bordered by stacked bales of hay.

I was halted by a kid I thought I'd seen around the butter sculptures. He and a few others — not necessarily kids — started unloading the pumpkins. I also saw Scott,

Ward, and Jerry the corn-dog vendor, who I thought was supposed to be at Bailey's today. Had Allison said anything about his start date? I couldn't remember.

I got out of the truck and pitched in to help.

"For an EMT, you sure do spend a lot of time doing other stuff," I said quietly to Scott as he and I both grabbed for pumpkins.

"I only do that part-time. Speaking of which, your chin is looking better."

I placed a pumpkin under one of my arms and touched his with my available hand. "Come on, Scott, what are you doing here? Your ties to this place have me both curious and concerned. Talk to me."

So much for leaving things alone.

He looked at me, the October sun making his blond-blond hair look golden and causing him to squint.

"Becca . . ." he began, but then stopped.

"What, Scott? What's up?"

"Nothing." He shook his head. "These pumpkins are great. Thanks for bringing them." He turned and hurried to the corral.

I almost had him. He'd almost told me something, but I doubted it was that he was a killer. What was he up to? I'd get it out of him by the end of the day.

"How's the kitten?" Ward asked as he reached into the truck bed.

"She's got a home where she'll be spoiled and loved and fed only the finest foods."

"Well, that's good news. See, I knew what I was doing." He winked.

I smiled.

"What are you naming her?" he continued.

"Something perfect, but her new owner hasn't come up with the right one just yet."

The corral had already been stocked with some pumpkins, but the addition of mine filled it to almost bulging, and it looked like there would be plenty for the kids who were scheduled to arrive at three o'clock. Even without the rides, they would have fun with the animals, the maze, and the pumpkins.

I was distracted by the scent of something spicy, and my stomach growled reflexively. I looked around to see a witch stirring a large cauldron. I'd forgotten that people would be showing up in costume to the maze-opening events. The witch was currently the only one dressed up, though, so maybe I could escape before the costumes took over.

"Mmm, what's that?" I said as I sniffed over the cauldron.

The witch looked up and smiled hesitantly. "Hi, Becca."

"Oh, hi, Dianna." I was startled by Dianna's getup. From what I'd observed, she wasn't exactly the fun type, the sort of person who dressed up in a great witch costume.

"It's Brain and Eyeball Stew. The dumplings make the brains, and the black olives make the eyeballs. Don't tell the kids, but it's just chicken and dumpling soup."

"Your secret's safe with me."

"Hey, I'm glad you're here. About the other day, I'm sorry I was being dramatic. I just wanted you to be aware. I didn't have your phone number, and I didn't want to just call your farmers' market out of the blue and warn them about Jerry."

"Oh. Well, it's all right. I appreciate the warning. I talked to my sister, the market manager, and his references came back glowing. Is there something specific you're concerned about?"

Dianna stirred the stew as though she'd done it a million times; the look on her made-up face was doubtful and perfectly sinister. The crazy gray-haired wig only added to the picture. "And that doesn't seem odd to you? Suspicious even? You haven't known him all that long, right? Well, you do know that he hasn't held jobs well. In fact, I think if your sister talked to people who he's worked for in Orderville, she might get a different story. He's not reliable, but that's not even the least of it." She pinched her mouth and then looked away. "I'm sorry again if I'm being dramatic, but maybe you should just suggest to your sister that she look a little closer at him."

"Got it," I said. "I will. And thank you." Dianna had vocalized exactly what I'd been thinking.

She looked at me again and nodded.

Dianna Kivitt and I would never be great friends. We were clearly very different people, but I suddenly wondered if that wasn't more about me than her. She was just who she was, suspicious by nature. I realized that perhaps I should have figured out by now that suspicion was sometimes a smart way to stay safe.

"Becca, yoo-hoo, do you have a minute?" Lucy said from the corral.

I excused myself from the cauldron and hurried back to Lucy.

"I can't thank you enough," she said. "You've been so kind and patient. I actually wondered if we'd see you this afternoon."

"Oh. No problem. My pleasure." I wanted to tell her that I wasn't the type not to hold up my end of a bargain, but that felt wrong.

"So, well . . ."

"What?"

"Well, I was wondering if you'd like to stick around and help with the festivities," she said so cheerily that I laughed in reaction.

"You don't have enough people to help?"

She shook her head. "It seems that that silly 'gypsy magic' rumor, legend, whatever, has grown so much because of poor Virgil's death and the roller coaster problem, most of my helpers have been scared away. Ward wasn't even supposed to be here, but he offered to help out."

That probably explained Jerry's participation.

I truly had nothing to do but go home, and Hobbit was spending the day with Mathis. If Hobbit had been waiting, I probably would have said no. But she wasn't.

"Sure," I said after only one deep breath.

The kids, who arrived loudly and via a big yellow school bus, clearly knew absolutely nothing about gypsy magic. Or they just didn't care. They ranged in age from five years old up to eleven or twelve. They stepped off the bus and into a world where they got to run around in costumes, yell, decorate pumpkins, and eat things that tasted good but were made to look gory. What wasn't to like?

I took up a post with the pumpkins and

helped dole out markers and stencils and glue and glitter. There were no knives, so carving wasn't a part of the decorating, and not one of the children complained.

During the crazy afternoon, Dianna brought me a bowl of the Brain and Eyeball Stew, telling me I'd been there a couple hours and should probably eat something, but other than that I lost all track of time. I lost track of Scott, Jerry, Ward, Lucy, and, eventually, Dianna. I played with kids, and ended up covered in marker and glitter and glue and even some stray yarn that someone had used to create a Raggedy Ann pumpkin.

I was a mess and I had a great time.

The kids finally left at about six thirty, and the corn maze began to transition to its early evening and nighttime audience. As it began to get dark, I thought I might be able to finally steal away. And I would have succeeded if only Lucy hadn't found me again.

"I didn't see you all afternoon," I said.

"Oh, I was around, here and there. I saw the fun you were having with the kids and I didn't want to disturb. I really can't thank you enough for your help. I promise I won't ask you to do anything ever again. Well, until next year when we need more pumpkins, I guess." Lucy smiled.

"No problem." I looked around. "Scott

still here?"

"Yeah, he's somewhere. I had him inside the maze with the kids. I think I've talked him into staying and donning a zombie costume for the nighttime crowd. I bet he'll be wonderful."

I was suddenly just plain tired of wondering. "Lucy, I've got to know something."

"Sure."

"What's going on with you and Scott? I mean, I saw the two of you disappear into the trailer and you didn't answer when I knocked. I know he's not my husband anymore, but that left me with a funny feeling. You do know he's married."

"Of course, I know," she said, but she blushed slightly. "I know . . . well, rest assured there's nothing illicit going on between Scott and me. He's helped out with the rides. He's good at fixing things. I didn't hear you knock and I don't know how I missed it, but our meetings have been about the rides."

I blinked. I couldn't tell if she was being truthful or not. Or was she telling the truth in a roundabout way? Had she and Scott been meeting about the rides but plotting to sabotage roller coaster tracks and such? She must have read my mind.

"Becca," she said as she put her hand on

my arm, "Scott and I didn't have anything to do with the coaster tracks breaking. In fact, and it might have been when we didn't answer your knock, he was adamant in telling me that some of the rides were far too dangerous to allow them to continue to run."

"And you didn't listen to him?"

She nodded. "Yes, we did listen to him, and we were considering it seriously, I promise you that. I wish we would have. Orderville is full of superstition and somewhat unexplained events, but plain and simple that track was weak. There's no gypsy magic at work there, and I don't think anyone sabotaged it. Scott caught it the first day of the fair. He asked for some blueprints or schematics of the rides, and he marked where he thought they might need extra work. He found the exact spot on the tracks that ultimately broke and drew it up for me, for us. He was trying to help."

"Then why didn't you listen to him?"

Lucy sighed. "Because the Bellings brothers are stubborn and wanted to bring in an expert. The fair was too important to . . . well, never mind that part. They didn't ask Scott to check the rides, he did that on his own. They wanted him to stick only to the job he was given and they'd find someone else to look at the rides."

"The shooting gallery?"

"No . . ." Lucy's eyes flashed, and she put her fist to her mouth. "I've said too much. I apologize but I can't continue." She moved her hand away and looked at me intensely. "I know Scott's wife, Susan. I know her well. It's not my place to tell you, but you should ask him what her maiden name is. Without telling you the secrets I'm not so good at keeping, knowing *that* might help you understand more." She turned and walked away, marking something on her clipboard as she went.

My plans to go home suddenly changed.

Dianna was no longer manning the cauldron; I didn't see Ward or Jerry either. In fact, other than Lucy, who hadn't donned a costume, none of the workers looked familiar. I suspected there were teenagers under all the fake gore and makeup, but if I had seen or met any of them before, I didn't recognize them now.

The next two things that happened were almost the last two things I expected to happen. I would have been less surprised to see my family or even Ian walking through the entrance of and into the corn maze. Instead, I saw Sam, or at least that's who I thought I saw.

Since the entire fairgrounds was in a valley, and the sun had mostly set, the maze, animal barn, and surrounding area were now lit with artificial light posts that had been dressed up to look like fire-burning torches. My eyes could have been playing tricks on me, but I was pretty certain I'd seen Sam disappear into the maze. The person had been classic casual Sam, dressed in jeans and a long-sleeved black T-shirt. And despite the full-coverage outfit, I could tell the guy was in great shape. And his hair was only slightly set free, making me think that if it was Sam, he had been at work earlier.

I wasn't ready to chase him into the maze. My curiosity hadn't caused me to lose all my good senses. But the next thing that happened changed everything again, and I do mean everything.

I had looked down briefly to make sure I didn't step on any small toes. I wanted to at least take a peek into the maze's opening to see if I could catch Sam. But when I glanced up again, I saw something that stopped me in my tracks.

Okay, to be fair, the area was crowded with people, many of them in costume. What I saw might have just been someone playing or pretending or acting a role.

A woman who looked almost exactly like the pictures I'd seen of Jena Bellings stood on the inside of the small roped-off entrance to the maze. She stared at me, specifically at me, through the crowd of people. She shook her head and held her hands out in a halt position. Apparently, this woman agreed with me about entering corn mazes.

I wanted to go talk to her, but as two large wolflike costumes passed in front of me, she disappeared. When I looked again as I hurried to the maze, she was gone.

"Hey, where did that woman go?" I asked the teenage skeleton who was taking tickets.

"What woman?"

"The one dressed like . . . well, a gypsy or a witch."

The skeleton laughed. "I'll need something more specific. There're lots of people like that around here, lady. Look around."

I did, and he was mostly right. There were a few kid witches here and there, most of them less realistic and much shorter than the woman I'd seen.

"She might have gone in there." The skeleton pointed at the corn maze opening. "I don't always pay attention to who I'm taking tickets from."

"Thanks."

I was *not* going into the corn maze.

Nope, not me.

I could just as easily wait at the exit.

"How long does it take to go through the maze?" I asked.

"Depends. If you just walk through, not long. But most people either get lost or like to get lost or like to goof around or like to be scared. That can take some time."

I gulped.

Why in the world would Sam Brion have gone into the corn maze? The more time ticked by, the more I thought I was mistaken about having seen him.

But who had I seen?

I'd hang out by the exit for a few minutes and then be done. Lucy didn't need me to do anything. I could go check on George and the kitten. I could make some preserves.

The exit wasn't all that far from the entrance, but it was surrounded by small food carts. Jerry's corn-dog trailer might have worked here, but it seemed this was more about sweets than anything else, specifically cotton candy, caramel corn, and kettle corn. Normally, I would have indulged in at least one of them, but my stomach wasn't on an even enough keel to add some sugar to it.

I'd been loitering by the exit for about three minutes when it suddenly occurred to me that I was being more than ridiculous. Small children were entering and exiting the corn maze and they all seemed to be fine, having a good time actually. If small children were going through it, surely I could handle it. I only saw one upset child and that was because she'd dropped her cotton candy.

Besides, I could always turn around and leave if I didn't like it.

I bought a ticket quickly and handed it to the skeleton before I could reconsider.

"Go on in," he encouraged me when I held up the line behind me.

Stepping over the threshold and into the stalks of corn turned out to be not so frightening. It wasn't the most enjoyable thing I'd ever done, but it certainly wasn't as confining as I'd thought it would be. Even though the corn was tall, the path was wide.

As I stepped just a little farther forward, though, I realized that my venturing into the maze was pure lunacy. It was a *maze,* with offshoot paths going every which direction. I would never be able to find Sam in here. Chances of running into him were slim at best, and that was only if I'd really seen him enter.

Nevertheless, I moved forward.

Scary masks hung from poles. People in costumes lurked in corners, but they seemed to be making an effort not to scare little children or the short grown-ups who crossed their arms in front of themselves and tried to look mean.

For a while I sauntered down the aisles with my arms crossed tightly, but it wasn't long before I was bored with the whole thing, and though I was battling well the sense of claustrophobia that was creeping up on me, I thought that I probably needed to find a way out sooner rather than later. Corn mazes just weren't my style.

Since finding the way out was supposed to be difficult, I tried to tell myself to just be patient and try each path. Again, though, since it was a *maze,* the paths were meant to be confusing.

I thought I heard movement in the stalks next to me as I turned a corner. I stepped back and peered into the gloom. It was difficult to tell, but I thought I saw someone in there. I crossed my arms again and scowled at the potential figure in the corn. No one was close by, so I leaned forward and said, "Do not jump out of that corn and scare me, got it?"

I received no response, but as I took a step forward, the stalks rustled. I didn't look back as I hurried forward.

I could hear other people in the paths nearby, but no one was close enough to witness what happened next.

The figure in the corn reached out, put one hand over my mouth and another around my waist, and pulled me into the stalks.

I panicked of course, but the first thought that went through my mind was "I knew I should have stayed out of the corn maze."

Twenty-Four

"Becca, it's me. Quit trying to bite me and don't scream," Scott said in my ear.

I turned my neck and looked at him. He was dressed all in black, including a black cap over his head.

I elbowed him in the gut.

"Ooomph," he exclaimed, but he pulled his hand off my mouth. "What'd you do that for?"

"Because you pulled me into corn maze, covered my mouth, and told me not to scream. I'm probably going to scream, too."

"No, don't. Please."

"Then you'd better tell me what's going on right this minute," I said. I was pretty proud of myself that I hadn't started crying. The terror of having been accosted was still crashing through my system; I was shaking and felt my throat tighten.

"I can't."

"What do you mean, you can't?" I swiped

a stalk out of my face. "Why not?"

"I'm undercover. And telling people you're a spy defeats the purpose."

Okay, you have to understand that hearing these words from Scott was akin to hearing them from a child pretending to be a spy. I didn't want to be patronizing and I didn't want to think he was being childish, but I'd spent a lot of our married years dealing with his childishness. Even though he'd become a part-time EMT, I had a hard time thinking of him as anything other than the guy I'd married and then divorced.

"Uh," I finally uttered.

"Yes, I'm undercover. I'm trying to catch a killer."

"In the corn maze?"

"Yes, I think this is his last chance to kill who he's come to kill. I want to catch him before it happens. It's easy to accost someone in here. I got you, didn't I? I saw you and was afraid he'd try to kill you, too. You've been too nosy."

"How do I know you're not the killer?"

"Come on, you know me well enough to know I'm not a killer. A lady-killer maybe, but not a real killer." His attempt to be charming in the midst of . . . everything that was going on was . . . so Scott.

I sighed. "Did I see Sam?"

"I think so. He's been trying to help me. We bonded over your cut chin. Since he's in law enforcement and the locals aren't much help, I asked him for his opinion and he's jumped in to help."

"Don't suppose you could give me a *Reader's Digest* version of what's going on and then get me out of here before you find the killer."

"There's not a lot of time, but the short, short version is that Virgil came to Orderville twenty years ago as part of WITSEC — the Federal Witness Protection Program or Witness Security Program. He and one other person had witnessed a brutal crime, and they were placed here by the program after they'd testified at the trial. Somehow the bad guys figured out where Virgil and the other witness were. They sent someone here to kill them both."

"I don't understand. How do you know Virgil was a witness, but you don't know who the other one was?"

"Virgil went to the Bellings brothers and told them he'd been receiving mail, notes from someone within the person's family he'd testified against. This person risked his or her own life to tell Virgil and presumably the other witness that they'd been found and they were in danger. Virgil told the brothers about his past, but he wouldn't give up who the other witness was, though he said he'd been trying to keep an eye on them."

"Randy or Dianna?"

"Yes, we think so. They're the only logical guesses, but they aren't telling either. The Bellingses sent me to the fair to watch over the three of them as best I could."

"You? Why you?"

"I'm part of the family, but no one really knows me. My wife hasn't been back to Orderville for years. The Bellingses needed someone they could trust, so they went to family. My wife is none-too-happy, though," he said.

"Susan Bellings?" I said.

"Yes, I thought you knew."

"I would only have known if someone told me." I paused. "Does Susan look like her grandmother? Is she back in town?"

"She's the spittin' image of Jena, but no, she and Brady won't come home until this is over."

"So you think you'll catch the killer here, this evening? Why?"

"Yes, the threats that Virgil received said that both witnesses would be killed by this night, this night of 'gypsy magic.' "

"Come on," I said, but a chill ran up my

336

spine nonetheless.

"I know, but it's something that feels real around here. Or that people say feels real. It's a big part of the reason Susan hasn't been back in years and doesn't ever want to come back."

"Did the killer sabotage the roller coaster?"

"No, no. That bucket of bolts was bound to fall apart. I tried to . . . well, it's not important now, but no, it wasn't sabotage. I'll deal with trying to help the authorities understand that later."

"What about outside of the corn maze? Who's watching for a killer out there?"

"Lucy, some local police officers and security guards. Look, you need to get out of here, get back home to Monson," Scott said.

"What about everybody else? Shouldn't the maze be shut down?"

"Sam tried to get the Bellings brothers to do as much, but they didn't think it was necessary — and they're superstitious. So Sam and I think that the killer will only try to harm those who are a threat to him. We don't think anyone but the remaining witness is in danger, and neither Randy nor Dianna is willing to hide. And maybe you're in danger, too since you've been snooping around."

"Is it just you and Sam . . . what, patrolling inside the maze?"

"Yes."

"There are children everywhere."

"I know. That's mostly why we're here, Becs. We're trying to do what we can."

I squelched the urge to yell "Fire!" and get everyone out of the maze. I had a very bad feeling about this sketchy plan, but causing a panic wasn't the right thing to do.

"So, there's a chance nothing will happen?"

"That's what we're hoping. You need to just go now," he said.

"Point me in the right direction."

"There's an orange string around the bottom of the stalks at each intersection. That will guide you. Stick to the paths with the strings."

"Great."

Somehow, Scott took me directly to an open aisle. We waited until there were no people close by before I erupted from the stalks. It was great to be free. I hurried to an intersection and looked down. About a foot into one of the paths and at the bottom of a stalk, I saw an orange string, and I scurried in that direction.

As I speed-walked along, I realized I

wished I'd asked Scott more questions, but I doubted he'd have answered them.

And then I stopped altogether.

What if I'd just been duped? Big-time duped?

I was in the middle of an aisle as these thoughts came to me. Kids, grown-ups, dressed in all kinds of costumes, ran past me in both directions, bumping into me without apology. A couple people probably told me to get out of the way, but I wasn't listening to anything except the reasoning tumbling around in my head.

Scott was the one hiding in the stalks. Wouldn't the guiltiest person be the one hiding? Scott was married to a Bellings, the Bellingses went ahead with the fair no matter the shape of the rides, and though he was gorgeous, Renard was weird.

I began to think that (1) I'd just had an encounter with the bad guy, (2) the fact that we'd once been married had blinded me to who he really was, and (3) his sentimental attitude about our past was the only reason he'd just spared my life. Despite the grave seriousness of these revelations, I couldn't help but be somewhat happy that our marriage hadn't been bad enough for Scott to want to kill me and leave my lifeless body in a cornfield.

But Sam hadn't been married to Scott.

I turned around and glanced in the direction from which I'd just come. Had I seen Sam enter the maze, really? I was pretty sure I had.

"Is he here to help Scott, or did Scott lure him here?" I asked myself quietly.

The two of them seemed to have hit it off. They'd been in cahoots when they were teasing me as they took care of my chin, and I'd watched them conferring outside the service station. I'd thought they were just being friendly, but had Scott been manipulating him? For what reason?

The only thing that came to my confused and scared mind was that Scott wanted to get someone in law enforcement on his side. Maybe then, he could commit whatever crimes he'd decided to commit more easily. Wait — that must have been it! Scott didn't need to worry about the Orderville police. Shoot, the rides hadn't even been inspected. The Bellingses had the police on their side. Sam, though not a local officer, had started snooping around, asking about fair-ride regulations and such. Oh no! Scott might want to get Sam out of the way, too.

Scott was the one hiding. He wasn't looking for the killer, he was looking to harm Sam. Lucy was in on it, too — oh, she'd lied so smoothly if that was the case.

Somehow, even though I was terrified by this point, in the very back of my mind my conviction that Scott didn't kill anyone truly wasn't weakening. That wasn't it at all, in fact. I was looking for an excuse, a reason to be worried about Sam, a reason beyond the real reason. If I'd taken just one more moment of thought I would have realized that it was okay to be worried about someone I cared for so much, maybe even as more than just a friend. I didn't need to lose faith in Scott just to care about Sam. But none of that rational thinking made it to the surface.

"Sam," I said as I turned down an aisle that didn't have an orange string marker.

I had to find him.

I hoped I wasn't heading back toward Scott, but there wasn't much I could do about it. I just started walking down random aisles, searching for Sam. It occurred to me then that the corn maze was a perfect location for committing a crime. If you could pull someone into the stalks, you could harm them in any way you chose without being seen. And any cries for help would likely be drowned out by others. As I trudged onward, I could hear the other maze visitors, but I couldn't tell where their shrieks of glee were coming from or if they were meant to be gleeful at all.

With every step, I felt my panic transforming from a claustrophobic need to get out of the corn maze to a heart-pounding desire to find Sam, but this was as close to the proverbial needle-in-a-haystack search as I'd ever experienced.

"Watch where you're going," snapped a costumeless man holding two small children by the hand.

"Sorry," I said as I skirted around them. Hopefully I wasn't leaving fallen characters in my wake, but I continued to hurry.

I came upon a big opening in the maze and beheld a most beautiful sight: a raised platform in the middle of a clearing, and only a couple of people were atop it.

I ran up the stairs and the world opened wide. I could see the entire maze from this vantage point: the snaking, curving aisles, the abrupt and cruel dead ends. I could see the tall billboard with the creepy house painted on it and realized that it bordered the maze, wasn't in the middle of it like it had seemed from the carnival grounds. The maze didn't spread as far as I thought it did. From here, I also noticed that it was actually quite well lit, with large floodlights around the far perimeter, a couple in this clearing, and several smaller lights strategically placed throughout. However, the maze was still too big and too crowded for me to pinpoint a specific person within its aisles.

I unconsciously put my hand to my forehead in scout mode and took my time as I turned and searched, turned and searched again. It was on my third circle around that I thought I might be seeing something important.

About fifty feet into the maze from the platform, I saw a flash of movement in the aisle and then activity moving through the stalks. It might just have been some kids fooling around, but the flash seemed . . . bigger than if some kids had just stepped through the wall of corn.

I tried to memorize the route I would need to take to reach the point where I'd seen the flash. I could still see movement through the stalks, a cartoonish flurry of activity.

I hurried down the stairs of the platform and took the path I'd scouted out. Once I passed one intersection, I couldn't be exactly sure I was headed in the right direction, but I just kept going.

As I took a left fork in the maze, someone said my name.

"Becca, what're you doing?"

I stopped, my feet skidding in the dirt, and turned to see Sam, dressed in exactly what I thought I'd seen him dressed in.

"Sam! Sam!" I said as I walked up to him and hugged him tightly.

"Uh, okay, what's going on?" he asked as I disengaged.

"I thought . . . well, I wasn't sure you were safe."

"Oh. How much do you know about what's going on?" he asked as he directed us to the side of the aisle.

I told him about my recent encounter with Scott. He nodded seriously as I continued.

"I thought that maybe I'd been duped, though, and that Scott was the bad guy and he was going to hurt you."

"No, no, I've been trying to help Scott. Scott's a good guy, Becca."

"Are you sure?"

"A hundred percent. He's just in over his head. I came here tonight to try to keep him out of trouble. The Bellings brothers should never have asked him to do what he's been doing. This is dangerous stuff. He could get hurt."

"I saw something. I think something's going on in the stalks."

"Where?"

"That way, or that way. I . . ." I had no

idea what made me look up, but that movement would change everything.

"Sam, lift me up."

"What?"

"Seriously, just for a second, lift me up."

Sam bent down, grabbed me under my knees, and lifted. I could see the lights, and when I did, I remembered that the scuffle had occurred at the second light over. I pointed. "That way, I'm sure."

Sam put me down and then grabbed my hand.

"Excuse us," he said as we threaded our way through a group of teens. "Emergency."

In only a few seconds we were standing beneath the light I'd pointed to. The stalks there were smushed and broken.

"Wait here," Sam said.

I squeezed his hand. "Not a chance."

If he'd had even a minute to spare, I was sure he would have argued with me to stay put, but fortunately for me, time was of the essence, so he just nodded, parted some of the stalks, and led the way.

Though my mouth wasn't being covered by a hand and I felt safe with Sam, my second time amid the stalks wasn't any more enjoyable than my first had been.

Sam didn't realize that his rushed steps were causing the stalks to snap back and hit me in the face. I didn't want to complain, so my only option was to keep my eyes closed and my head down, hoping that I wouldn't trip over something and he wouldn't suddenly let go of my hand.

The sounds of our own movement must have muted the sounds from the ruckus ahead because I didn't even realize we'd come upon the exact trouble we'd gone looking for.

"Stop!" Sam suddenly yelled as he did exactly that.

I stopped, too, opened my eyes, and peered around him.

We'd come upon another clearing, a much smaller one this time. The clearing I'd been in earlier, the one with the platform, had been made by cutting all the cornstalks from that part of the field. This space was a fifteen-by-fifteen-foot area in which someone had smashed down all the corn and, apparently, set up their own living space. There were two lawn chairs on either side of what looked like a huge metal toolbox. Sitting on top of the box was an old transistor radio, its antenna extended straight up in the air.

I didn't know who Sam was talking to. It was either Jerry or Scott. They had their hands on each other. It looked as though

Jerry was trying to choke Scott and Scott was trying to punch Jerry in the gut.

"It was him!" Jerry said. "He's the one who killed Virgil and who was going to kill Randy tonight."

Scott, his eyes bulging from the pressure on his throat, turned toward Sam and me, but I couldn't tell what he was trying to communicate.

"No, Jerry," Sam said. "I know better. Come on, let go of him or I'll have to jump in, and I'm on his side."

Jerry looked at Sam a long time before he finally let go of Scott, who fell to the ground and struggled to find his breath again.

"He's the one," Jerry insisted.

"Sam knows about Virgil and the other witness. I told him," Scott choked out with a raspy voice.

"What did he tell you?" Jerry asked Sam.

"That Virgil and the other witness testified against someone twenty or so years ago. That someone from the convicted person's family had come to town to get revenge. They thought it was you, Jerry, but they couldn't prove it until now," Sam said.

"They? You mean the Bellings brothers, right?"

"The family, yes."

"No! The person they testified against was

a Bellings. Well, it was a distant cousin. The brothers made sure that Virgil and Randy . . ." Jerry was suddenly quiet. He'd said the other witness's name twice now and I could tell he wished he hadn't, but he continued. "They came to Orderville. They've been waiting all these years for the opportunity to kill the other Bellings."

I shook my head and tried to understand what he was saying, but plain and simple, it didn't make sense. Jerry was beginning to ramble.

"No, Jerry, it was your father, not a Bellings, that they testified against. I'm certain of that," Scott added as he stood on shaky legs.

"No!" Jerry looked at Sam. "You've fallen for their tricks — their lies, too. Don't listen to him."

"Has the killer been hiding here, in the corn maze?" I asked. I'd come around Sam and wasn't as frightened as I should have been. It was three against one, after all, though I wasn't totally sure who Sam's and my third ally was; I hoped it was Scott.

"Yes!" Jerry said. "That's what I think, at least. This is a good place to hide. No one would even consider the possibility that someone was here, waiting, watching, hoping for the right opportunity. Scott's a crafty guy."

"There's one way to know for certain," I said to Sam.

"How's that?" he said, but I could tell he wasn't happy that I'd jumped into the conversation.

"Well, I'm sure that Scott has a toolbox like that . . ."

"Becca . . ." Scott said.

"But, if he does, he'll have used every tool inside it. There will be fingerprints all over the tools. Unless they're brand new, there would be no way to clean all the prints. We just need to get out of here and have the tools looked at more closely. That'll tell us what we need to know."

"Unless the tools were stolen," Scott said.

"We'll figure it out," Sam said. "It's a good idea. Let's just get out of here and we'll send some people back here to gather ev . . . gather the stuff. We'll get it worked out. Jerry, Scott, let's go."

Sam was a good police officer, one of the best from all I'd seen. I didn't know much about being a law enforcement officer, but I knew they liked to have their weapon with them when they came upon potential killers. Sam didn't have his gun. And we were in the middle of a volatile situation. He was just trying to get us all out of there. My contribution about the prints was something he'd, of course, already thought of and probably wished I hadn't brought up.

For the briefest of instants, I thought he'd accomplished his goal. It looked like both Scott and Jerry were just as ready to get out of there as I was.

"Let's go," Sam repeated with a calm and even tone.

Scott made a small motion that showed he was turning to walk away — and this move probably saved his life.

Because, from what must have been his back pocket, Jerry pulled out a short-bladed but sparkly sharp knife and hurled it at Scott, then ran into the stalks opposite from where Sam and I had entered the clearing.

The knife embedded itself in the top part of Scott's arm but would have landed close to his heart had he not turned only a second before. Scott yowled and went back to his knees.

Sam and I ran to him as he struggled to stand up again.

"No, don't!" Sam said. But it was too late; Scott reached for the knife, yanked it out of his arm, and threw it to the ground. In the dim light of the corn forest, I could see the dark stain of blood ooze quickly through his short sleeve, down his arm, and in between his fingers. We needed to stop the bleeding, and quickly.

"Come on, Sam, let's get that SOB," Scott said.

"Your arm!" I said.

Scott held his hand over the cut, but the blood still oozed. "The sooner we get him, the sooner I can get some medical attention. I'll be fine." He stood surely and disappeared into the stalks.

Sam glanced at me.

"Go, go, I'll get out the other way and meet you out front. Go!" I said.

The two of them took off. Having a dangerous and violent man on the loose was enough to make them believe I could take care of myself from there. I hoped they'd find Jerry quickly so that Scott could get the medical attention he needed.

Being alone in the small clearing was more unsettling than I'd anticipated it would be. The path Sam and I had taken into it was evident, though, and I'd be able to find my way out easily. I thought about picking up the knife or grabbing something else that might serve as evidence or a weapon, but I was too spooked to follow through on those inclinations. I just wanted to get out and get away.

As I stepped one foot over the threshold from the clearing to the path, I thought I saw movement about ten feet ahead. Though we'd worn a decent path, there were still plenty of standing stalks obscuring the lights.

"Who's there?" I said stupidly.

Just then, the figure came more fully into view, except it wasn't much of a figure; I could make out only a deeper darkness, cloudlike but in the shape of a human — a human with long black hair, actually.

"Go the other way, Becca," said a voice that seemed to come from the figure. The voice was female, though deep and thickly southern.

"Excuse me?" I said, again stupidly.

"Go out the other way. This way is dangerous," the voice insisted.

And then the figure seemed to dissipate, and I saw only dead stalks of corn ahead.

I didn't think about it, I just did as the voice had commanded. It took me only about thirty seconds to find my way out and into the open.

It was as if I joined the party about those thirty seconds too late. I missed what must have been a struggle between Sam and Jerry, and I only caught the part where Sam was clicking handcuffs in place onto Jerry's wrists as Jerry lay face down on the straw-strewn ground. A uniformed police officer stood next to them and observed. Either Sam had been prepared enough to bring his own handcuffs or the police officer had supplied them.

Scott was still bleeding, though another police officer or perhaps a security guard was guiding him somewhere, hopefully to get his injury cared for.

Lucy and others were in the process of getting people out of and away from the maze. I chose to hurry to her, offer my assistance, and see if she could give me more answers.

"Hey, did you see a grown woman dressed in black and with big black hair exit from the maze?"

Lucy, who was grateful that no one else had been killed and that almost no one had noticed what had really gone on at the corn maze, laughed lightly. "Becca, there are a number of people dressed as witches around here."

"But grown women?"

"I don't know. Dianna maybe, but I thought I saw her leave. And I thought she had a gray wig." She looked around; though the crowd was dissipating quickly, costumed characters roamed here and there. She gestured toward the faraway sign with the painting of the old house. "There's a legend around here, though, about Jena Bellings."

"I might have heard."

Lucy shrugged. "Well, I don't give much credence to that silliness, but maybe you experienced a little gypsy magic."

"Yeah, maybe." I turned and faced the maze, and for an instant that was shorter than a blink I thought I saw the figure in the corn. I thought she smiled and nodded at me.

"There, right there," I said as I pointed.

But Lucy and her clipboard were gone. In fact, I didn't see them anywhere, but I assumed they were off doing important things for important people.

TWENTY-FIVE

TWO WEEKS LATER

The results from the evidence testing were conclusive, and put Jerry, the corn-dog vendor, away for a long, long time.

His fingerprints were all over everything: the tools, the lawn chair, the radio, the toolbox, and the gun that had been used to kill Virgil — the cops found it in the toolbox. There was also one wrench inside that had Scott's fingerprints all over it, but the police concluded that Jerry must have stolen it from Scott. Scott confided to me that he didn't remember owning such a wrench, but he had so many tools, maybe he forgot about it.

After all the facts were put into place, it turned out to be a pretty simple story. Twenty years earlier, Virgil and Randy had helped put Jerry's father in jail. They'd been innocent bystanders to a crime, a Mafia murder, though disappointing to me only, not Russian mafia.

Orderville, South Carolina, was, in fact, a great place to hide witnesses. In what I thought was the most unusual twist, the Bellings family knew about the witness protection program and knew that at least one person had been relocated to their town, but they weren't sure who until Virgil told them about himself. Virgil's real name was Darrell, and Randy's was Aaron. It wasn't until the night of the maze opening that the Bellings brothers and Scott figured out the other witness was Randy/Aaron, but Scott and Sam and I intervened before Jerry could commit another murder. Randy/Aaron had to be relocated again, just in case there were others searching for him. None of us knew where he'd been sent.

A few weeks before he was killed, Virgil had received written threats; so had Randy. Jerry's research had led him to three "Outsiders" via a twenty-year-old archived newspaper article and picture he'd come across on the Internet. It talked about the three new citizens of Orderville, South Carolina, and how well they were fitting in. If the picture of Virgil, Randy, and Dianna hadn't been enough, the article's mention of Virgil's tattoo confirmed to Jerry that he'd found who he was looking for. Before Jerry's father died in jail, he'd frequently told his son to be on the lookout for the man with the spider on his neck. Jerry had moved to Orderville six months ago, but had bided his time, figuring that if he waited until the fair started, he'd be able to kill the witnesses and have his actions diluted by what he termed "those people's stupid gypsy magic."

According to Sam, Virgil and Randy's biggest mistake was not contacting WITSEC marshals. Virgil had gone to Renard Bellings, but though the Bellings brothers were powerful, they weren't able to stop Virgil's murder. As with many too-powerful people, they'd been arrogant and thought they could handle the situation on their own, so they'd called in their brother-in-law, Scott.

The Bellings brothers had told Scott about Virgil. Scott, wasn't, in fact, the owner of the shooting gallery after all, but just pretended to be so he could place himself at the fair, where he could keep an eye on Virgil and try to figure out who the other witness was. He'd hoped to use some of his Scott charm to get Virgil to confide in him, but that plan had quickly gone awry, and I'd been there to witness it. After Virgil's death, Scott decided he needed to aggressively try to figure out who the other witness was so he approached both Randy and

Dianna and asked them outright. Randy remained calmly mum, but Dianna became agitated and worried about her fellow Ordervillains — yes, that's what they call themselves. I find it an appropriate name. She, suspicious by nature anyway, started to put the pieces of the puzzle together and she figured that the newest newcomer Jerry was up to no good. Ian and I weren't the only ones she warned. We should have all listened to her, but it was difficult for anyone to think Jerry, the nice-looking young man with the shaggy hair, could be a villain.

Ethel wasn't Virgil's aunt, but it was the story he'd stuck to even long ago when people wondered how it was possible that Ethel had a nephew. Soon, no one cared and they quit asking about the house. No one else claimed it, so it didn't matter much. Virgil *had* served twenty years in the military — under his real name, Darrell Sulich — and thus qualified for retirement pay. WITSEC had arranged for his checks to be written out to "Virgil Morrison," though the army had no record of him. Virgil had been proud of his service and occasionally talked about it even though he'd been instructed not to. The authorities suspected that Virgil, in an attempt to throw off the killer, had put the feminine furniture on his porch about a week before he was killed. No one knew what happened to it after I mentioned it during my and Ian's visit to Bottoms Up.

Once Scott got involved deeply, he knew things weren't being handled properly, and when I introduced him to Sam, he figured he'd found someone he could confide in. Sam had, in fact, contacted WITSEC on his own, but not until after Scott talked to him, which was after Virgil had been killed. The marshals arrived about the same time Scott got the knife in his arm.

The sticky note I'd seen was Scott's writing. He still wasn't sure why he'd written it; he thought maybe he'd done it in a moment of despair over his failure to prevent Virgil's murder.

As for the ledger I'd seen listing which fair workers owed what, Scott said he'd picked that up accidentally in Lucy's trailer. When he tore down the shooting gallery, he found it and returned it to Lucy. It was fair business that was no one else's business.

The morning after my snooping excursion at the shooting gallery, Scott had noticed a puddle of blood on the ground under the table; he'd assumed it had come from an injured animal. I wanted to punch him when he burst out laughing as I told him the real story.

Scott and Lucy's meetings in the trailer had nothing to do with romance: they'd been trying to figure out how to save the other witness and convince the Bellings brothers to either close the fair or at least have the rides more closely inspected. Scott was head over heels for his wife, Susan, someone I still hoped to meet someday.

None of us ever learned *why* Virgil had a spider tattoo on his neck, but I'd become attached to the idea that it was some sort of symbol about hope and fate. I'd likely never know for sure, though.

It occurred to me that the woman in black was, indeed, Dianna Kivitt. It could have been. It might have been. She denied it, though, so I guessed I'd never really know that for sure either. I couldn't quite make myself believe in gypsy magic, but I didn't quite disbelieve it either. I also don't know exactly why the woman diverted me; maybe she thought I'd get lost the other way. I didn't think I'd ever venture into a corn maze again, so if she was still somehow lingering there, I wouldn't get the chance to ask.

As for my personal life, well, Ian and I easily transitioned into being just friends. In fact, in the weeks following our breakup, we'd spent more time together than we had when we were more than friends. Business at the market had slowed, so I'd been helping out a lot at the lavender farm. George's living space was finished, so we'd moved him and his kitten in, and things were going even better than I'd expected. George named the kitten Gypsy, and the two of them were crazy about each other. Gypsy still wasn't so sure about me, though. Maybe in time.

And now, I found myself sitting in my truck in front of Sam's small house. Actually, I'd been sitting there for forty minutes, trying to summon my courage to go knock on his door. I'd brought Hobbit along for moral support, but she'd grown tired of my behavior.

Finally, Hobbit sighed heavily and turned her back to me to look out the passenger window.

"All right, all right, I'll go."

I hopped out of the truck and walked to the front door. I hadn't seen Sam since the night at the corn maze, and I was nervous about what I was going to do.

As I reached up to knock on the door, it opened wide.

"I wondered how long you were going to

361

sit out there," Sam said with a smile. He was in jeans and a sweatshirt, and his hair was one hundred percent free of gel. He must not have had to work today.

"You saw me?"

He raised his eyebrows. "Even if I didn't have the observation skills of a police officer, I'd have to be blind not to notice your orange truck."

"Oh."

"What can I do for you, Becca?"

I cleared my throat. I'd thought long and hard about how I was going to handle this moment. I knew he knew about Ian and me. Everyone knew about Ian and me. I didn't want Sam to think I was acting on a rebound. I wanted him to know that what I was about to do was genuine and real. I'd waited awhile, but only because I thought that's what I was supposed to do. But during the last couple weeks, I'd thought about him. I'd thought about our kiss from a few months earlier. I'd thought about a lot of things, one of them being that I had a bad record of choosing men, but I realized that Scott had been right — I hadn't been wrong about him, just premature. And I hadn't been wrong about Ian either. Ian was great, but we just weren't meant for each other. My track record wasn't all *that* bad. And finally, I thought about the fact that maybe I should just stay out of relationships for a good long while. Some time alone might be good for me.

But there was that kiss, and it deserved to at least be explored a little.

Sam smiled, waiting for an answer to his question, and when I didn't say anything for a good few seconds, he repeated, "Becca?"

"Sam, I'm here to invite you out on a date," I blurted out. "I'd like to take you to dinner and maybe a movie. What do you think?" I sounded awful, like a programmed robot.

Fortunately, Sam continued to smile. "I'd love to go out to dinner and maybe a movie with you. But, why don't you grab Hobbit and come in for some coffee or tea or something right now. It's a little cold out there."

I was nervous, but I got Hobbit and we went inside. Sam and I had some coffee and some stale cookies that had been in his pantry, and we talked for a long, long time.

And then the next night we went out on our first real date.

And then we went on many, many more.

RECIPES

Strawberry Syrup

2 pounds strawberries
1 1/2 cups sugar
1 cup water
1 tablespoon pectin
2 tablespoons lemon juice

Hull and clean the strawberries, and then pulse them in a food processor until mashed or thoroughly mash them with the back of a fork.

Place the prepared fruit in a large pot and sprinkle with 1/2 cup of the sugar; let stand for a half hour to draw out the juice.

In a smaller pot, combine the water, pectin, lemon juice, and remaining 1 cup sugar. Bring the mixture to a boil over medium heat; boil for 5 minutes. Add this simple syrup to the pot containing the fruit and bring to another boil, stirring while cooking, for 3 minutes. Skim off any foam that forms.

Pour the syrup into prepared jars, wipe away any drips from sides or rims, and seal. Hot-water process.

Makes about 7 half-pint jars.

Thanks to the fabulous Laine Barash and Bonnie Mills Schelts for giving Becca the idea to add syrups to her repertoire. And thanks to Laine for sharing this delicious recipe.

FUNNEL CAKE

2 quarts vegetable oil for frying
1 1/2 cups milk
2 eggs
2 cups all-purpose flour
1 teaspoon baking powder
1/2 teaspoon ground cinnamon
1/2 teaspoon salt
3/4 cup confectioners' sugar
Funnel cake pitcher or plastic zip bag with
  1/2 inch cut from the corner

In a deep fryer or heavy skillet (cast iron is ideal), heat oil to 350 degrees F.

In a large bowl, beat together the milk and eggs. In a separate bowl, combine the flour, baking powder, cinnamon, and salt. Add the dry ingredients to the egg mixture, a little at a time, stirring until smooth.

Pour 1 cup of the batter into the funnel pitcher or the plastic bag. Starting from the center of the fryer and using a swirling motion, let the batter flow into the hot oil to form a 6- or 7-inch round cake. Fry the funnel cake on both sides until golden brown. Remove the cake from the oil and place on paper towels to drain. Repeat the process with the remaining batter.

Sprinkle the funnel cakes with confectioners' sugar and serve warm.

Makes about 7 cakes.

DEEP-FRIED SNICKERS BARS

8 Snickers Bars, frozen
Funnel Cake batter from previous recipe
1 quart vegetable oil for frying
8 Popsicle sticks

When the candy bars are frozen, prepare the Funnel Cake batter.

In a deep fryer or heavy skillet (cast iron is ideal), heat oil to 350 degrees F.

Push a Popsicle stick into the bottom of each of the candy bars, then dip the bars in the batter. Drop the bars, a few at a time, into the oil and fry until golden brown, which will take only a minute or two.

Remove the bars from the oil, and drain and cool slightly on paper towels. Serve.

Makes 8 bars.

JERRY'S CORN DOGS

1 quart vegetable oil for frying
1 cup yellow cornmeal
1 cup all-purpose flour
1/4 teaspoon salt
1/4 cup white sugar
4 teaspoons baking powder
1 egg
1 cup milk
2 (16-ounce) packages beef frankfurters, rolled over paper towels to dry
16 wooden skewers

Preheat oil in a deep saucepan to 350 degrees F.

In a medium bowl, combine the cornmeal, flour, salt, sugar, and baking powder. Stir in the eggs and milk. Chill for 30 minutes.

Insert a wooden skewer into each frankfurter, and dip the frankfurters in the batter until well coated.

Fry the corn dogs in the oil, 2 or 3 at a time, until lightly browned, about 2 to 3 minutes.

Drain on paper towels and serve.

Makes 8 corn dogs.

STELLA'S CINNAMON BREAD

5–7 cups flour (sometimes Stella uses all white flour, sometimes half whole wheat, half white)

1 1/2 tablespoons active dry yeast

1/2 cup sugar

2 eggs, lightly beaten

2 cups warm water

1 1/2 teaspoons vegetable oil

2 teaspoons salt

1 1/2 cups cinnamon chips (available at some grocery stores, or baking specialty stores, these are like compacted bits of cinnamon — sometimes called "cinnamon-flavored bites" — or see recipe on next page to make your own, my preferred method)

In a large mixing bowl, combine 2 cups of the flour with the yeast and sugar. Add the eggs, water, and oil. Beat well until the mixture resembles cake batter. Stir in the salt, cinnamon bites, and 3–5 more cups flour to create a bread-dough consistency.

Using a stand mixer with kneader attachment, knead the dough until it reaches the right thick bread-dough texture, when it holds together smoothly and pulls away easily from the side of the bowl (add up to 1 more cup of flour if needed). Place the dough in a greased bowl, cover with plastic wrap, and let rise for 1 hour. Divide the dough in half and put each loaf into a greased bread pan. Cover again and let the loaves rise for another hour, or until doubled in size.

Preheat the oven to 375 degrees F and bake for about 30 minutes. When the loaves are done, let them cool just slightly, then slice thick and serve warm with butter, or toast the slices in the toaster. This bread also makes delicious French toast.

Makes 2 loaves.

CINNAMON BURST CHIPS

1 cup granulated sugar
4 1/2 tablespoons cinnamon
3 tablespoons solid all vegetable shortening
3 tablespoons light corn syrup

Preheat the oven to 300 degrees F. Mix ingredients together with fork and fingers until uniform and crumbly. Spread thinly on foil-lined baking sheet and bake until melted and bubbly, about 30 minutes. Cool completely and then break into small pieces with a small kitchen mallet.

Makes the correct amount needed for 4 loaves of the previous Cinnamon Bread recipe.

ABOUT THE AUTHOR

Paige Shelton spent lots of years in advertising but now writes novels full time. She lives in Salt Lake City, Utah, with her husband and son. When she's up early enough, one of her favorite things is to watch the sun rise over the Wasatch Mountains. Visit her website at www.paigeshelton .com.

The employees of Thorndike Press hope you have enjoyed this Large Print book. All our Thorndike, Wheeler, and Kennebec Large Print titles are designed for easy reading, and all our books are made to last. Other Thorndike Press Large Print books are available at your library, through selected bookstores, or directly from us.

For information about titles, please call:
  (800) 223-1244

or visit our Web site at:
  http://gale.cengage.com/thorndike

To share your comments, please write:
  Publisher
  Thorndike Press
  10 Water St., Suite 310
  Waterville, ME 04901

CPSIA information can be obtained
at www.ICGtesting.com
Printed in the USA
FFOW051155040713
1350FF

9 781410 458407